SHERLOCK HOLMES
VS.
CTHULHU

THE ADVENTURE OF THE
INNSMOUTH MUTATIONS

SHERLOCK HOLMES VS. CTHULHU

THE ADVENTURE OF THE INNSMOUTH MUTATIONS

LOIS H. GRESH *NEW YORK TIMES* BESTSELLING AUTHOR

TITAN BOOKS

THE ADVENTURE OF THE INNSMOUTH MUTATIONS
Print edition ISBN: 9781785652127
Electronic edition ISBN: 9781785652134

Published by Titan Books
A division of Titan Publishing Group Ltd
144 Southwark Street, London SE1 0UP

First edition: July 2019
2 4 6 8 10 9 7 5 3 1

This is a work of fiction. Names, places and incidents are either products of the author's imagination or used fictitiously. Any resemblance to actual persons, living or dead (except for satirical purposes), is entirely coincidental.

Visit our website: www.titanbooks.com

A CIP catalogue record for this title is available from the British Library.

Printed and bound in the United States

Did you enjoy this book? We love to hear from our readers.
Please email us at readerfeedback@titanemail.com or write to us at
Reader Feedback at the above address.

To receive advance information, news, competitions, and exclusive offers
online, please sign up for the Titan newsletter on our website:
www.titanbooks.com

PART ONE

INNSMOUTH

CTHULHU

January 1891

Filaments brushed his flanks and spun circles before his eyes, before sinking into the crevasse—a hole so deep that no human had ever ventured into it. The water swirled with microscopic creatures and vegetation, some of this world and some from the other dimensions. Fish etched in glowing color swept past him. Some darted into the hole, others swam too close to him, and he sucked them into his feeding tubes.

Cthulhu ruled here, and soon, he would rule all of the oceans, the lands, and the air. His hunger hurt. It was a hunger born from loss, an ache that flared to fiery pain and never burned out. A hunger for what *was*, for what had come *before*, for what *must* come again.

Like a giant star, I spread my tentacles across the hole, I latch my suckers onto all, I writhe, I feel the trembling of the earth, I hear the stirring of those who have awaited me for eons. Rising from R'lyeh beneath the Pacific Ocean, I swam long and hard and claimed my home here, deep

9

beneath the crevasse beyond Devil Reef, Dagon, and Innsmouth. I call to Yog-Sothoth, to the Elders, to the Deep Ones, to the believers.

Cthulhu rumbled, his vast body quivering over the ocean floor, his tentacles stretched taut, their tips probing for food. Sorrow, pain, *unbearable*, and with no end.

Green phosphorescence rippled up from the crevasse, slashed the black water, split it. He felt the invisible creatures tumble from the dimensions beyond human knowledge. Following them were creatures of great and varied scope. Nyarlathotep, the crawling chaos, changing shape, slipped into and out of view. Azathoth, he of tentacles and eyes and mouths, shrilled his cosmic flutes and drummed his hide with muscular appendages, his sound killing sea beasts hundreds of miles away. Yog-Sothoth, ever-faithful keeper of the door to the dimensions, he of the glowing spheres, showed them the way.

The weak race on shore—the humans—recoil in fear from us. They've seen those unleashed upon the River Thames, those of Dagon and the Deep Ones at Half Moon Bay in far-distant England, and nearby, at Devil Reef off Innsmouth. The weak race rages, it loves, it hates. Jealousy, greed, ego. The weak race kills to satisfy its emotions. Those of us from beyond: we feel only the need to exist.

Ah, to reclaim the Earth, where eons ago we ruled.

Anticipation sparked, and Cthulhu's spirit lifted. He felt energized, ready to take what had been his all along.

Miles above on the ocean surface, a huge boat fought

the waves. Cthulhu sensed the human fear onboard, felt the movement of tides and sea. The fish fled, dove deeper. Many slammed up and down on the waves along with the boat. Cthulhu smelled excitement. He knew that Dagon and his worshipers upon Devil Reef felt the human fear, as well.

Cthulhu had waited long enough. It was time to show himself to his followers. It was time to take the Earth back from the humans, who had been destroying it for centuries.

Calling to those who had broken through the dimensional void, he released his suckers from the ocean floor. He unfurled his tentacles and surged upward. The crawling chaos followed him, as did Azathoth, Yog-Sothoth, and the others. Hundreds of creatures rose from the depths.

On the surface, the waves rose sixty feet and thundered down. Cthulhu tightened his tentacles and rode a wave up, and at its crest, he looked down at the boat, saw the humans scream in horror and point at him before toppling over from the impact of the crashing wave. Cthulhu was bigger than the boat. His eyes swiveled, magnified the human faces, saw the blood, the broken bones and bodies. Hunger gnawed, but he had no taste for human flesh. Bugs, all of them. Disgusting.

The glowing spheres of Yog-Sothoth billowed into the sky. Azathoth's tentacles flailed, his mouths opened to reveal teeth longer than the tallest humans. His flutes shrilled, bursting their eardrums.

Come, let us swim to Innsmouth, where Dagon and his followers await. Finally, we will live as we did before humans swarmed over the Earth, defacing everything with their filth, their trash, their very presence.

A wave lifted both Cthulhu and the boat. He would swim toward shore, get as close as he could without injuring himself in the shallow waters.

As the wave crashed, Cthulhu tensed his muscles and fell full-force upon the boat, flattening it. The wood broke. The metal broke. The humans broke. Splinters and flesh and blood and all the debris of humanity surged up with the next powerful wave. Cthulhu broke free of it all, dove beneath the heavy waves. The others came with him. Together, they swam toward Devil Reef, Innsmouth, *humanity.*

1
PROFESSOR MORIARTY

Innsmouth, Massachusetts, January 1891

The fog settled like scum on my shoulders. My gloves were slick with it. The dirt road had turned to mud, and my shoes stuck with every step.

Pulling my hat low, I shivered as the fog leaked a freezing drizzle that pooled in the mud, and farther out, fell like nails into the black water. A screech shattered the night, and I almost jumped but kept my nerves under tight control.

Devil Reef lay a half-mile off shore. I couldn't see it in the darkness, but I knew it was there. Craggy, the holes and the tunnels beneath the reef filled with bizarre beasts, its pointed rocks jutting—*daggers*—and dripping with the flesh of those who had been stupid enough to swim out there. The locals had warned me: *Do not go into the water. You are not of the right kind. Your race is ill equipped.*

But someone lurked by the water tonight. From the shadows of an alley, I watched him: a tall figure, slender, with a long face beneath a gentleman's high hat. Professor Henry Fitzgerald, my prey. He slipped from a lopsided structure with a roof that sloped toward the sea. Another screech shrilled through the fog, and Fitzgerald halted. His head jerked toward Devil Reef, then over his shoulder at the misshapen building, which twitched, shaking rain as a bird shakes its feathers to remove dander.

Innsmouth. Devil Reef. Not much frightened me. Not much surprised me. I'd thrown off the tales about this place as the nattering of idiots. But now, confronted with the eeriness, the sick air, the foul smells—a cross between rotting fish and garbage—I realized that I'd underestimated my sources. If anything, my men had toned down what they'd told me, most likely out of fear that I would think them fools.

A light shot up from the reef and illuminated the dense fog. Odd shapes fluttered, merged, splintered back apart, and formed even stranger shapes in colors I'd never seen. Glowing colors, greens and oranges, mixtures that made my stomach knot. The shapes had ridges, teeth, wide-open mouths, leering eyes, and millions of tendrils.

I forced my eyes from the scene, and again, controlled my nerves. I'd seen plenty of hellish and bizarre formations, creatures that killed, *things* that seemed from another time and place—all back in England before I'd made the journey to Innsmouth.

When I looked up again, I focused on Fitzgerald, and shocked, saw two females with him. My heart raced. How would I infect Fitzgerald in the presence of *these* two? It would be so much easier to attack him if he was alone. And I wanted their powers to help me, not my nemesis.

One was small, young, and ran across the long sheet of rock that edged the water. *Maria Fitzgerald.* Henry Fitzgerald believed that she was his own daughter, although he cared nothing about her well-being. Actually, she was the child of the dead soprano Lucy Anne Nolande and the French leader of a Dagonite gang.

And the other female? I would never forget her. *Amelia Scarcliffe.* Even at this distance, I could swear that I saw her webbed fingers. Her hair was matted and thick like tangled netting. She was near-bursting from pregnancy, yet she gripped the slate with her toe suckers, racing after little Maria and Henry Fitzgerald. Her gills glowed with the nauseating colors of the creatures over Devil Reef. Her neck flaps were no doubt pulsing—I knew this because I had seen them up close—and they emitted high-pitched treble notes that skittered over my nerves. As she had done in London in one of my Eshocker dens, Amelia shrieked words that made no sense.

Courage, I told myself, *be strong, Moriarty. You are their equal, if not their superior. You conquered these females in England, and you will conquer them again. This time, it will be permanent.*

Fitzgerald swiveled to face his two companions. His hand waved them off. He barked something in his baritone voice, but I couldn't make out the words.

Maria stopped short with Amelia behind her. They huddled together, then raced past Fitzgerald toward a broken pier that my sources had explained creaked halfway to Devil Reef in one direction and to an abandoned fish-processing plant in the other. I supposed that Amelia and Maria, gleeful and giddy that they were in Innsmouth, where their kind thrived, were heading to the fish plant, and from there, possibly to the village.

I didn't care where they went, not for now. I wanted Professor Henry Fitzgerald to myself.

You will die, I thought, *but first, you will unwittingly kill Olengran, the worldwide leader of the Order of Dagon, he who is so revered by those in Innsmouth, he who dwells in that lopsided building you just visited. How perfect. You will do my bidding, Fitzgerald, without knowing it.*

I smeared the fog scum from my glove onto the lining of my coat pocket. *Cautious.* I didn't want the knife to slice my fingers.

Fitzgerald paused in the rain and gazed at the dwelling again. I wondered what had transpired when Fitzgerald had attempted to gain access to the building and to Olengran. Had he succeeded in seeing the great leader? A loyal servant of Dagon and the head of a major Dagonite gang in London, Fitzgerald stood a good chance of accessing Olengran, certainly a far better chance than my own.

My fingers curled around the knife handle in my pocket. I stepped from the shadows.

You are my toy, Fitzgerald. I will smile, and you will yield, dropping your guard for a few seconds, which is all I need to infect you. I could almost feel the thrill I'd get when my knife, slathered in a new and particularly virulent strain of smallpox, ripped into him. My mouth went dry from excitement. My nerves tingled. *I'll infect you*, I thought, *and through you, I'll infect Olengran and kill him.*

Sloshing through the mud, I displayed a smile, hoping Fitzgerald would view it as sincere. But he must have sensed the menace, the coldness behind my façade. Seeing me, he gasped and shrank back, and his arms rose to shield him from me.

The drizzle slashed. Above the reef, colors sizzled down like lightning. Beasts screamed, flared into view, shimmering and then fading back into the fog.

With my free hand, I reached for Fitzgerald and grabbed his elbow.

"Come, old friend," I said. "It's cold and wet out here, and the rock is dangerous. It's time for us to talk. Let's go somewhere and sit together, shall we?"

He wrenched his arm from my grasp, slid on the rock, then steadied himself.

"W-what are *you* doing here? How did you find me? How did you *know*?"

I laughed.

"It was *my* men who broke you out of jail, Professor. Surely, you didn't think that I would lose sight of you, did you?"

"*Your* men? It was *you* who freed me? I don't believe it!" He staggered back from me, and as he lurched and fell sideways, I grabbed his arm again and pulled him up so hard he winced.

I released him, and he rubbed his injured arm.

"Leave me alone," he hissed. "Leave me to my business. The Order of Dagon is not your affair. Go back to London, Moriarty."

"Come, be reasonable," I answered. "The weather couldn't be worse, old fellow. Let me buy you a drink and some dinner. Surely, there's a pub in this town...?"

"Ha!" he spat. "There is no place in this town for an ordinary man to find ordinary food. You are a ludicrous fool, Moriarty. I tell you—for your own sake—leave this place at once and return to London." Beneath his hat, the brim dripping with rain, his huge, black eyes glittered with hatred.

"Did you see Olengran?" I asked.

"No," came the fast response, "and if I had, it would be none of your business."

"And why do you consider it none of my business, Fitzgerald? I control the Dagon gang in England. You went to jail, and I took over."

"I went to jail because of Sherlock Holmes. My motives with Dagon have always been pure. Yours are based solely on greed. You understand nothing of what you tamper with. You 'took over'—as you put it—something that will destroy you."

"Did you see Olengran?" I asked again. "He *is* my business. I own the Eshockers, which control entry of Olengran's followers into our world." It was a stretch, I knew, but there was some truth to my statement. The Eshockers, as reported throughout London, had cured Dr. Watson and many Londoners of the microscopic creatures that had infiltrated their brains. Holmes and Watson had used a modified version of the Eshockers to destroy the creatures in the Thames. I still owned hundreds of the machines, though I had yet to get my hands on Dr. Sinclair's hospital and extreme treatment versions, much less the killer version built by Willie Jacobs, Holmes, and Watson.

"Sherlock Holmes shut down all of your Eshocker dens," Fitzgerald said. "You know that, and I know that. You destroyed my London operation. You and that dreadful Holmes with his chemistry—he stopped the Jacobs tram machine from pumping out my gold, he stopped me from bringing forth Yog-Sothoth, the Old Ones, and Great Cthulhu. And you—what was your role in all this, but to step in, kidnap Amelia Scarcliffe and Maria, and *try* to take over the Dagonite gang? Yes, sir, that's what you did, and I have forgotten nothing."

My hand tightened on the knife handle. I'd hoped to ease the man into a more agreeable position before infecting him. I'd hoped it would be less painful for him to do what I required. I ached from the cold and wet. I wanted to find shelter. I'd arrived in Innsmouth, by boat, mere hours ago. I needed a meal and a warm bed. My patience was wearing thin. I would try once more to reason with him.

"If you're willing to help me with just a little information," I said, "I'll go easy on you, and I won't hurt your daughter."

"You are a liar, sir."

"And you, Fitzgerald, are the biggest fool I've met in a very long time."

I whipped out the glistening knife. *I dare not delay. The rain, the smallpox on the knife. I must act quickly.*

"What—!" he cried, but too late. I lunged, not to kill him, not to injure him unduly, but rather, to infect him. The knife slashed his right cheek. He fell backward, this time landing on the rock, and he screamed in pain.

"Idiot," I said.

He rose, his face mottled with fury. Blood flowed from the gash on his cheek. He threw himself at me, and for a moment, we grappled. Then I shoved him off and held up the knife, still dripping with his blood.

The fog had grown thicker, the night darker, the rain heavier.

"I'll kill you!" he screamed, balling his hand into a fist. He lunged, and I stepped to one side and blocked the blow to my face with the knife. I felt the blade plunge into soft flesh, then I yanked it out. He winced and clasped his fist with his other hand.

"Damn you, Moriarty!"

"It is not I who am damned," I whispered.

Before me stood a dying man. He was simply unaware of the fact.

I turned and walked away, glancing over my shoulder a few times to make sure he didn't follow and attack me again. But he remained standing on the rock, glaring at me. Eventually, as I moved farther off, his figure disappeared into the fog.

He would lick his wounds, I felt sure, and return to wherever he dwelled in Innsmouth. And I would wait. The smallpox would do the work for me. Fitzgerald would get past Olengran's guards. Infected with the deadly disease, Olengran would die, and I would assume control of the worldwide headquarters of the Dagon gang with all its powers from the great beyond. The murderous creatures, the gold-cranking machines, the addiction dens: all would be mine. Not only would I control the criminal underworld of London, I would control crime, money, and power everywhere.

2
DR. JOHN WATSON

January 1891, Innsmouth, Massachusetts

Sherlock Holmes leaned on the ship's rail and gazed at the choppy waves. Hugging Mary closer, I shuddered when I remembered my last journey with Holmes on a boat this size. My wife, in turn, clasped our infant Samuel more tightly as if guessing my thoughts.

"We're almost at port, John. We'll arrive safely," she said, and then added, "I'm sure."

"Of course, we will," I replied, but my voice trembled. The Belle Crown incident on the Thames haunted my dreams. Incident, I thought, is a sterile term for what we'd endured. Thankfully, whatever had infected my brain was gone. Holmes had cleansed London of the near-invisible creatures that had penetrated our brains, driven many insane, and left a lot of Londoners broken in spirit. "We will consider this a holiday by the sea for you and Samuel," I told Mary. "We will make the best of it. Together. I'm so happy that you have returned to me. I was desperately lonely without you."

Samuel gurgled, and I stroked a wisp of hair from his tiny gray eyes. His mouth sucked the air, reaching for my fingertip, making me laugh. He was always hungry, this one, born prematurely but growing sturdier by the day.

The sky hung low, a darker gray than Samuel's eyes. Clouds threatened to burst, and the wind whipped, picking up speed. In the distance, where our ship, the *Elysium*, was headed, the sky formed a thick black mat from which a curtain of rain fell.

The ship pitched, and Holmes's fists tightened on the rail. Tall, leaner than usual due to our battles against the Order of Dagon these past months, he appeared gaunt, and I worried about his health. But his penetrating gaze told me that his mind was as sharp as ever.

"Soon, we'll be in Innsmouth, at the headquarters of that nefarious Order of Dagon," he said. "The fools who follow Dagon claim that he is some form of god. A ludicrous notion, Watson. I'm anxious to find Dagon himself or the man who leads his organization. We must destroy them once and for all."

I nodded, my attention on Fortuna, Samuel's nurse, as she eased him from Mary's arms. Next to Mary's delicate features, blue eyes, and blonde hair, Fortuna appeared dark and dangerous, but I knew her well—she was loving, kind, and incapable of disloyalty. She had been a patient of mine for years. Widowed in her teens and without children of her own, Fortuna devoted herself to Mary and Samuel. Her hair, black and curly and hanging to her waist, flew in all directions as the wind grew stronger and howled. Casting me a worried look, she carried Samuel down the stairs to the lower cabin. Mary followed, grasping the rails as the ship heaved. We careened down the side of a steep wave, and icy water splashed over me, soaking my coat, trousers, and shirt. With the waves getting higher, blasts of air pounded the *Elysium*. I could barely remain upright. Holmes merely laughed and flipped his wet hair off his face.

"When the British government requested that we travel to America, specifically to Innsmouth," he yelled over the wind, "they said that the weather would remind us of London. From what I see ahead, Innsmouth will be damper, colder, and even more bleak. Finally, a place with weather worse than our own."

Shrugging and giving Holmes a brief smile, I neglected to share his amusement about heavy rain and winds. As the ship clanked and soared up the side of another steep wave, I grabbed the rail next to him. We must have shot fifteen feet into the air. My stomach churned, and I groaned as the ship smashed down the other side of the wave.

"Apparently, there's not much demand for holidays in Innsmouth," Holmes yelled, "as we are the only passengers onboard."

It's no wonder, I thought. *Who would willingly go to Innsmouth?* The Pinkertons, American detectives who would be meeting us on the dock, had forewarned Holmes that the shanty town offered nothing but filth, foul odors, and weird people.

"What do they mean by weird people?" Holmes had asked the British official who escorted us to the *Elysium*.

"If I tell you, Mr. Holmes, you might refuse our assignment," the man had responded. "When you arrive in Innsmouth, you will see for yourself what the Pinkertons mean. Just go there, and get rid of this plague that has infested our good lands. Get rid of Dagon, and get rid of this Cthulhu monster... whatever they are and wherever they come from."

The Dagonite gang in London worshiped Cthulhu, a gigantic creature that had been spotted lurking in the waters near Innsmouth. I prayed we reached shore before it rose from the depths and killed us. I didn't want to see Cthulhu, didn't want to confront Cthulhu, yet Holmes and I had no choice. Nobody else would handle this case but Holmes. As for me, I had no clue how we would outwit Dagon, much less Cthulhu.

The waves pounded us a few more times, then subsided into ten-foot rolls that hit us with less frequency. The wind eased.

"The only good thing about the waves and the wind," I commented drily, "is that they carry off the stench of our cargo."

Holmes chuckled.

"Fish and fish bait," he said. "If we don't eat or smell fish again for another year, Watson, I won't miss it."

Thankfully, the ship's cargo also included Killer Eshockers built in London. We might need them, along with the electrified torpedoes that killed the monsters and sealed the dimensional rifts.

"I do wish we had Willie Jacobs with us," I said. "His expertise would come in handy. After all, he helped us build the first Killer Eshockers."

"Indeed. It was a sorry day when Jacobs died in the equipment room while we took down those Thames creatures. A true loss to the world. He was a good man."

"The best," I said.

Jacobs had been our first client in this case against creatures from an unknown place and time. With his father, Theodore, and funded by Professor Henry Fitzgerald, Willie Jacobs had built a tram machine that used Dagonite arithmetic and design to produce gold—but the machine had brought forth terrible creatures from another dimension, and so had cost Theodore his life. Willie Jacobs had first come to Holmes after the police accused him of the murder. And even after we had cleared his name, and Holmes's chemical knowledge had reduced the machine to what he termed "a simmer," poor Willie had seen the nightmarish creatures everywhere he went. Committed to an asylum, he had been forced to build Eshockers by the dreadful Dr. Sinclair—but his knowledge had proved invaluable in building the Killer Eshocker and freeing London of the creatures. He had given his life to end the suffering of others.

How many more would die? I wondered.

"Holmes, we must close this case. We must get justice for Willie and his father," I said.

"And don't forget Moriarty, Dr. Watson. We must stop him. Once he found out the tram machine produced gold beyond his wildest dreams, he became a man obsessed—we saw how that turned out. Now he lives only to control the immense powers of these monsters. If ever a man wanted to control the world, it is Professor James Moriarty."

Riches and power, greed and egomania. What drove a man like Moriarty, with his vast intelligence, to go down the evil path? Holmes's path had been the opposite. He'd turned his intelligence to solving mysteries and crimes; in all the years I'd known him, Holmes had displayed no interest in riches and power. Certainly, he knew he was smarter than the rest of us, but egomaniacal? No.

A ridge of craggy rocks jutted half a mile offshore, and as it came into view, the waves eased into choppiness; and relief washed over me. The ship would not split down the center as the *Belle Crown* had done; Mary and Samuel would not drown in the ocean. My stomach still churned, and dizzy, I leaned over the rail.

"Steady, old man," Holmes said, then pointed at our destination. "We'll board the ship's smaller boat to take us past Devil Reef and into port. The ship will drop anchor here."

Down below, the crew ground the ship to a halt, and we lurched a final time. I squinted at Devil Reef. Swirling around the rocks was an oddly hued fog—or was it foam?—that sizzled, bubbled, and disappeared, only to form spheres and boxes and complex shapes of many sides and angles. The shapes whirled and coalesced into tendrils, and what I swore looked like eyes, mouths, teeth, claws, suckers, and tubules.

"What *is* this?" I whispered harshly.

"John?" A soft voice.

I turned from the rail. It was Mary. She clutched her skirts with one hand, Samuel with the other. Climbing the stairs from the lower bunk behind Mary, Fortuna carried a Moses basket and a bag.

"Don't let anything frighten you," I told them.

Mary laughed. "Whatever do you mean?"

From below, two crewmen emerged with our luggage. We'd brought little with us to Innsmouth. Hopefully, our stay would be brief.

Suddenly, Mary cringed and shielded Samuel's eyes with his blanket. She pointed at Devil Reef, as a large translucent orb bubbled up from the rocks, burst, and sprayed hundreds of creatures into the wind.

"They're like the ones over the Thames!" she cried.

Fortuna dropped her things, and crossed herself, murmuring a horrified prayer. She'd grown up in a traveling caravan of gypsies, and while she believed in more superstitions than I thought possible, she also swore by a deep faith.

As the crewmen lowered the smaller boat into the water, our little group huddled together. I tried comforting Mary as best as I could, while Fortuna muttered, "The devil, *the devil*."

"It's not the devil," I said. "These creatures are from

another place and time. We'll make it past the reef and safely to Innsmouth. You will all be safe, tucked away and guarded."

Holmes picked up Fortuna's basket and bag in one hand and put his other arm around her shoulder. He squeezed, then released her. Both stared at Devil Reef and the equally jagged outline of Innsmouth beyond. Dreary, dark shapes— the buildings, I presumed—looked as ill-formed and bizarrely clustered as the rocks of Devil Reef. As they did on Devil Reef, strange hues sparked in the black clouds, fog, and rain of Innsmouth. I stared, mesmerized, as the colors illuminated the coastline—a flash of dilapidated ruins.

Holmes addressed Fortuna.

"Madame, you must be strong. You're here to protect Mrs. Watson and little Samuel. Let nothing distract you from your purpose."

"Yes, yes, Mr. Holmes. I saw these horrors in London, but this—this is of the devil himself."

Indeed, as she spoke, a green gas rose from the rock spikes of the reef and formed a flute at its top. From that flute soared a monster with a spiked tail, wings, and at least a dozen mouths drilled into its body.

"Whatever it is," Mary said, "it is not of this Earth. Fortuna, it is not the work of the devil." She broke off and eased slightly from my embrace. "John, I want life to be simple and *firm*, as it was before... I want to know that what I see is *real*. Please, let's get off this ship and let's get this *done*."

Holmes handed Fortuna's belongings back to her, then

climbed down the rope ladder onto the small boat. He gestured at me to follow. I helped Mary and Samuel onto the ladder. Holmes grasped Mary's waist and helped her down, and she settled on a wooden bench. Her face clouded, she glanced nervously at me. I managed a faint smile. I *had* begged her to stay in London with Samuel.

"There are dangers in Innsmouth," I'd said back in the safety of our sitting room. "It may be worse than what we saw in the Thames. Holmes and I must journey to the center of the creatures, Mary, the center of all the horror. I don't want you there."

With Samuel sleeping in her arms, she'd frowned at me as she did now.

"Samuel and I have only just returned. I am frightened, John. Of course, I am. That's why I left London, and you. But I fear that if we part again, our marriage will weaken. Another parting might be our last. I missed you too much when we left. I can't bear to miss you like that again. It's breaking my heart. It's more than I can bear. I'd rather risk going with you than losing you."

I'd jumped from my chair, exasperated.

"But Mary, you won't lose me. I'll be gone a short while, then I'll return safely to you, and forever."

"London is still not safe," she'd answered, lowering her eyes. "What's the difference if I'm here *without* you or there *with* you? Frankly, I'd feel safer with you than alone in London with Samuel."

She'd had a point. During our earlier investigations

into the deadly dimensions and the neural psychoses that had gripped London, Holmes and I had relied upon both the police and Willie Jacobs to protect Mary and Samuel. Jacobs had almost died saving their lives in our own lodgings. And the police, what good had they been? Even Mary had been able to slip past their guard when she left me and ran off terrified with Samuel tucked beneath her coat. Perhaps my family *was* safer with me and Holmes than without us in London.

Holmes and I gathered the luggage from the crewmen, who hoisted the rope ladder back onto the ship. With a brief salute, they departed, presumably to begin collecting the fish cargo and transporting it to shore after us.

Thankfully, the small boat had an engine and power, relieving Holmes and me of the task of rowing through heavy waters and over killer rocks. The engine was a Priestman Brothers, a new model, powered by kerosene or some other form of ordinary lamp oil: I'd seen plenty of these boats transporting cargo in London. The engine sat in the middle of the boat, a huge contraption with many pipes and tubes, and with cables coiled on the floor. Near the engine, Holmes sat on an overturned box, steering us toward our destiny.

I shivered from the water soaking my clothes, as did Mary and Fortuna, who were huddled on either side of me. *It could be worse*, I told myself. *After all, it is January, and we could be in the midst of an ice storm or a blizzard.*

Yards from us loomed Devil Reef. As it grew closer, the

rocks looked higher, more jagged, and more deadly. The monsters looked bigger and stranger. I saw intelligence behind the hundreds of eyes that peered at us from all directions. I also saw claws, pointed teeth, bat wings, bodies of grotesque shapes riddled with suckers and with cavities that oozed viscous substances.

Samuel wailed, making the creatures around us jitter, bounce, and howl. Mary soothed him and held him closer. On my other side, Fortuna hid her face against my shoulder.

Holmes steered the boat horizontally along the reef, which towered over us, the tops of the rocks hooked like claws. Sprouting from the rock, gelatinous strands and multi-flowered globules glowed.

Hundreds of eyes, maybe thousands, watched our every move, as they swiveled on fleshy stalks or from body recesses to follow us.

"Do you have your gun, Watson?" Holmes asked.

Nudging Fortuna off my shoulder, I slipped my hand into my pocket and fingered the weapon. What good would it do against all these creatures? God help us, what if they infiltrated our brains, our bodies, and drove us mad? What if they killed the baby? *What if, what if...*

My mind whirled with the horrors, the possibilities.

"I have the gun, yes," I murmured.

"Keep it at hand, Watson," Holmes said. "Up ahead, I see an opening. Get ready. We're going to speed up, and I'm going to take us through as fast as I can."

At that moment, the monsters of Devil Reef screaked

and burred, yammered and skirled, and vaulted from the rocks. Others splashed up from the depths, whisked into the wind, tentacles lashing, mouths gnawing at the air, bulbous bodies descending...

Plunging right at us.

3

I yanked both Mary and Fortuna down, and the three of us slid from the bench to the floor of the boat. Then I stood back up, fumbling for my gun, as a winged beast—as fat as a cow—shot from a rock and almost slammed into my head. It missed me by an inch or two—so close that I smelled it, and ducking, I tripped over Fortuna's legs. She sat closest to the reef and shifted toward Mary. Samuel cried steadily—I knew not whether from exhaustion, from the noise around us, or from the fear emanating from Mary. The boat tilted up at the far end that held our luggage. Holmes wrenched the steering mechanism—a small wheel embedded atop a large box—to the left.

Whipping off my coat, I covered Mary, Fortuna, and Samuel with it.

"Get down," I ordered them, "and stay down."

I pulled out the gun, no fumbling this time, aimed, and shot at the larger creatures flinging themselves at the boat. Bullets blasted into hide but seemed to have no effect on the creatures, which continued to flail tentacles, snap jaws, and dive at me. By now, monsters of all types had attached themselves to the coat, suckers pulling at the cloth, teeth ripping at it.

"Holmes," I screamed, "get us out of here!"

He didn't answer. His back to me, he swung the wheel steadily as the boat angled into a clear waterway between the rocks.

I swatted at one of the monsters nearest me, a beast with dozens of mouths and numerous clawed feet. It was thick with muscle, covered in bristles, and heavy with tentacles, all coated with suckers. When my left fist tightened on one of the tentacles, I recoiled but made sure to hold on. Beneath the bristles, the flesh was slimy. Before I knew what was happening, the creature attached two suckers to my palm, and I felt the burn of bleeding pain.

My bullets were spent, and besides, had done no good.

Recovering slightly, I shoved the gun back into my pocket, and then I punched the creature as hard as I could. I got it between two eye stalks. It screeched and clacked, and several other creatures detached from the coat and flung themselves at me.

Meanwhile, the boat zoomed through the opening between the rocks. On both sides, Devil Reef stood tall and ominous, all spikes and barbs woven with nettle, its lances dripping with ichor. The rock itself was an unearthly hue: specks of color merging into charcoal and ash, pulsing with a sickly tinge. The reef was a cancer.

As we cleared it, the boat rose on a giant wave then fell, and Holmes steered us past looming boulders and slabs of sheer rock. Waves thundered over the rocks and broke, a dark froth under the swarthy sky. The creatures that had flung themselves at me fell to the rocks, piping and warbling in octaves well above the range of the human voice. Although they seemed to melt away, I told myself that they had instead disappeared beneath the water.

With no help from Holmes—he was occupied keeping the boat afloat—I had to cope with the remaining beasts on my own. I whipped out my gun again, and using the butt, hammered at the one whose suckers still grasped my other palm. Fortuna slid from beneath my coat, and half of the creatures fell back into the water. I wobbled and fell to my knees. Fortuna yelled at Holmes to get off the steering box, and he did as told, sitting instead on the boat's edge. She then lifted the box—and I knew that it was heavy from the way she struggled with it—and slammed it down on the hideous thing that held me captive.

The suckers popped open. I jerked up my hand. The palm a bloody mess, I wriggled my fingers—they could still move—and then beat on the monster while Fortuna battered it with the box.

Samuel was still crying, and I could hear Mary whimpering beneath my coat, as well. I knew she would have jumped up and helped us if it were not for Samuel. She would protect him at all costs, even if it meant sacrificing her own life.

The boat careened off a small boulder and crashed

through the surf toward shore. With Fortuna bashing the creature, I lifted my coat off Mary—she stared at me with a look on her face as if she were screaming, *What are you doing, John?*—and I threw the coat into the water. With it went the creatures, still shrieking and clacking and clawing at the air. Mary's face softened, and she turned her attention to Samuel, cooing at him and holding him close. I nearly wept from relief.

I had to dispense with a final creature with eye stalks and suckers and with tentacles flailing on the floor of the boat.

"Lift it!" I cried, and together, Fortuna and I hoisted the monstrosity up and flung it overboard. It hit a spike, but bounced off and splashed into the sea spray, which carried it over a jutting rock. The creature fell off the far end, and by the time our boat got there, the monstrosity had disappeared.

Fortuna and I both sank to the wooden bench, moaning and holding our heads in our hands. My injured palm would require bandaging once we got to shore.

Lifting herself back onto the bench and hugging me, Mary kissed me. I embraced her and stroked Samuel's head beneath his wet baby blanket. He was so tiny, still so fragile, and I feared for him.

"That was much too close, Mary," I said.

She paused for a long time before answering me.

"Soon we'll be guarded by the Pinkertons," she finally said, and then, "I still feel safer with you, John, than back in London without you. I don't know if there *is* a safe place in this world with those creatures loose."

I assumed she was putting on a brave front. What other choice did she have at this point?

"Yes," I replied, matching her tone, "the Pinkertons will protect you at our little hideout in the countryside."

But I wasn't so sure about that.

Holmes steadied the boat, and we cruised over moderate surf to a dilapidated pier. Fishing boats bobbed in the water, tied to splintered posts poking from a near-slatless walkway. The wood was gray from rot. At the end facing the ocean, the whole pier slumped into the water as if trying to drown itself.

Holmes called over his shoulder.

"The Pinkertons are well respected here in America, I assure you. They can't solve complex mysteries, but I understand that they are quite successful with ordinary crime, and with criminals, in general."

"The Americans have told us that the monsters don't venture inland," I assured Mary, "at least, not yet."

Cold rain welcomed us to Innsmouth. The fog billowed in places, roiled in others, occasionally parting to show us the hovel of the town. A few glimpses were enough to dishearten me. The worst slum of London would be a paradise compared to this place.

Crumbled buildings crouched by a black-mud beach that stretched to a large expanse of rock serving as the shore. The buildings were indistinguishable from one another, gray with rot, their windows shuttered. They were unlike any place of habitation I'd seen in England. Just jumbles of wood nailed together to form shack-like barriers from the wind and mud. Lopsided messes, some roofless, others with sides missing.

What must have been a door swung open from one, catching my eye. Like the others, the shack was a crumbled mess. The roof was a thicket of mud and driftwood thwacked into a thirty-degree angle. What emerged from the dwelling was someone barely recognizable as human. Perhaps it was the distance, for after all, we remained in the boat at the end of the pier.

The Innsmouth resident differed from the oddly shaped Dagonites I had come across in London. This fellow, or perhaps, woman, had a multi-humped back, causing him... it... him... her... to bend at the waist and totter rather than walk. One leg was at least a foot shorter than the other.

He... she fell into the black mud and shrilled loudly, then rolled like a pig, coating him... herself with the muck. The keening continued, as he/she hurled gobs of mud into the air.

"What is—" I started to say, pointing, but the fog roiled over the shore, obscuring my view.

"I saw it, too," Holmes said, his voice sharp. "Come along and help, Watson, would you?"

The boat had bumped into the rotting pier next to a craft filled with fish heads. The stench was unbearable. I almost lost my last meal of... fish.

"Let's get away from here, and quickly," Fortuna insisted. Poor woman, she looked exhausted. She'd been in our employ for only a day or so before we had left for

Innsmouth—not exactly a holiday resort. To my credit, however, I had been honest and told her about the trip before she signed on with us.

"I have nobody in London, sir," she'd said, "and I have no other work. Not many will hire a gypsy to watch over their wee ones. You've been kind to me over the years, and I am honored to work for you, Dr. Watson, and for your wife."

"We will treat you like family," I had responded, "I promise."

Her smile had filled my heart with warmth. It was true that I had always been kind to her—treated her illnesses for free and listened to her problems. I understood her loyalty. But in doing kindness, I always felt that I was more the recipient, for to see such a smile was a gift worth more than anything. Perhaps this was why I had become a doctor, to help people, to put kindness into the world.

On the other hand, I knew of no other way to earn a living.

Holmes led the way down the pier, carefully stepping across broken slats and holes in the wood. Mary was holding Samuel, and I hovered nearby to make sure she didn't fall. Fortuna followed us. We moved slowly, and every time a plank rattled, fear bolted through me.

As we neared the shore, the pier shook with our every step. The planks wobbled, cracked, and splintered off. With a loud sucking noise, the water strained up and pulled the slats beneath the surface.

Reaching the sheet of rock, we jumped from the pier, which continued as a walkway toward a low building in the distance. The fog swirled and settled on my already wet shirt and trousers. As we tottered toward the mud beach, Holmes wiped scum off his coat and flicked it to the rocks. The stench of dead fish rose and merged with the foulness of excrement and garbage.

Samuel, quiet at last, slept in Mary's arms.

I pointed at the multi-humped person squealing and tossing sludge into the air. *Who rolls in the mud?* I thought.

"Is that a child?" I asked Holmes, and he squinted through the fog and drizzle.

"It is hard to tell exactly what..." he said, and then, "Ah, he's standing, hunched over with multiple lobes jutting off his back. One leg appears significantly shorter than the other. His odd caterwauling reminds me of our stay at the *Loggerheads*, when we were surrounded by Dagonites who shrieked and clucked all night. I would say this is a Dagonite, Watson."

"Like those poor fellows at Swallowhead Spring," I said, referring to the worshipers of Dagon—deformed and squealing nonsense in high octaves—who had gathered for a bizarre rendition of Bellini's *Norma*.

"Do you think he's a man or a woman?" Fortuna asked.

As if on cue, the Innsmouthian plucked something out of the mud and placed it on his back between two of three humps.

"I'd say this is a woman," Holmes said drily. He led us into the mud. My foot sank several inches into the muck, and I had to wrench my leg up so as not to lose my shoe. With each yank of my foot from the sludge, rancid air bubbled up.

"But why do you say that it is a woman?" I asked.

"Look closely," Fortuna answered.

"Yes, dear fellow, do look," Holmes said with a chuckle.

In that moment, I knew why we were looking at an Innsmouthian female. Her *child* clasped one hump with both arms and sucked on the tip of a second hump. The child was feeding.

As we passed the mother and her child, Mary and Fortuna tried not to stare at them, and I recoiled from the sight. Holmes also observed them but displayed no reaction.

The child slurped from the hump tip, its face streaked in mud and green goo. Fur resembling rat hair covered the entire head—face and scalp—and where there should have been a nose and two eyes, three additional mouths sucked at the air. As for the mother, she was no beauty queen. The odd fur covered her head, as well—perhaps it was a family trait—and she brayed and whistled from four mouths bored into what might have been her face. Her arms were longer than her legs and hung to the ground, and her fingers were snakes. Both she and her child wore mummy-like swathes of cloth caked in mud. The mother growled, then looked over her shoulder at the child and blurted out words that sounded like gibberish. She sloshed backward and lowered herself as if preparing to leap and attack. The child clung more tightly to the humps.

I wrenched my eyes away.

"Nothing like a day at the beach," Holmes muttered.

Mary and Fortuna scurried past us, slopping mud—or

was it offal?—all over their skirts, coats, and fine shoes. After struggling up a jumbled array of alleys, we came to the edge of the village, where a buggy waited. A man—*a normal human man*—held open the door and called out to us in an American accent.

"I'm your Pinkerton, Mr. Holmes! Welcome to Innsmouth and to America! We've been awaiting your arrival with much anticipation. And this must be Dr. Watson, with your lovely wife and baby, and—"

"Fortuna, who is my best friend and Samuel's nurse," Mary chimed in.

"Harry Rinsdale," our new friend replied, "at your service." The Pinkerton was a bright sight, indeed. Clean clothes, top hat, no-nonsense features. His mustache was old-fashioned, long and bushy, curled at the ends. He had chubby red cheeks and wore spectacles. I liked him immediately.

While he helped Mary and Fortuna into the buggy, Rinsdale chattered amiably with them. Then he helped Holmes into the vehicle, and I climbed in last.

"Don't mind what you see here," he said, his accent so strong that I found it a little difficult to understand him. "Innsmouth is its own little corner of the world. Most Americans are folks just like you and me."

My mood lifted. Our long voyage was over. The nightmarish trek from the boat to the shore was over.

"I must say it's blissful," I said to Holmes, who was crammed next to me on the seat, "to be in a warm, dry buggy, looking forward to an equally warm and dry room with a comfortable bed."

"A hot bath," Mary sighed.

"Food," Fortuna said.

"As long as it's not fish," I said.

Rinsdale chortled. "I'm afraid, sir, that fish is all they serve in these parts, so you'll have to make do."

Closing the door, he climbed onto the driver's seat and snapped the reins, and the horse trotted off at a snappy pace.

I must have dozed, for the next thing I knew, the buggy jerked to a halt, and we were in a forest with mature pines and oak trees. The sky was a slumped shadow. The rain had petered to a drip. The fog had cleared. As Harry Rinsdale opened the buggy door, a gust of refreshing air hit us, and collectively, we sucked it into our lungs. My hand hurt from the sucker attack, and I noticed that it had swollen. It would probably ache for a day or two, I thought as I inspected it, but it wouldn't bother me much after that.

We clambered from the vehicle and thanked Rinsdale, who gestured at a large house with framed windows and wood siding painted blue.

"Your lodgings," he said.

"Very nice," Holmes said. "Notice the steep gabled roofs, the round right side extending three levels up, the section jutting from the left side, the profusion of porches—that small one on the third floor, the half-wraparound on the main level. How old is this magnificent house, Mr. Rinsdale?"

"I'd say, fifty years," he answered, "but fully modernized.

I'll be staying here with you along with several other Pinkerton detectives."

Indeed, it was an elaborate house, and I brightened to think of my family here. A wide lawn separated the back from the surrounding forest, and on both sides of the house, bushes and evergreens made the place welcoming.

"Thankfully, quite different from the dwellings in Innsmouth," I said. "Mr. Rinsdale, how far are we from town?"

"You were sleeping, Dr. Watson," Holmes said. "Not far at all. We're near the village, perhaps thirty minutes by buggy."

"It's almost the only residence in these parts that is *not* in Innsmouth," Rinsdale said. "There are no hospitable accommodations in town that I would recommend for a family, or... anyone, to be frank. It wasn't easy, as it were, to persuade the owners of this place to let you stay here."

"No?" Holmes raised his eyebrows. "And why was that?"

Harry Rinsdale carried our luggage, and with Holmes and me hauling the rest, we headed toward the mansion. The front door was curved with Gothic angles and had an octopus knocker. A flurry of panic ripped through me. I'd seen such knockers before—on the homes of the Dagonites.

Rinsdale turned and answered Holmes.

"Let us say, sir, that Frederick Cararo and his wife, Hortense, aren't the most normal Americans you'll meet. They're not quite like you and me—if you get my gist."

4

Are Frederick and Hortense Cararo deformed, I wondered, *like the Dagonites, like the Innsmouthian mother and child?*

"Do you mean to say—" I started, when Holmes interrupted me.

"Mr. Rinsdale, I assume that our hosts look like ordinary humans. I assume that they have two arms and two legs, one head with a mouth, two eyes, and so forth. Otherwise, the Pinkertons would have found another place for us to stay. I know, you say that there is no other place, but surely, the Pinkerton detectives are staying in the village."

"You are correct," Rinsdale replied, as he swung open the front door, "that we would *not* have acquired rooms for you in the home of a villager. However, you are incorrect to assume that my companions and I have taken lodgings in Innsmouth. We most certainly have not."

We all followed Rinsdale into the house, and I gazed at the room to our left and the hall in front of us. A carved wood arch with matching columns separated us from the room. The hall led to a curved staircase winding up to a landing that stretched across a hexagonal room. Halfway down the hall was another carved arch supported by columns and topped by red-and-blue stenciled trim. The stenciled pattern also extended along the tops of the walls in the room to the left.

"An odd pattern for this style of house," Mary said, following my gaze. "I would think that any stencils would be of flowers and leaves, something to do with nature. But this pattern, hexagons and tendrils, lovely as it is, seems out of place."

"Decorating issues aside," Rinsdale interrupted, "you are lucky to be in the Cararo home."

"Yes," Mary said, "of course. I didn't mean to imply otherwise."

"The family is a bit odd. You may find the household habits and decor somewhat outré. I understand, believe me." Rinsdale smiled at my wife, who reached for my hand and squeezed it. "My agency has no presence in Innsmouth. My own home is in Boston, for example. I'm here, as are my companions, to be of service to Dr. Watson. Only to protect your family," he added quickly.

Rinsdale was a grown man, a detective in an elite agency. Yet he was afraid of something—the horrors of Devil Reef, the Innsmouthians, Cthulhu? All shook me to my core, and we'd only just arrived.

Feeling it best that we all bathe, eat, and rest before further discussion, Rinsdale rang for servants. Two women in aprons scurried from a rear recess of the house and down the main hall. I realized the hexagonal room was not the back of the house, that the building extended more deeply beyond the hexagon before opening to the rear gardens.

The evening passed quickly. I requested bandages and ointment, which the two women helped apply to my injured hand. Then we dined on fish broth, fresh bread, and apple cobbler, and before I knew it, Mary, Samuel, and I were fast asleep.

Other than baby feedings, we slept soundly, and by morning, our wretched journey through Devil Reef felt almost surreal, as if it hadn't happened. Mary remained visibly shaken but didn't want to discuss what we'd seen. She did ask once if there was anyone else who could handle the case with Holmes other than me. She knew my answer, and I didn't have to state it. The case of the deadly dimensions, of the neural psychoses, of its conclusion in Innsmouth required more of Holmes than he'd ever faced. I had to be by his side to see the case through to the end. Should I leave Holmes alone, and should something happen to him, I wouldn't be able to live with myself. I also couldn't imagine a world in which Mary and Samuel and other decent, normal people lived alongside the likes of Cthulhu, Dagon, and those monstrous creatures that seemed to kill with neither reason nor motive.

In our room, one would think the world was fine and without care. The fire crackled with warmth. The bed, surrounded by velvety peach curtains, was plush, and the linens were fresh. I opened the shutters and peered out the window. The rear gardens did indeed reach to the forest, but the plantings were meager, just a few random bushes and trees. Perhaps there had once been a pattern or a beauty to the gardens, but the owners had neglected them for decades.

After a breakfast of salted fish in various sauces, which I thought peculiar and Mary did not like, the women and Samuel returned upstairs. Holmes and I remained in the dining room, sipping strong coffee, which I deplore, at a table designed for thirty. Four candelabra with half-burned candles were set along the table's length. Stale smoke filled the room from the near-dead fire. Servants bustled in and out, feeding us, taking away our dishes, and then refilling the fireplace with logs and fanning the flames.

"Will the master of the house be here soon?" Holmes inquired of a young girl placing cakes—exactly two cakes—on the table. She curtsied, telling us that Mr. Cararo would join us shortly.

"I don't suppose you have come across cakes like these before, Doctor," Holmes said lightly. "They call them muffins in this country, though they are rather different from our own. Would you care to try one?"

"No," I said. "I'm afraid, dear fellow, that the herring has taken away my appetite."

"It's no great deduction," he said, "that Rinsdale was right about the fare here. We'd best get used to fish at every meal, or we'll starve." He pulled out his pipe, filled it, and lit it, rapping the table impatiently with his fingers. "I'm anxious to get moving on the case. We rested enough last night. Where is this Frederick Cararo? Blast it, Watson, where are Rinsdale and the other Pinkertons?"

At that moment, Rinsdale entered with two other men, one heavily muscled and tall, the other slender with red hair and sharp blue eyes. All three nodded at us, then to my astonishment, stood on either side of the doorway and bowed slightly.

I half-rose, as did Holmes, and we exchanged a glance before returning our attention to the doorway. An ancient man, leaning on a cane, hobbled into the room. His hair was a mass of white curls, his face angular with a fat, battle-scarred nose. His eyes were huge, black, and fierce: they lashed around the room, as if he sought evidence of wrongdoing. Thin lips formed a straight line over which an even thinner mustache was etched. He wore a blue velvet waistcoat with black satin lapels over black flannel trousers. A chiffon shirt peeked from beneath the waistcoat, with ruffles at his wrists.

Taking their places at the dining table, the Pinkertons avoided each other's eyes. *This man must be very rich and powerful to make three detectives bow at his presence,* I thought.

His cane jabbed the air, pointing at Holmes and then at me.

"Mr. Sherlock Holmes and Dr. John Watson," he rasped. "I am Frederick Cararo, your host. Sit. We're all friends here." As we returned to our seats, he cleared his throat and the withered voice croaked, "May I introduce my wife, Mrs. Frederick Cararo, or as I call her, the lovely Hortense." He gestured at a woman, who entered behind him.

Holmes's eyes widened and glittered with interest. Mrs. Cararo was in much better condition than her husband. I put her at forty or perhaps fifty years his junior. She was neither a beauty nor lackluster. Oddly, her movements and demeanor were overtly sensual. She swiveled rather than walked. With a flip of her hand, she tossed her hair over her shoulder and coyly looked first at Holmes and then at me. She was well endowed, as it were, with an ample chest and a small waist apparent beneath the long-sleeved satin gown slinking down her body. *Was this appropriate attire for an American lady?*

"Pardon me," she said, her voice sultry, "are you gentlemen startled by me?" She emitted a slight giggle, which made Holmes's eyes widen yet more.

He stood, straightened his jacket, tipped his chin up, and took her hand.

"Mrs. Cararo," he said in a formal tone, "it is a pleasure to meet you *and* your husband." He turned and bowed briefly at the other. "You have our utmost appreciation for extending your gracious hospitality to us."

"Harrumph," Frederick Cararo snorted. "The government insisted. Prattled on and on about the country, the government, dire urgency. Don't think for a second that we *wanted* you here, Mr. Holmes."

"Speak for yourself," his wife said.

Holmes withdrew his hand, as another fellow sauntered into the room. He was impeccably groomed and dressed: wool flannel trousers and coat, starched shirt, brown hair trimmed to perfection. A handsome man in his mid-years, he introduced himself as Dr. Jacob Dragoon.

"I'm a friend of the Cararos," he said, "as well as the family doctor. How do you do? Jeffrey, their delightful little boy, fell ill in the night, and Mrs. Cararo called me over. I'll be on my way soon but wanted to meet the famous Mr. Sherlock Holmes first. We hear much of your adventures from overseas, sir, thanks to your friend, Dr. Watson."

"You have read my accounts of Holmes's work?" I asked.

"We have indeed, sir, and if anyone can get to the bottom of this nightmare, it's Mr. Holmes. This monster, this Cthulhu, terrifies us all. He lurks right off our shores. Innsmouth has been isolated for decades: those strange folk keep to themselves, don't cause us any trouble, never come into Boston or Plymouth. You might say they're like a separate colony," he chuckled.

"Jeffrey is how old?" Holmes asked.

"Eight," Mrs. Cararo said, "and my daughter, Sylvia, is six."

"You stayed overnight, Dr. Dragoon?"

"I did," Dragoon answered. "I often do, when one of the family takes ill, and it's late. Jeffrey is... weak, the poor little fellow."

"The doctor is ever so kind. My son was born frail, and without Dr. Dragoon, why, I don't know how we'd manage." Mrs. Cararo settled herself into a chair at the dining table. The doctor held her husband's elbow and eased him into the chair next to her, then sat to Frederick Cararo's right.

"Yes, yes, all very fine," Harry Rinsdale interjected, "but let's move on to business, shall we? Our government has enlisted the aid of Mr. Holmes. He's here. Let's use his services."

Holmes snapped his fingers.

"Right to the point," he said. "I like that!" He turned to Frederick Cararo. "I do apologize if our presence disturbs you. I promise that we'll be discreet. I ask that you indulge us with information about Innsmouth and its inhabitants. In particular, I'm interested in finding the man who leads the Order of Dagon. What is his name? Where does he dwell?"

"We've always handled our own affairs, Mr. Holmes. Why our elected officials have thrust you upon us and forced you into my home against my will, I do not know," our host answered.

"It is true," Dragoon interrupted his patient's tirade, "that traditionally, we have handled our own affairs." His demeanor was that of a compassionate and caring doctor. He clasped his hands on the table. "But let us try," he continued, "to help our new friends from England, shall we? They've had a long journey. I'll be honest, Mr. Holmes. What Mr. Cararo means is that we know little about the Order of Dagon, as you call them. We think of them more as a tribe of in-bred families with strange habits."

"Order of Dagon! What utter nonsense!" Frederick Cararo grumbled.

"Innsmouth," the doctor continued as if he hadn't been interrupted, "is a quaint seaside village that provides us with fish. It's old-fashioned economics, really. The fish-processing factory is abandoned for the winter, but once the weather warms, trade will pick up. We supply flour, milk, cloth, building materials."

From what I'd seen of Innsmouth, they had received little in the way of supplies or materials of any nature for centuries.

Harry Rinsdale crammed one of the muffins into his mouth and gave the other to his slender red-haired associate. The beefy Pinkerton cleared his throat and addressed us.

"We've done background work, of course," he said, "and know the location of the Order of Dagon's headquarters as well as its leader's name."

"And you are?" Holmes asked, extending his hand for a shake.

"Mr. Moe Smith." He shook Holmes's hand, and his thick lips spread into a grin. "Some people call me Knuckles. I'm good at busting down doors and extracting information from uncooperative people." He tilted his head at the red-haired Pinkerton. "He's Terrance McCole. And you already know Harry."

"And the name of the Dagonites' leader is—?" Holmes said.

"Olengran. Just the one name. Olengran."

"His physical appearance?"

"Unknown, sir. We've never caught a glimpse of him. We've questioned the Innsmouthians, but nobody will tell us anything."

"They're loyal to each other. They're a tribe, like I said," Dragoon murmured.

"Yes," Holmes said abruptly, then asked Moe "Knuckles" Smith, "and where exactly is Olengran's headquarters?"

"Go down the street with the tallest building, which is to say the building that hasn't collapsed as much as the others. All the streets and buildings are unmarked. No names. No numbers. Just look for the tallest building. Facing the shore, the street will be to the left of Innsmouth. Follow that street to the mud beach. There you will find Olengran's headquarters."

Mrs. Cararo let loose a flood of giggling, and crossing her legs, stroked the satin gown over her thighs. Limp brown hair slipped from a bun and straggled to her shoulders.

"This is ridiculous. Olengran doesn't really matter, does he?" she said.

"Be quiet, Hortense!" her husband snapped.

Instead of being offended, she giggled again. I wondered if she was drunk.

Harry Rinsdale and Terrance McCole stood and signaled at Moe Smith to get up, as well. The three Pinkertons—those who would protect Mary, Samuel, and Fortuna, I presumed—gestured at us to follow them.

"We'll point the way," Rinsdale said, "then you're on your own. We have to get back to your family, Dr. Watson. That's our watch during this business."

"Yes, you have work to do. Please do go," Frederick Cararo grumbled.

"I will tell you this," Rinsdale continued. "It's extremely dangerous to go to Olengran's headquarters. It's heavily guarded. Be aware, gentlemen, that it has impenetrable ten-foot-thick walls. If the guards don't kill you, and if you find a way to break into the place—and good luck with that—we may never see you again. According to what little information we could get from the villagers, there's an impenetrable locked room inside the building, and this is where Olengran sleeps. His room also has ten-foot-thick walls. The building has no windows."

Moe Smith cracked his knuckles and headed toward the hall with Terrance McCole.

"Also," Smith said, turning briefly, "it's said that Dagon himself lives at Devil Reef."

"In the water?" Holmes asked.

"Indeed," Rinsdale replied. "This Olengran might be Innsmouthian, we don't know. But Dagon, that's another matter entirely. We don't know what he is. Human? Probably not. He's a monster, Mr. Holmes, and nobody I talked to would admit to ever seeing him."

"Come, Watson, no time to lose." Holmes leapt from his chair, and I jumped up. I knew where we were going— to Olengran's headquarters. Before we could dash off, however, Mrs. Cararo had a final word for us.

"Don't worry, gentlemen. We'll do all we can to help you." Her voice was more flirtatious than serious.

"Make it quick," her husband said, "and leave us in peace, would you? Dagon. *Harrumph*. Don't take this personally, Holmes, but we don't need you here."

"One final word of warning, gentlemen," Rinsdale said, as Holmes and I stood by the door leading to the hall.

"Yes?" Holmes prompted. I could tell that he was

struggling, as was I, to remain dignified in the face of Frederick Cararo's rudeness. I wondered if all Americans were as offensive as Cararo—was it enough for these people to *pretend* that they had honor and compassion, or that they had a sliver of sensitivity beyond their own needs; *did they actually believe their own nonsense?*

"Moe, Terrance, and I have seen and heard plenty of strange doings in Innsmouth," Rinsdale said. "At night, the villagers howl and scream in a foreign language for hours. They cavort in gruesome and deranged parties on the shore, on the pier, and by Olengran's place. The point, they tell me, is to bring forth mighty Dagon from Devil Reef. They believe that Olengran is the key to Dagon's rise. They believe that Dagon is a Deep One from the Great Beyond, that Dagon and the even more powerful Cthulhu will take over the world, and that the faithful Innsmouthians will rule the world with these Deep Ones. It's all rot, just like the village itself."

5

"I wouldn't mind having Moe Knuckles Smith with us," I muttered to Holmes, as our buggy halted at the outskirts of Innsmouth. Holmes passed a few coins to the driver, Mr. Hagley, an employee of the Cararo residence, and requested that he return to collect us four hours hence. With a curt nod, the driver shook his reins and guided the horses away from Innsmouth.

"One muscleman wouldn't help much, dear fellow, should we encounter what we battled last night," Holmes said. "I need information, Watson. Logic and science will defeat these monsters, not one man with thick fists."

My mind drifted to the *Elysium* and the Killer Eshockers in its hold. I hoped we'd brought enough Eshockers to do the job.

"If only we could return to the ship and blow up Devil Reef and then make a quick escape," I said, resigned to the fact that such a simple solution wouldn't work. Holmes was squinting at the skyline of Innsmouth.

"The Americans have set dynamite and cannons to that reef over and over again with no luck," he said. "The rock withstands all assault. Ah, *there*, Watson." Holmes pointed at a tall building to the left of the village. "That must be the street we take to get to Olengran's headquarters. I must say, this place looks much smaller in the day."

The fog had lifted, though a brown drizzle misted our faces and clothes. We both wore thick boots and rain cloaks over our woolen garb. When I wiped my cheek with the back of my hand, my glove removed a rusty trace. The stench of fish and garbage rode the stale air. In the light filtering from the glowering clouds, Innsmouth poked up like a field of scabby weeds about to die. Each building drooped, listless and decaying amid heaps of trash. Starving cats and dogs dug through the piles, baring teeth as we passed them. *God help us if they bite*, I thought. All were mangy, their fur a patchwork of scabs, some of the mouths foaming, some of the eyes red.

"Also," Holmes said, his voice distant as if his mind were on other things, "even if we could do it, blowing up the reef would make no sense." He flung a piece of trash aside with his walking stick to remove it from his path. Carefully, we shuffled down the still-muddy street. "The opening between our world and the creatures' world would still exist, as evidenced by attempts to do this very same thing in London. As we saw, the creatures lived on, despite the firepower of cannons and other artillery. Only the Killer Eshocker could destroy them." Abruptly, he stood still. I said nothing, unsure what he was thinking as to how we might proceed with the case. On either side of the narrow mud street, the buildings pitched, the wood wheezed. From shuttered windows came the morning chatter of the Innsmouthians, though in their case, the sounds consisted of clucking, shrilling, and clacking interspersed with guttural moans.

"No," Holmes frowned at me, "our method is clear. We shall confront Olengran, try to reason with him and gain the information we need. If that fails, we must turn our attention to Devil Reef and its occupant, Dagon. How we dispose of Dagon, I do not know."

"Are you worried?" I asked.

"No," he answered curtly. "I never worry. Given time, the answers will come to me. They always do, Doctor. Now come, before these poor souls leave their homes to find out who we are, and before these dogs and cats decide we might make a fancy meal."

Heart pounding, I slogged after him, wiping my face with a cloth from my pocket. The street, which had been gently sloping thus far, took a sudden dip straight down, requiring that we slide down the mud to continue toward the shore. Holmes gingerly hopped to his feet at the bottom. Mud clung to the back of his rain cloak. He helped me up, and we continued the steep descent to Olengran's headquarters. As we neared the bay, the dwellings became increasingly dilapidated, and the shrills and clacks emanating from the windows picked up pace.

We entered an area of one-room shacks smacked together at odd angles and built from driftwood and bones. Esoteric symbols were etched upon the doors, reminding me of the symbols on the bone spheres we'd found in the Jacobs tram machine building in London, and the Beiler barn in Wiltshire. A head popped up at an open window, making me jump. Five eyes goggled at me, two mouths opened and long tongues flopped out, salmon pink.

I clutched Holmes's arm and he swiveled, pointed his walking stick at the creature. "Let's say hello," he said grimly. "Perhaps this fellow can help us."

Horrified, I followed my friend to the window from which the creature stared at us with its five eyes. The tongues slapped back into the mouths, which emitted an excited series of staccato trills interspersed with squalls of clanging and cracking.

A door banged open, hitting the front of the shack. An arm protruded, the width of my large toe but as long as my body. At its end, where a hand should be, a frill of multicolored tendrils quivered, arched outward, then sucked in the drizzle with a loud slurp. The frill blossomed again, its tendrils twitching, and after another slurp, a body followed it from inside the house.

The head disappeared from the window, and reappeared on another body that followed the long-armed creature from their home. The first creature was in charge, the leader or the father, I assumed; the second creature was smaller in height and possibly a child or mate, I could not tell.

The leader, as I shall refer to him, swept over Holmes's body and face with several of the multicolored frill blossoms. Feeling his dimensions? Smelling him? Tasting him?

Shuddering, I backed away, for I had no desire to be examined in a similar manner.

"You are aliens," the leader said in broken English. "I am Taumo family. You are who?"

"I am Mr. Sherlock Holmes, and this is my companion, Dr. John Watson. We're from London, England, and have arrived only yesterday to Innsmouth, Mr. Taumo. I am pleased to make your acquaintance." Holmes tipped his hat, and the frill blossoms withdrew.

Taumo's long arms coiled like snakes at his sides and on his back. Along with five eyes, his head had one slit that might have been a nose and two mouths, each with one of the long tongues. The head was misshapen and propped on a segmented stack of three oval body parts clad in rags. Rope belts secured the rags between the ovals. Four legs kept him upright. They were short, furry as far as I could see from where the rags hung, and supported by stubby bare feet. His toes were clumps of tendrils much like the frills that fluttered on the ends of his arms.

Taumo introduced his family member as "Taumo-mate." Holmes murmured additional pleasantries, and Taumo-mate bent at the waist and gazed up at him with two eyes while her other three eyes swept over my body. She clucked her hellos, apparently less well versed in English than her husband. She had but one body segment, which was spherical, and two legs with two feet. Also clad in rags of indeterminate original color, she squished her frill toes into the mud as an arm suddenly jutted from a hole in the front of her belly. Holmes and I both leapt back this time, then he burst out laughing.

"You gave me a start!" he cried, and I could tell that his friendly manner was forced.

Her arm ended with an actual hand, and her fingers poked at my hat. I fumbled for her arm, turning red, and gently pulled it down. It was slimy and cold, mottled with the brown scum that fell from the sky. I held her hand for a few moments.

"Madam, it is a pleasure," I said, emulating Holmes's forced politeness.

A few smaller Taumo family members popped out of the house and huddled near their mother. All were ill-shapen in some way or another, though the deformities differed somewhat among them. I could see characteristics of both parents in their offspring. *These aren't monsters*, I thought. *These are grossly deformed people. But interbreeding alone, even for centuries, wouldn't have deformed a population to this extent.*

"We are seeking Olengran," Holmes said. "Can you introduce us, or perhaps point us in the right direction?"

Taumo's eyes narrowed, and he shook his head. He gestured at his wife, and she herded their children back into the shack.

"You are aliens. It's best that you leave. Do not come

again. Consider this a warning." He spoke with a heavy accent, and I could barely recognize his words as English.

By now, other Innsmouthians were appearing at doorways and windows, anxious to watch the scene. Apparently, they didn't get many visitors, as Harry Rinsdale and Dr. Dragoon had pointed out. It was frankly beyond my comprehension how a population such as this could exist. It was the stuff of nightmares, particularly given my medical training. I'd never seen such people. Part of me wanted to help them. Part of me wanted to run away.

"We want to speak to Olengran about matters in England, where we live," Holmes said. "We mean you no harm, sir. We are not dangerous."

"If you value your life, then go," Taumo insisted.

"Come on, Holmes," I said, and to Taumo, I added, "We'll be on our way, sir, and thank you for your time."

Taumo grunted and shook his head again. He warbled and croaked, his voice skittering up and down raucous scales. I assumed he was telling us about the dangers of staying in Innsmouth, but of course, I couldn't understand him. Finally, he returned to his family, slamming the door, and Holmes and I ventured forward, sliding down another incline, this time by accident. Eventually, we reached the end of the street. My hand throbbed, reminding me to be more careful about sliding, falling, or God forbid, getting into a fist fight.

Yet another lopsided building, with a roof angled toward the water, tottered before us. It was windowless and covered in what might have been whale hide. I had never seen leather of this nature—mottled, gray, and puffy as if stretched across mounds of flab. Flies buzzed and clung to the building, only to be swept away by gusts of air blowing in from the sea. The stench of the place overpowered the gusts of air, and it reminded me of battlefields covered in corpses, and of my most horrible memories of war.

To our right, the beach sloped up to the slate rock, and in the distance, Devil Reef flashed its warnings: a haze of colored light, the screeches of its creatures. At this distance, the clouds appeared to cling to the reef.

Holmes headed to the building and probed the whale hide, as I chose to think of it. I turned from the stench and stared at the pier, remembering Mary, Samuel, and Fortuna on those broken slats.

"Blast it, Watson, are you coming?" Holmes called, jerking my attention away.

Over Devil Reef, the clouds bulged and split, and out tumbled enormous clusters of color that I guessed were creatures from the deadly dimensions. Thunder bellowed from offshore and lightning cracked.

I wiped scum from my face, forced my boots through the mud, and found Holmes on the ocean-facing side of Olengran's headquarters, where a guard confronted him.

A guard with a Winchester rifle.

"Halt!" the guard commanded Holmes. "No further."

Holmes raised his hands.

"No harm, no harm," he said. "Just here to see Olengran.

Mr. Sherlock Holmes at your service, with my associate, Dr. John Watson."

I was shocked to see that the open door was twice my height and several feet thick, and its outer surface was also covered in whale hide with blubber insulation. The ocean was strong, the waves kicking, and it crept and splashed at us from boulders only yards away. Another guard joined the first one, aiming two revolvers, one in each hand, at us. Both guards bore more resemblance to humans than the Taumo family. But both were deformed, nonetheless.

The one with the Winchester was twice Holmes's height, and each of his arms was the size of an ape's. His head was a bloated monstrosity, wobbling as if a carnival balloon had been filled with gas and set upon a spikey neck. He had two eyes, a nose slit, and a mouth slit—similar to Taumo. He also wore rags but of a less worn nature. His were stained with blood and wrapped mummylike around his body and legs but had fewer holes in them.

The guard with the two revolvers had four legs and feet that ended in toe frills—also Taumo features.

Were these two related to the Taumo family? I wondered, then chided myself. Of course, they were. Probably everyone in Innsmouth was related.

"You will not see Olengran. Now, go!" the Winchester guard commanded, shoving the rifle into Holmes's side. His Innsmouthian accent mangled the words more than Taumo's voice, making him nearly incomprehensible.

Holmes winced but held steady. His eyes motioned at me

to move aside, which I did. Was he planning to storm the place? Dear God, I hoped not.

"Just a few words with Olengran, I promise," Holmes said. "We've traveled from far away, from England, to speak with him. We're associates of the followers of Dagon, and we have much respect for him."

Such lies coming from Holmes, I thought.

Both guards loomed over him. Three weapons pointed at his chest. Meanwhile, the door remained open, the entranceway clear.

Holmes's eyes motioned at me to go into the building.

I shook my head. I was not entering that building on my own.

"Go, or I will kill you," the Winchester guard said.

With his hands still raised, Holmes backed toward the rocks and the waves.

"Just a few words," he repeated.

"No!"

Just as I feared the worst, that these two would kill us, another creature emerged from Olengran's headquarters. This one also carried two revolvers, and a fishing pole was strapped over his back. He looked fairly human, except for the gills flapping on his neck, the scales clittering on his flesh, and a fish tail protruding from his mummy-rags. He appeared to be in charge. He told the other guards to lower their weapons. His English was the most precise I'd heard from any of the Innsmouthians.

"Follow me. You will come to the alien room," he said in

a guttural voice. "We will talk there. I am the manager of the building."

Dread filled me. "But Holmes...!" I cried. My protest died on my tongue; rather than answer me, Holmes glared at me. He had come to Innsmouth to get inside Olengran's headquarters, and we both still had our heads intact and our hearts still beating.

As I was closest to the building, I had to enter first, with Holmes behind me, followed by the two guards and the fish-tailed manager. I stepped onto a spongy floor. Dim lanterns hung on what I thought was sinew dangling from a blubber ceiling. I could barely breathe, and nausea gurgled up from my stomach. Groaning, I turned, but there was no way back. The manager had already squeezed into the room. The tall Winchester guard collapsed into four or five ratcheted pieces—reminding me of the snake that Fitzgerald had built in the London warehouse. He settled by the now-closed door, blocking any exit.

To say the room was uncomfortable and uninviting is to do it a service. Compared to Olengran's "alien room," the Stranger's Room, designed to discourage visitors to the Diogenes Club, was luxury at its finest.

Stuck into the fatty floor, three stools jiggled on splintered legs. Even in the thready light, I could see the sheen of slime on the seats. My feet unsteady, I grasped Holmes's arm to keep my balance.

"Steady, friend Watson," he murmured.

The fish-tail manager ruffled his scales, reminding me

of a molting bird, and he rasped something to the shorter guard, who exited via a door whose outline I had failed to notice in the blubber walls. With the door ajar, I could see that the walls were indeed as thick as ten feet, and from the corner of my eye, I saw Holmes flinch. The door itself was perhaps two feet thick, and while it was coated in a fat-like substance, I suspected the core of this entire structure consisted of hard and very thick bullet-proof metal.

With a whoosh of dead fish and excrement, the door shut.

"Sit," the manager told us, waving his two revolvers at the stools. Supporting each other, we made our way to the stools, which were sticky to the touch, and complied with his order.

"What is your business with Olengran?" the manager asked Holmes. "Nobody sees Olengran. Most who try die." He paused, then added, "We kill them."

"I seek a manner in which we can coexist peacefully," Holmes said, which was not entirely untrue. "I am trying to understand how your kind come to be here, and how we can get along. To do this, I need information, and most important, to talk to the leader of your people."

The manager slipped his revolvers into pockets hidden beneath his rags and unhooked the fishing pole from his back. He propped the pole by the collapsed guard at the exit door. The guard hissed through his mouth slit. His carnival-balloon head bobbled on his neck spike. The jiggling floor, the balloon head... the stench...

I doubled over on the stool, clenching my stomach, trying

unsuccessfully to control the dry heaves. Holmes clasped my shoulder.

"Perhaps another time," he said to the manager. "My friend here, as you can see, is unwell. Do you mind terribly if we leave now and then return when it's more convenient for Olengran?"

The manager stared at Holmes as if the latter were an idiot. Rarely had I seen anyone look at Holmes with such an expression.

"Olengran never leaves his room. Only I am permitted to enter his private domain. He locks it from the inside." The manager pulled out his revolvers again and aimed them at us. "No entry, nothing, not ever. Understand?"

"Yes, yes." Holmes nodded his head vigorously. Watching the scene, I continued to hold my stomach and dry heave.

"Please let us leave," I retched. "I'm not feeling well."

"I have nothing against you," the manager spat. "It was you who came to me. You tried to find a way into Olengran's room, didn't you?"

Holmes rose from the stool and took a few steps toward the creature. As he spoke, he jabbed the floor with his walking stick.

"I assure you, sir, that I did not attempt to break into this building. You must understand that, where we come from, there are no buildings resembling this structure. I was startled, yes, by the lack of windows and ordinary doors. Certainly, the interior is unusual, as well. Tell me—" suddenly Holmes switched the topic "—how does

Olengran eat if he's always locked in his room?"

"It is time. You must go." Two revolvers waved us toward the guard at the exit door. "No more questions."

"What does he eat? Do you all eat fish here, and nothing else?" Holmes pressed, but he hauled me off the stool and toward our escape.

In my current condition, the last thing I wanted to talk about was the consumption of fish. Should we conclude this bizarre case and return to England safely, I swore that I would never eat a fish supper again. Nor would I take for granted the pleasures of my simple life. Only a month or two ago, I'd felt bored, without direction and true purpose. I'd needed this adventure, this case, with Holmes to feel alive. I doubted that I would ever feel that way again.

As Holmes opened the door, fresh ocean air blasted into the fetid room, along with a tremble of light from behind the clouds. I sucked in the air, and it quelled my nausea.

"Do not return," the manager growled. "Do not try to poison Olengran's fish. Tasters ensure safety in the kitchen. Cooks and maids ensure safety. Olengran knows you are here. We told him. You will go. Now. Next time you come, you will die."

"Small-town hospitality at its finest," I muttered to Holmes, as the door shut behind us and we stood before the jumbled rocks and the ocean beyond. The scum-drizzle was almost a relief after being in what had felt like the belly of a whale.

Holmes's eyes flashed, and he gave me a broad grin.

"Come along, Watson. We shall return, and no, we will not be killed. Fear not. That fellow gave us more information than he intended to, possibly even a means for getting into the building."

"But how can you be so positive, Holmes, given the circumstances?"

Holmes slogged through the mud up the street where the Taumo family lived. Wearily, I dragged along behind him.

"Holmes, wait. I need to know. Surely you owe me an explanation? What is this information?"

"Simply this: that there are people who go in and out of this dwelling; it is not entirely under lock and key. Kitchen staff prepare fish for Olengran's meals. Servants must go in and out of Olengran's room. Someone brings him food." He narrowed his eyes. "As that fellow said, 'cooks and maids ensure safety.'"

"But I cannot see how they would provide a way in."

We stood before the first mud slope we had slid down on the way to Olengran's headquarters. Now we pondered how to climb back up and regain our footing.

"Come." Holmes swiveled abruptly and headed toward Olengran's headquarters again. "We have to find another way up. We'll walk across the beach, find another street, try to go that way. Or perhaps get into the village and beyond via the extension of the pier, the walkway stretching to the long building we saw when we arrived."

This time, I kept quiet and didn't repeat my question. I stared at the mud, and occasionally, lifted my head to look at the waves breaking upon the rock shore. The pier creaked. The village ached. The sky cried.

What a miserable place, I thought. *These poor creatures who live here, their poor children. To be born into this existence. What do they do with themselves all day, the parents and children? Fishing, cooking, worshiping Dagon—anything else?*

Again, I thanked God for my former life in England; mundane as it had been, Mary, Samuel, and I had been safe, warm, and comfortable with plenty of food and drink. My medical practice enabled me to care for other people, which I felt was important, and once in a while, scientific advancements in my field infused me with that spark of life I craved. Where I once considered Willie Jacobs downtrodden and born into a sad and sorry life with no hope of escape, I now knew of those born into a much worse world.

Holmes helped me onto the pier. I wished that we were with my family, about to head down the pier into the water, where a landing boat might take us to the *Elysium*, and from there, far away from this horrible place.

But our journey was in the other direction, away from the ocean and back through the squalid stench of Innsmouth.

"At least one servant goes into and out of Olengran's room," Holmes said abruptly. "While, as that 'manager' just told us, *poisoning* him might prove difficult via the food and the cooks, we might find another way to gain access."

"Via his laundry service?" I asked.

"Someone washes his sheets, towels, and clothes, and returns the clean articles to that room."

"Are you suggesting that we disguise ourselves as Olengran's maids? They must surely be Innsmouthians as deformed as the ones we have seen today! Holmes, I seriously doubt you can pull that off, despite your theatrical skills."

"And he spoke of poison, Watson," Holmes went on, as if he hadn't heard me. "For now, I merely seek knowledge and understanding from Olengran. I need to permanently close the rifts between the dimensions. I need to kill off all the creatures from beyond and make sure they never enter our world again."

He touched my arm, his eyes soft.

"In time, Watson. I will find a way. Then you will see."

6
MARY WATSON

"Let me tend to Samuel. He'll be fine with me while you stroll in the gardens." Fortuna dangled a ball of wool in front of Samuel, who gurgled in delight at the sight. Eagerly, he grasped the wool and batted it against his cradle. "Go on," Fortuna urged. "The Pinkertons are here to keep us safe, after all."

With John and Holmes in Innsmouth, seeking the leader of the Order of Dagon, I was restless. A holiday in a deserted mansion on the edge of Innsmouth didn't quite measure up to being in London. So I thanked Fortuna and headed into the hall, where Terrance McCole and "Knuckles" Smith guarded the bedroom.

McCole jumped up from the chair where he'd been lounging and reading a newspaper. I shuddered, as I saw that it wasn't a newspaper, but rather, the *Innsmouth Fish Heads Trade Index*.

"Nothing else to read around here except the fancy books in the library," McCole said, clearly noticing my reaction to the *Fish Heads* listings. "I never was one for *Moby Dick* or Shakespeare or those Greek hero stories."

"No, I suppose not," I said. "And I'm sure it doesn't hurt to keep up with the local trades. Mr. McCole and—" I nodded at Knuckles, who had also stood up "—Mr. Smith, I'm going outside for some air. I'll remain on the grounds, where it's safe."

Moe Smith settled himself back on his chair, shuffling playing cards in his thick fists. He spread the cards on a marble table that would have been more at home in the Queen's drawing room than in Innsmouth. He flipped one card, then another, grunting as he revealed the other side of each card. His eyes flicked my way, then back to the cards.

"You be careful, Mrs. Watson," he said. "Make sure Mr. Rinsdale has a watch on you out there. You never know..." He didn't finish the sentence. He didn't have to finish it. I understood. Innsmouth was nothing but danger, even here at its farthest edge, in the forest, in a mansion with three guards. The last thing I wanted was a tentacled monster with a squashed head and twelve mouths jumping out of the bushes at me.

"I'll do that. Thank you," I said, and leaving them, made my way down the curved staircase to the hexagonal room. Unlike the estates of England, where the upper crust hang in their houses portraits of family members ranging back hundreds of years, the hexagonal room's walls displayed paintings of coiled shapes and patterns that seemed to change as I stared at them. Somehow, the paintings were linked, but I couldn't determine how. In one painting, a thick coil wound endlessly around dozens of cubes that shifted in my view as I moved around the room. *Impossible!* I thought. *And yet I'm seeing it, and I'm quite sane.* In another painting, cylinders swallowed endless streams of dots, as throats might swallow, contracting at one end, releasing the stream, contracting again, releasing again.

"I suggest you look away."

I swiveled to see Harry Rinsdale at the end of the hall leading into the hexagonal room.

"You gave me quite a start!" I said, my right hand on my chest, as if that would slow my racing heart.

He fingered the twirled ends of his mustache and looked at the carpet.

"Sorry, Mrs. Watson. I didn't mean to scare you." He came over to me, gently took my arm, and led me from the room and away from the paintings. His eyes, warm and brown behind his spectacles, calmed me. You can tell a lot from looking at a man's eyes, and I could see that Mr. Rinsdale was kind and honest and had my best interests at heart. Briefly, I wondered if a man could tell the same thing about a woman from looking into her eyes.

"Who painted them?" I asked the detective. "Why are they so strange? How did the artist achieve such an unnerving effect?"

He shrugged.

"Don't know, honestly. Mr. Cararo tells me that they've been in his family for centuries, but there are no known paintings that I'm aware of that compare to his little collection. Believe me, Mrs. Watson, I've done some research into the issue, too."

"I imagine you have, sir. Tell me," I said, switching the subject, "what's wrong with the Cararos' son, Jeffrey? And where are the children? I don't hear them playing."

"Ah, the children," he answered. "Now that's a story, dear lady. Shall we sit somewhere while we talk? Perhaps the library or drawing room?"

"I'd hoped to go outside."

"Fine, then," he said, smiling and steering me back toward the hexagonal room. "You might as well enjoy the outdoors while you can. Any day, the place might be buried in snow. You never know. Unfortunately, we'll have to return to the room with the paintings to get to the rear door. Focus on the carpet, and you'll be fine."

At that moment, Frederick Cararo stumbled into the hall from the dining room, dropping his cane. Mr. Rinsdale bowed deeply—out of habit, I supposed—while I rushed to Cararo's side and helped steady him against the wall. I retrieved his cane. His black eyes lashed at me.

"I can get my own cane!" he snapped.

Not only was I shocked by his manner, I was equally shocked by his appearance. Up close, Mr. Cararo looked too ancient to still be alive. I'd known elderly people, plenty of them, but I'd never seen a person with such translucent and deeply wrinkled skin. I could see the veins throbbing in his forehead, cheeks, nose, and chin. I could see the angular

78

bones holding up his eyes and mouth, the ridge undercutting his jawline. It was as if his skin might rip if I simply touched it. The smashed nose flared, and he snorted air through his mouth. The mustache, which had appeared etched earlier, was actually a thick vein over his lips.

"I know that you can take care of yourself," I said gently. "Perhaps I'm being excessively helpful. I'll try not to overstep again in the future."

The forehead creased, and the eyes peered at me as if trying to determine the validity of my statement.

He drew up his shoulders and lifted his chin. *Such arrogance.* Or was this a man who had always been self-reliant and in charge, who could not bear to lose his independence and control in any way? Either way, I didn't like him. Yet I was beholden to him, for he'd taken my family and Sherlock Holmes into his house. For that, he required my respect.

As I mused on all this, Mr. Rinsdale piped up.

"Mrs. Watson and I were just about to head into your delightful gardens, sir. Would you care to join us?" he asked.

"Harrumph. I have important matters to attend to. Business... papers... meetings... important..." he drifted to a halt.

Dr. Jacob Dragoon strode into the hall from beyond the hexagonal room. Wearing a charcoal suit cut to perfection, he was freshly shaved and smelled faintly of cologne.

"Why, I thought you'd already left!" I exclaimed, noticing that his suit differed from the one he'd worn at breakfast.

Perhaps he'd not yet prepared for the day before meeting us earlier in the dining room. He took my hand. His skin was softer than John's, and his nails were trimmed and smooth. John was in the same profession, yet by comparison was a ragamuffin. The elegant Dr. Dragoon clearly had a lot more time to pamper himself, and the money with which to do so.

"Mr. Cararo's heart condition has flared," he said, "and I want to monitor him for a few hours before I leave. It's a perk that you're here, Mrs. Watson. You brighten our little world with your presence. So lovely." The man was as smooth a talker as he was handsome. My cheeks grew warm from the flattery, but I didn't take him seriously. Some men—typically those who considered themselves attractive—flirted with every woman they encountered. Dr. Dragoon had no clue that, behind his handsome face, I saw a shallowness that drained him of appeal.

"Enough pleasantries," Frederick Cararo barked. "There are important matters, I tell you, and I must be ready for them."

Clutching his cane, he jabbed it at me, and I jerked back to avoid injury. He grumbled and I thought I heard him curse at me, as he hunched over and shouldered his way past.

"Surely, sir, you can be respectful of Mrs. Watson," Harry Rinsdale said, stepping between me and Cararo. "I'm here to make sure no harm is done to her. We don't expect *you* to harm her."

"Stand aside," Cararo snarled. When Rinsdale didn't move,

he added, "You're in my home, and you will do as I say."

"But what have I done wrong, sir? We've only just arrived." I tried to remain calm. My body tensed, and I could feel my blood pressure rising. "It is not my intention to put you out," I said. "We're here on government business of a most critical nature."

"I don't want you here," Cararo snapped. "Who invited you? Not me! Now be off, and leave me be, why don't you?"

Mr. Rinsdale led me away from the old man, who tottered to a room on the other side of the hall and shoved open the door with his cane.

"You must forgive him," Dragoon murmured. "He is not well. You shouldn't worry your pretty head…"

I didn't listen to the rest of the doctor's greasing. I was much too stunned by Mr. Cararo's behavior. John would probably have diagnosed him with senile dementia. As the old man disappeared into the room, leaving the door wide open, I saw a billiards table alongside a doctor's examination bed, the type used by John in his London offices. *How peculiar*, I thought. *Does the doctor examine family members while playing billiards?* I couldn't picture either Mr. or Mrs. Cararo playing the game on any evening. Their son, Jeffrey, was only eight and sickly, and the daughter, Sylvia, was six, no age for billiards.

"Madame, please excuse me, as I must attend to him." Dragoon bowed and started heading after his patient, but I touched his arm, stopping him. "Yes?" he inquired, his eyes widening, and as I removed my fingers from his jacket sleeve, he cast me a smarmy grin. "*Yes?*" he repeated, and leaned toward me.

"Doctor, where are the children? What is Jeffrey's illness? Is his sister similarly afflicted? I am concerned for the family, and if I can help, I am most willing to do whatever I am able. Also, my husband might be able to help. He is a medical doctor with some experience, you know."

"I see, I see." Dragoon gave me a dismissive wave. "You want to help. That's most charitable of you. Jeffrey was born with mental afflictions and bleeding that does not clot."

"Hemophilia," I said. "Where is his room, sir? Might he like some company?"

"I really must go," the doctor said. "All this chattering... The children reside in the nether wing. The girl, Sylvia, is in good health. She's with her nanny."

"Dr. Dragoon's room is in the same wing," Mr. Rinsdale told me. "This is a big house, and you've not had a proper introduction to it. I'll show you around, at your convenience, of course."

"You have a room here?" I asked the doctor. "Where is your own home located? We've been told that the Cararo home is almost the only one anywhere near Innsmouth."

The doctor glared at me, all pretense of warmth and charm gone. His eyes flashed.

"You, madam, ask too many questions! These matters are none of your business. You should tend to your own affairs, those of your baby and your husband. Do the English have no manners?" He fumed into the billiards room, leaving me alone in the hall with Mr. Rinsdale, who shoved his hands in his jacket pockets and rocked on his heels.

"I suggest you avoid your hosts as well as the doctor," he said. "They're most unpleasant people, but I believe them to be harmless. Think about it. Who *decides* to live near *Innsmouth* rather than near normal people? They are cracked, no doubt about it. Cararo's ancestors had close associations with the villagers, of what nature I don't know. His wife, a former dancer in the burlesque, married him for money. Dragoon, a quack who *also* chooses to be near Innsmouth, lives off the family. A simple arrangement." He nodded toward the hexagonal room. "Shall we go outside, madam?"

"Outside. Yes." As we walked side by side through the hexagonal room with our eyes focused on the carpet—a dreary gray that reminded me of the sky—I asked, "But how did Hortense meet Frederick, and how did Dr. Dragoon know of them, to come here and dwell here as their family doctor? It's all so strange, Mr. Rinsdale."

Halls branched in several directions at the rear of the hexagon. The Pinkerton pointed at one and told me it was where the household staff slept, at another, which was reserved for family use—the "nether wing," he said—and yet a third, which served as Mrs. Cararo's private quarters. A final hall would lead us to an outer door, he said, steering me in the correct direction.

Here, the carpet was richly hued again, in greens and blues, and adorned with tendrils and motifs that reminded me of eyes and of sea creatures. The elaborate weaving left me breathless, much as the hexagonal room had swept my senses. Briefly, I stopped and placed a hand on the wall to steady myself. Paintings on the walls matched the weavings of the rug. My head whirled. I shut my eyes.

"Give me a moment," I said, a flush sweeping through me as sweat broke out on my forehead.

"Mrs. Watson, are you well?" The detective's words floated, sing-song and as if from afar.

Pulling my kerchief from a pocket on my dress, I wiped my forehead and cheeks. "This place is dangerous," I said.

"The Pinkertons don't live here. Now you know why. You don't want to venture anywhere. Even in the house. I hope you and your family will be safe at home very soon," Rinsdale said, his words becoming sharper and clearer as my dizziness passed.

"Why are the people of Innsmouth so odd?" I asked.

"If you want to believe the myths told late at night in saloons, it started when ordinary people had... relations, madame... with a deformed people that migrated somehow from the South Seas. The resulting generations merged man and... deformity. What we see now is something unnatural."

He chose his words carefully. Mr. Rinsdale had an intelligence and a sensitivity that Dr. Dragoon could but imitate poorly.

With my head no longer in a fog, we walked rapidly to the rear door, and the rush of cold air hit me. "Oh, that feels good," I said.

"Indeed, it does," he agreed. "Some days, I think this house will kill me." Directing me to a bench beneath overgrown pines, he sat, and I followed suit. He crossed his legs and gazed at a tangle of weeds and bushes that bounded the property, where the forest loomed high and thick. In the dead of winter, the trees were a twisted mass of branches sprouting from ancient trunks. The sky was a tumor. Wind wailed and swept across the grounds, carrying the decay of brown leaves, twigs, and dust.

Changing my mind about walking in the gardens for fresh air, I asked my companion again to tell me what little he knew about the family.

"Other than the gossip of the household staff, I've not been able to learn much," he said. "Supposedly, Frederick's family was in the fish head trade, and he grew old with a fortune but no heir. He sent Mr. Hagley, the buggy driver who also repairs and paints the house, into Boston. Hagley's mission was to find a doctor willing to move to these parts—a tall order, indeed—but also to find a wife for Frederick. *Imagine.*"

"And so he found Hortense dancing in her burlesque club. And Dr. Dragoon... where?"

"Same place—it was a saloon rather than a club. Apparently, it was a rough part of town, a lot of fist fights, shootings, stranglings. Dragoon was known in the underworld as a healer of anyone who had the money to pay."

"And so Hortense and Frederick married and had the two children?"

"Yes. Very quiet children." Rinsdale paused, considering his words. "Jeffrey never speaks. He remains in his room, playing with toy soldiers and gazing at a book about trains. His education is minimal. The Cararo heir is not expected to live to maturity."

"The hemophilia?" I asked.

"Yes, but he's also mentally... shall we say, *unaware*? I have rarely seen him. He takes his meals in his room. The nanny, who is actually just a maid, is under strict orders never to speak about the heir."

My heart clenched. I was so lucky that Samuel was a healthy child, and suddenly, I desired nothing more than to be with him, tucked away in our safe room.

"Sylvia," Mr. Rinsdale rumbled on, "is also a quiet child; her intellect and health are both as one might expect in a girl her age. The nanny-maid provides her with *some* instruction, I am told, but the girl is favored neither by her mother nor her father."

My heart breaking and my eyes beginning to well with tears, I asked the detective if he minded sitting alone while I returned to the house and to my child. He shook his head, firmly against the idea, and reminded me that I must return via the hall with the strange carpet and the hexagonal room.

"Regardless, I'm freezing out here. My coat isn't heavy enough to withstand the wind, and the dust is burning my eyes."

He seemed only too happy to go inside himself and return to his position in the dining room, where it was warm, and tea and biscuits awaited. After we had shuttled quickly through the hall and the hexagonal room, he set off for his repast. All was quiet in the billiards-examination room, and after checking on Samuel—he was sleeping near Fortuna, who was knitting a blanket—I slipped out of the bedroom and down the curved stairway again. I was restless, curious, *horrified* by the thought of the two Cararo children, hidden away somewhere in this house, where they were abandoned, neglected, and most likely, miserable. I would find them. I would comfort them. Surely, even if Jeffrey was in no state of health to receive a visitor, the *girl*...

Heading down the hall to the "nether wing," where Rinsdale had told me the children resided, I was thankful to see that the floor was made of oak planks, the walls were also of ordinary wood, and there were no paintings. At the end of the hall were three closed doors: I assumed one led to Jeffrey's room, another to Sylvia's, and the third to the maid-nanny's. But where was Dr. Dragoon's room, which he'd said was in the nether wing? Possibly, his was the third room, while the maid-nanny slept with one of the children or perhaps in the staff wing; after all, according to Rinsdale, nobody really cared for the children, so the maid-nanny's might not be a full-time position. This unknown woman was probably folding sheets or dusting bannisters.

Halfway down the corridor, another hall opened to my left. Were the children tucked down this even more remote hall, or imprisoned in the three rooms of the main corridor? I opted for the remoteness, and swung left, my heart beating rapidly, a peculiar fear rising in my chest. What would I find? Would Jeffrey and Sylvia be chained to their walls, would they be dead, their little corpses rotting away, unnoticed for weeks?

Get a hold of yourself, I told myself. *You're letting your imagination run wild.*

Still, this was not an ordinary family. This was not an ordinary house. Innsmouth was a disease. And my husband and Sherlock Holmes were there, right now, in Innsmouth, hunting down a bizarre creature, Olengran, who might lead them to the horror of all horrors, the monster Cthulhu.

I had such little courage. *I must summon my strength*, I told myself, *and all of it, for Samuel and I are stuck here by my decision.* London was defiled by the same creatures. The world was collapsing around us; terror reigned over the sightings of Cthulhu and his hellish menagerie.

The left-hand hall was short, a stump compared to the other corridors. It was more cheerfully decorated here, and my nerves settled a bit, though I remained on guard and in a general state of agitation. There were only two doors, separated by two statues, one on either side of the hall: one of Mr. Cararo in his younger days—possibly at age ninety— and one of Mrs. Cararo in revealing lingerie. The sculptor had done an excellent job, capturing yet enhancing their images. Frederick appeared dashing and powerful, while Hortense looked beautiful and alluring.

I peered into the first room: it had rich furnishings, a

damask sofa, a piano, a harp. The walls were deep pink, the curtains pink gauze. Carefully aligned on a white table, perfume bottles and cosmetics suggested that the room might belong to Hortense Cararo. A dainty chair, draped in white lace, was tucked beneath the table. An open wardrobe displayed dozens of slinky gowns, as well as the types of outfits burlesque dancers might wear: garters, underthings, and the like. While I hardly thought of myself as prudish, the display left me vaguely nauseous. Did the lady of the house entertain her husband, or someone else?

I was walking past her statue, when a voice made me stop and duck behind the figure.

"Be brave, my sweet. Let me soothe you. Let me give you bliss."

It was Dr. Dragoon.

Apparently, he'd left Frederick Cararo to tend to another family member, and it couldn't be Jeffrey, the hemophiliac child. No, I was clearly in Hortense's private quarters, and Dr. Dragoon was treating her.

I peeked over my shoulder, then around the Hortense statue's garters.

"Gentle. Oh, and more..." The sultry voice belonged to Hortense. Thankfully, she was attired in another long-sleeved satin gown rather than her underthings. Hair straggled limply over her shoulders to her chest. Almond-shaped eyes, the same dull brown as her hair, were slits, the irises hazy as they gazed at the doctor.

That's when I saw that the sleeve on her right arm was rolled to her elbow. Dr. Dragoon removed a hypodermic needle from the crook of her arm.

"You'll be fine, my sweet," he said. "This is enough for now. It will tide you over."

"Not enough," she whispered.

"More is dangerous. A seven-percent solution is best."

Cocaine, I thought. *He's giving her the abominable dose that Sherlock Holmes injects into his forearm and wrist.*

Dr. Dragoon tucked the needle into a padded case. He delicately kissed her cheek, and her eyes fluttered briefly; and they had the dreamy, vacant look that came over Holmes when he used drugs. The doctor rolled Hortense's sleeve back down to her wrist and arranged the lace frills.

Her other arm languidly moved to her chest, where the satin gown dipped to show off her cleavage. She moaned and smiled coyly at Dr. Dragoon.

"Stay longer," she begged.

"No, sweetness. I must be off. Now that I've taken care of three of the four Cararos—"

"One in a most special way," she whispered, "but you can have more, if you want..."

"Next time," he answered. "Jeffrey won't bother you today. Not at all. I dosed him well. Sylvia required more, but no mind. She won't bother anyone, either. Enjoy the day, sweetness."

"But why leave?" she asked.

"My dear, the house is too full of nosiness. Those

Pinkertons, and now Holmes and his pack of intruders. The wife is prowling about somewhere, too."

So they had drugged the children. This is why I hadn't heard the chatter or laughter of little ones. *Such evil*, I thought, *it is perhaps worse than the evil we confront with Cthulhu, Dagon, and their pack of monsters. Human evil exists with purpose, with intent to inflict harm and pain. The creatures possess a different type of evil.*

As Dr. Dragoon packed his medical bag and rose to take his leave, I hurried away, cringing as the floorboards rattled. God help me if he caught me in that hall.

Terrified, I ran up the staircase to the bedroom and past the surprised Pinkertons. I fumbled with the door knob and entered.

"What is it?" Fortuna asked, dropping her knitting, and as I held Samuel close, I told her all.

7
PROFESSOR MORIARTY

I slept in an alcove in the recesses of the fish factory. When I awakened, with a start, the fish scales, the filth, and the odors reminded me that I was no longer in my plush London bed. Using a table to support myself, I stood and rubbed my eyes. The table ran the length of the room. Its splintered surface was maroon—*dried blood*—and littered with stained butchers' knives and fish remains. Several covered barrels stood around the table. I lifted one of the lids and peered into a barrel, then instantly regretted it. I shoved the lid back onto the barrel, shut my eyes for a moment, and let my head clear. Eyes, gills, tails, bones, the reek of death, and fat black flies, several of which had escaped from the barrel and now buzzed around my head.

The sooner I got out of here, the better.

As I pushed past the door—a cracked and blood-stained mess hanging by rusty nails—I felt dizzy, and once outside, leaned against the building. The disgusting morning air of Innsmouth was refreshing compared to the stench of the fish plant.

My eyes ached as they adjusted to the fog. In the distance, Innsmouthians sprawled in various heaps on the beach. Some played in the mud, others just lay there as if basking in the sun. Several villagers clambered into the small fishing boats tied to the decaying pier. They piped and squealed at each other as they hoisted supplies onto the boats and then floated out toward sea. In the mist, Devil Reef jutted from the water, a gauzy look to it, which shifted both in color and shape. What appeared sharp and pointed one moment looked bloated and smashed the next. What appeared orange and green shifted with bright yellow slashes into a purplish hue. Breaking from the top of the reef, froth sprayed in all directions, and creatures flitted and dove, apparently plucking morning meals from the surrounding sea.

A figure rose to its feet on the rock slab edging the waves. *Professor Fitzgerald.* My luck could not have been better. I'd assumed my first hours this morning would require that I look for him in the village. But there he was, in a location near the one at which I had left him last night. Had he slept on the rock? I couldn't imagine it. No, he must have sloped off to his temporary lodgings then returned this morning, just as I had done.

My mind surged through the options. Was he waiting for me to return so he could attempt to kill me? Was he waiting for someone else? Or was he anxious to beg admittance to Olengran's headquarters again?

I decided on the third option. Fitzgerald was in town

to see Olengran. Right now, he was slipping over the rock toward Olengran's building, and thankfully, Amelia and Maria were nowhere in sight. I didn't want those two getting infected, nor did I want them harmed. I needed Amelia and Maria to help me gain control of the Dagonites and to permanently make those Eshockers and that tram machine building provide riches for my coffers.

The only human who *looked* like a human, I stood out here. Fitzgerald might easily notice me. Quickly, I ducked into the alley that ran behind the shacks edging the mud beach. What I presumed to be a child gnawed on a fish head by a pile of bones. Tiny, crouching on six legs pocked with open sores, the child's cylindrical body was horizontal to the ground. The head sat, neckless, on the top center of the cylinder. Four skinny arms with claws held the fish head to a giant mouth with the teeth of a mountain lion. She, or he, or *it* peered up at me as I scooted past, and a cold fear trembled down my body. I broke into a sweat.

Acids churned in my stomach. My hunger had given way to a total lack of appetite. I'd have to force myself to eat at least once a day while in Innsmouth. Where and what I would eat was unknown. I'd certainly not succeeded last night in finding lodgings and a meal. Fitzgerald's words rang in my ears: *"There is no place in this town for an ordinary man to find ordinary food. I tell you—for your own sake—leave this place at once and return to London."* He'd given me good advice, and as soon as I dispensed with him and this Olengran, I'd be on my way at once.

My nerves jittered from the discordant shrieking that came from within the shacks. Tuneless and harsh, interposed with chittering and clucks, it was like walking through a cloud of noise whose sole purpose was to break my eardrums. Hands clamped over my ears, I picked up my pace. At the end of the alley, I turned toward the sea. To my left stood Olengran's headquarters; to my right, Fitzgerald gazed to sea at the very place where I'd knifed him last night. Waves battered the rocks where he stood, and they muted the cackling, cawing, and shrilling of the villagers.

Dizzy from lack of food and water, I stood, trembling, wavering, with floods of color washing over me. I hung back as Fitzgerald swiveled, eyed Olengran's headquarters, and began limping toward it.

He was attempting to infiltrate it again. *Please let him succeed*, I thought, my heart hammering wildly, *so I can return to London on the next ship. Please!*

His coat whipped around his legs. One hand clamped his rain hat to his head. Despite the haze and the distance, I could see the long slash of dried blood upon his cheek. Our encounter had not gone as smoothly as I'd hoped.

Fitzgerald swung behind Olengran's headquarters and disappeared from view. I crept closer and circled the building, steeling myself from the stink of it and from the flies buzzing around my head. I held onto the blubbery and slimy exterior, and beneath my touch, the building jiggled like a huge slab of fat covered in animal hide. I poked my head around the side to see what was going on. Fitzgerald faced a blubber-and-hide wall, where a door suddenly flew open and out came an Innsmouthian twice his height and pointing a rifle at him. Fitzgerald jumped back, both hands raised, and his hat was whisked to sea by the wind. His eyes widened and glittered with mingled fear and audacity. I admired his spirit, I must say. In another time and place, Fitzgerald and I might have been the best of friends and cohorts in crime.

Wrapped in filthy rags, the guard—for what else could he be?—poked at Fitzgerald's knife-slashed cheek with his rifle. Fitzgerald winced but stood his ground.

"I am Professor Henry Fitzgerald of the Order of Dagon. Olengran knows my name. Please tell him that I've traveled from afar to seek his advice."

The guard's head, mounted on a spike of a neck, bobbled in the wind.

"No entry." His words were guttural but recognizable as English, which surprised me.

"But why? I demand an audience. Give him my name, I beg of you. He will want to speak with me. *Professor Henry Fitzgerald,*" he enunciated his name slowly and carefully.

The bobble head dipped in agreement, and the guard lowered his rifle. He repeated Fitzgerald's name, posing it as a question.

"Yes, yes," Fitzgerald said. "That's correct."

Leaving the professor on the rocks, the guard retreated inside, and before long, emerged with his answer. I noticed that he no longer held a rifle. *So they trust Fitzgerald on some level,* I thought. *This could prove useful.*

A wave crashed on the rocks and jetted high, soaking Fitzgerald and the guard, neither of whom cared. Like everyone else in town, the guard seemed to be a form of half-fish or marine life. As for the professor, my respect for him rose another notch.

"Sorry," the guard said. "Olengran says, no. He says, 'Come back.'"

"But why and when? I demand—"

"Just, 'Come back.'" As Fitzgerald's shoulders slumped, the guard, in broken English, explained, "Two others like you were just here, forced out, bad men, bad motives."

"What men?" Fitzgerald pressed, his eyes narrowed and filled with fury.

"Men. Two. One was half as short as me. One was a tiny bug."

"Do you have their names?"

After hesitating, the guard answered; friendly, I assumed, because Olengran had declared Fitzgerald a Dagonite dignitary or leader of some sort. Despite the guard's broken English, I could not mistake the names that rushed from his mouth in a click-clack guttural stream.

"Sherlock Holmes. John Watson."

The professor cursed at the news. As I slunk off, I heard him tell the guard never to let Sherlock Holmes and Dr. John Watson into Olengran's building, not under any circumstances, for they were dangerous to the cause and should be killed on sight.

If only I could be so lucky, I thought, as I scurried up

the main path leading into the village. *Let Fitzgerald take care of business for me with Olengran. In the meantime, I must attend to Amelia and Maria, protect them from the infected professor.*

I didn't know their hiding place, but I am not a man without intellect and determination. Fully confident that I would achieve my objective, I stopped short upon reaching a high mud wall. I could see no way to scale it, and had to return and find a more winding path back to the main road. Partly to tune out the grating racket that passed as Innsmouthian conversation, I indulged myself and allowed my mind to float into the past—specifically, early 1890, when I'd paid my doctor a fortune to do as I asked and to keep his mouth shut.

It had been worth the skin rash and the sore throat. It had been worth the pustular lesions where Dr. George had infected me with the cowpox—lesions that had spread from my thigh down my leg, had ulcerated and developed black eschar before healing.

I remembered the doctor's face when I'd first requested the treatment.

"But *why*, Professor Moriarty? You are not at risk of contracting smallpox. I inoculated you against it years ago." He'd leaned back on his examination room stool, cupped his chin in a hand, and stared at me with disbelief. "Once is enough," he'd said.

In the 1850s, England had forced smallpox vaccinations upon the public, causing anti-vaccination demonstrations despite the fact that smallpox deaths began to decline. Nonetheless…

"It wasn't that long ago," I'd said, "in the early to mid 1870s, as I recall, when ten thousand people a year were still dying from smallpox."

"But it's 1890 now! Only a few hundred a year are getting the disease. Why are you suddenly so afraid of it?"

"I'm not afraid of anything, Doctor," I'd said coldly. "You should know that." He had shrunk back slightly, his face flushed, as I continued, "I have my reasons. For example, should I travel overseas, I may be exposed to dangers we can hardly imagine. It's well known that other parts of the world are still infected, and heavily. May I point out that, since 1868, British India has reported ten years of smallpox epidemic with millions dying. Some medical experts claim that one incidence of cowpox long ago might not suffice to protect a person from contracting smallpox. Perhaps repeated inoculation is wise, Doctor."

While Dr. George did not have cowpox on hand, he had obtained some for me and did as I asked. Later, before my journey to Innsmouth, he'd also slipped me a few vials containing smallpox. Money had changed his attitude.

"I have no desire to know why you want these vials, Professor. Do me a favor, and never tell me."

A screech snapped me back to the present. Several Innsmouthians burst from a tiny shack, nearly shattering the door. Mold grew all over the bones and driftwood from which the shack had been constructed. Indeed, upon first glance, the Innsmouthians appeared to consist primarily of mold, as well.

I flattened my body against a shack on the other side of the road as the moldy group flailed about and slashed each other with knife-tipped appendages and bit hunks of flesh off each other. I couldn't tell one creature from another: all had too many arms and legs and mouths and humps and assorted eyes and tentacles. Everything was tangled up and rolling in the mud, as the villagers squealed, bayed, barked, and clacked... while jaws snapped, teeth ripped into fleshy blobs, and throats swallowed meat.

Edging away, I noticed a few smaller creatures toddle from the shack onto the road. Another larger creature followed, trying to push the little ones back into the dwelling. One of the fighters embroiled in the mayhem broke free, and I realized that what I'd taken to be mold actually was greasy body fur.

"Taumo-mate!" it shrieked, and then in half-English and half-Innsmouthian clack-shrills, something sounding vaguely like, "Cl-fuh-*ring* shree shree *ring* baby-bo!" I had no idea what the thing was screaming, but the creature by the door scooped up the tiniest one, and just in time; as a tentacle from the fighting pack suddenly swung up, curled, and smacked the baby-carrying figure, knocking the pair down. The Taumo-mate had at least five eyes, and in place of fingers and toes, its appendages all terminated in frills that fluttered in the air or mashed into the mud.

The baby-bo wailed from several mouths, while its

appendage frills swept over what I took to be its mother. She rolled to her side, and an arm whipped out from a hole in her stomach. With an actual hand—a humanlike hand—she snatched up the baby-bo, a formless fleshy blob with miniature multiple heads and tentacles—and draped it on her back. The thing began sucking from a small hump covered in fur and barely concealed by filthy cloth strips.

Claws dug into the creature who had yelled at the mother, and yanked him... her... it back into the fray. Stooping behind a mound of rubbish—decomposing flesh, gnawed bones, and human waste—I watched, with my head splitting from the discordant keening and yammering. Eventually, they pushed apart from one another, spitting shrieks back and forth, and I saw that there had been only three of them in the fight. Green ooze curdled their fur. The one who had screamed at the mother kicked at the others, bellowing and shrilling at them, and it gestured with two long tongues and an arm that was longer than my height. The others slithered away in various directions, leaving me with the two-tongued fighter, the Taumo-mate, and the baby-bo.

Had someone told me that he'd seen such creatures, I would not have believed him, and in fact, I would have punched and kicked him for blatant lying and disrespect. Innsmouth was no place for the faint of heart. Innsmouth was an infestation, a scab on the Earth, a pestilence worse than any pox.

The two-tongued brawler swiveled its head, and five eyes

stared at me. A frill of tendrils, dripping green, swept over my face and torso. Cringing, I wiped my face on the sleeve of my shirt.

"Taumo," the thing said firmly, and then, "Taumo-mate," while fluttering the wet tendrils at his... *wife?* Satiated, the baby detached itself from the exposed hump, and Taumo-mate lifted it and stood by the door to the... *what?* I thought wildly, *the family home?*

"Sampson," I said, giving a fake name. "I'm visiting Innsmouth, looking for two friends, both girls." I gestured at Taumo-mate to provide an example of the word "girl."

"Leave. It is best," Taumo said, while Taumo-mate retreated inside with her infant. "The baby-bo is not well," Taumo explained.

"Your baby is ill?" I asked, wondering why he was telling me about the health of his child.

Coiling his arms both on his back and at his sides, Taumo nodded. He spread his four legs, and where toes should have jutted from feet, dozens of tendrils sank into the mud, keeping him upright. His body consisted of three ovals wrapped mummylike in rags, with ropes tied at the two "waists."

"Enemies came and attacked my family. They injured us. They fed rancid fish oils to the baby-bo. It was done on purpose, no accident." The man, as I now thought of him, was furious, remembering what his enemies had done to his infant. Further broken conversation informed me that Taumo was a major figure in Innsmouth and controlled much of the fish trade with humans. He maintained power using the strength of his huge, extended family, all natives of Innsmouth. Other groups occasionally fought him for control.

"They never force me out," he clacked. "Taumo is the master of Innsmouth. No other."

"What about Olengran?" I asked.

At that, Taumo glared at me.

"Do not speak of that!" he spat.

"Would more human money help you and your family?" I asked, already knowing the answer.

He didn't let me down. He nodded vigorously.

"You are an alien, a human. You will give money to Taumo? Why?"

I told him that I needed the Taumo family's protection for my two friends, the girls.

"If you find the two girls and treat them well, protect them from everyone, keep them out of sight—if you do this for me," I said, "I will give you more human money than you've ever seen at one time. Think what you can do for your family. A bigger home. Better food. Full-time protection for your Taumo-mate and baby-bo."

"I will find them, yes, and then, you will come and pay me."

We reached an agreement, and I left Taumo, feeling that I had found a business partner in the criminal underbelly of Innsmouth, one that I could control. All it would take was a small amount of cash. To Taumo, even twenty dollars would be a fortune. In return, I would make sure that Taumo and his family—a huge contingent of Innsmouth—

kept Amelia Scarcliffe and Maria Fitzgerald safely tucked away and hidden from Professor Henry Fitzgerald. They, in turn, would be safe from his smallpox infection, nor would they know that I was in town. As far as Taumo was concerned, his benefactor was named Sampson.

If things kept going this well, I would be home in London before I knew it. I would take Amelia and Maria with me, of course, and use their powers to get the tram machine to crank out gold.

Before leaving Taumo, I also had him give me directions to a family member, who he promised would give me a bed and food during my stay in Innsmouth. Everything would remain confidential, private, unknown to the world around us.

While I knew that Sherlock Holmes was also in town with his idiot friend, Dr. John Watson, I wasn't worried. What did I care about those two, really? By the time they caught up with me and got a clue as to what I was doing here, it would be too late.

As usual, I had all the control.

The shack where I would be staying—owned by Taumo's family member—was on the other side of Innsmouth, higher on the hill from the fish-processing plant. Anxious for a decent meal, I hurried through the side streets, and before long reached the fish plant. To my left was the wrecked pier, its wood riddled with holes as if rats had gnawed at it for centuries. Its rickety legs wobbled in water the color of dung. Stepping from the pier onto the shore was a character I knew well, and suddenly, my good mood shattered.

Anger flooded me.

Of all the—

Koenraad Thwaite? I'd recognize *him* anywhere: short, froggy body, neck flaps, toe suckers. Thwaite possessed intelligence as well as strange powers beyond my understanding. He was a Deep One from another time and place. The leader of the Dagon gang in England, he had almost destroyed my London enterprise. He was more dangerous than Sherlock Holmes.

He'd escaped my men in England. No longer my prisoner, he'd disappeared. And now he was *here*, no doubt ready to hunt down his beloved Amelia Scarcliffe, the mother of his as-yet unborn offspring.

8
AMELIA SCARCLIFFE

"I want to be one with the others. I want the reef." Maria Fitzgerald, six in human years but eternal in space and time, lay on her stomach, head over the side of the pier, staring into blackness.

At the tip of the pier, where the wood crumbled, mold sweet, and ached to fall into the water, I sat beside her, with my legs dangling and my mind soaring. My toe webs tightened. Trills of excitement shot up my spine.

"He's here," I whispered harshly. "*Mau fetia,* the stars, they align, and they embrace me. Can you not feel him?"

She lifted her round head, tilted it toward me. Her green eyes glazed, and she trembled. The flesh bubbles on her neck jiggled with the pulse of Koenraad, rocked in harmony with his essence, with mine. Yes, we both felt Koenraad.

In my belly, Koenraad's spawn wriggled. They would be born at Devil Reef, here with me and Koenraad. They would emerge potent and powerful, more so than even Maria, whose power eclipsed my own in many ways.

"He swims at Devil Reef with Dagon," Maria said. "All who live in these waters swim to their beat."

"You feel Dagon?" I tried to hide my surprise. I couldn't sense Dagon's presence, although I did feel the surge of Yog-Sothoth at sea—straight out beyond the reef.

"The door is open," Maria said, a direct reference to Yog-Sothoth. Again, I was startled by her powers, so vast…

"Such ability," I said. "When you are much older and choose a mate, my offspring will be eclipsed by your own, I fear."

"You know so much." She wrenched her gaze from mine, and stared at the water swirling by the posts of the pier. "Yet you know so little. You still think of me as more similar to you than I am. Have you not realized it yet, Amelia? I am incapable of reproducing. While I may appear more female than male, in actuality, I have no reproductive organs. I cannot bud. Nothing. I am one. I am static. I continue."

"I have no purpose *other* than to reproduce," I said.

"I am aware," she said simply.

To fulfill the final rule of the Order of Dagon, to bring forth the Great Old Ones and unleash them upon the Earth, I had to give birth to Koenraad's young. I was a vessel. Before he took me upon the slab of open waters at Half Moon Bay, I had been a shopkeeper, serving teas, cakes, and flowers to old ladies. My friends were the mistletoe and the scabby undergrowth of the forests. From time to time, to stifle the boredom, I mixed the mistletoe with the old ladies, never to the benefit of the latter.

Touching my neck flaps, which were hot and swollen with blood, I wondered what would happen after I gave birth. I supposed that Maria would continue serving Dagon and Cthulhu, and as for me, I would cease to serve any purpose.

Did I care?

No. Only humans care about life and death. Even if I died, my existence would continue. It would be in another form, of course, somewhere in another dimensional plane. Possibly, I would float as molecules or embed myself into the darker parts of the universe. Possibly, I would exist as particles so minute that mankind would never notice me.

The human form was finite. Once the body died, the person reached its endpoint. But for Deep Ones, our forms were infinite, and bodies meant nothing.

I'd almost given birth back at Half Moon Bay, but Koenraad had arrived and disrupted the event. *There is always a reason*, I thought, *for everything. Now, we're both at Devil Reef, the most potent place on Earth for our kind. I will give birth here, and Dagon will emerge from the sea to claim my children as his own. Cthulhu will rise from R'lyeh and reclaim the waters, the land, the air. All will bow to Him.*

"Cthulhu has already risen," Maria murmured. "Nyarlathotep, the crawling chaos, has come from the void, as has Azathoth, whose flutes bring the waters alive with music and kill those who cannot hear. Our time is near, Amelia."

Aauhaoaoa demoni aauhaoaoa demoni aauhaoaoa demoni. Ch'thgalhn fhtagn urre'h nyogthluh'eeh ngh syh'kyuhyuh, we thought in harmony. Maria didn't need to hear my words. She knew them, instinctively. They punctured the air between us, entered her flesh, rode her brain waves.

Her hands caressed the water. Fingers stroked the wavelets, and they rose in response to her touch. I gazed at the Innsmouthians in their tiny boats. Not many were in the bay today. Harsh weather kept them indoors, though today was mild enough to bring them out to the mud for play. The few who bobbed in boats couldn't resist the lure of the water, I knew, for I felt the same. I needed the sea. I needed immersion. I cared nothing for the nonsense of humanity, of what they'd brought to this Earth. My mind was tuned to the universe, the stars, the interdimensional interludes, the other times and spaces where colors spoke, shapes breathed, and dimensions slipped into vast whirlpools. The surface life of this planet bored me, as it bored all of my kind. With one exception: Cthulhu slept here, in its depths, and had been here before the first cells of life crept from the seas. Of all times and spaces, this planet demanded that we claim it as our own.

I lost myself in the rhythm of Koenraad and Devil Reef. Shut my eyes, drifted into the lifeblood of the sea. Felt the lush algae, the jagged rocks, the flit of fish against my skin. Cool water flowed past me, under and over me, bubbles of interdimensional time flooded me, enticed me. Maria's fingers fondled the water, and the water fondled me. Koenraad kicked his legs, and his strong arms pushed against the flow of sea. He was with another presence—

Dagon, I assumed—and as they rode the waves beyond the reef, fish died, and in their little boats, the Innsmouthians screamed. There was another presence farther out, yes, I felt it, too...

Koenraad called to me.

"*Aauhaoaoa demoni aauhaoaoa demoni aauhaoaoa demoni. Ch'thgalhn fhtagn urre'h nyogthluh'eeh ngh syh'kyuhyuh.*"

I bolted up, grabbed Maria's arm. She flipped to her back, then sat beside me. Her eyes bored into mine, a mirror reflecting back the knowledge.

Behind us, the pier groaned. Footsteps approached. Without standing, Maria and I both swung around to face the interloper. We feared nothing, and we feared nobody. Indeed, the Innsmouthian who approached was one of our own kind: a worshiper of Dagon but not born of pure Deep Ones. Everyone in the village, interbred for hundreds of years yet spawned from the mating of humans with Deep Ones, worshiped Dagon, but some bore more power than others. By the way he carried himself—not subservient, but rather, confident yet respectful—I sensed that the male before us held a position of authority. He proved me correct.

He spoke in the old language, not in the broken English that Innsmouthians used with outsiders. With a series of clicks and squeals, he told us his name, Taumo, and that he came to offer us protection and shelter.

"We are honored to have you in our village," he said from one of his two mouths, while the other chimed in, "yet your esteemed professor might be in danger, under the grip of maladies unknown to you. The Taumo family is powerful here. I lead the most powerful worshipers of the Order of Dagon. Here. Tightly. At the locus. At Devil Reef."

"What maladies, and what danger?" I asked, also using the old language. "Who sent you?"

Taumo uncoiled several long arms from his back and gently placed the frilly tips on the pier. Easing himself onto his four knees, he sat with us. Tiny feet poked from beneath his rag-robe, and his toes were like his fingers: tendrils that flitted and twitched, flicking the air and absorbing nutrients, dangers, and other sensations. Two eyes looked warmly at me, two others at Maria, and a fifth eye focused on Devil Reef.

"He wants to protect us from Professor Fitzgerald," Maria said. "We are not completely removed from human illnesses and crime. We *were* kidnapped by Moriarty. Even Koenraad was held against his will for a while."

"Never!" I retorted. "Koenraad cannot be held captive. He has his methods."

"And yet," Taumo said through both of his mouths simultaneously, "there *is* danger here. Humans are in town, requesting access to Olengran, who answers only to Dagon Himself. Even I cannot see Olengran. As for who sent me, I can only answer that I sent myself. I sensed that you were here, at the end of the pier, and so I came to find you."

Maria and I locked eyes and transmitted our thoughts, that we both believed Taumo. We would stay with members of his family, as he suggested. He was a devoted servant to our people. While we feared little, timing was everything. The universe was like a clock: when the pendulum swung, click clack, worlds changed; when time thinned or stretched, worlds disintegrated, grew lush, or exploded with violent storms.

From out at sea, the waves rumbled, and the current changed. Koenraad swam toward the reef, and from there, toward shore.

Heat shot up my spine and rushed to my head. Maria pulled me to my feet.

"He comes," she said softly, as Taumo rose and bowed toward the sea.

Claws reached up from the water. They grasped the edge of the pier, which heaved and sank farther into the water. Lurching, I clutched at Maria, who propped me up. We shifted back from the edge of the pier, as green-slime planks swayed and cracked beneath our feet. Decayed wood splashed into the water, which surged up, spraying us with sea nectar. Honey honey honey. Take me take me take me. Now now now now now.

Maria shook my shoulders. Taumo's long arms wrapped around my gigantic, pregnant torso. The world whirled.

Webbed feet slopped onto the broken pier. Slime upon slime. Must and mold greased his neck flaps, which opened and closed as he sucked in air rather than filtering water through his gills.

I gripped Taumo's arms, which quivered. And then

Koenraad's hand rose, and his webbing fluttered across my cheeks. Taumo released me and fell to his knees again, this time with his head on the pier.

Koenraad's thoughts melted into my own. *I found you*, came his words, *through the void, I found you. Interdimensional space. The homelands. I swam, a long journey. We still stay together, you and I, dear Amelia. Our spawn will be born at Devil Reef, with Dagon Himself at our side. Our spawn will flood Innsmouth, they will swim the seas, multiply, and take over all lands. Cthulhu has risen and awaits our spawn, his army.*

"I-I didn't know—" Taumo's voice cracked. "P-please let me help—"

Breaking from me, Koenraad lifted the trembling Taumo to a standing position.

"You need not fear me," he said. "Dagon tells me that you are to be trusted."

"H-he knows of me?"

"Dagon knows all. Olengran knows all. I know all." Koenraad shrugged. "We take your offer of protection, Taumo."

"But... but how did you know that I—"

"What, that you offered to keep Amelia and Maria safely hidden away?" Koenraad asked. "I just answered you. Don't ask stupid questions. Now, leave us here. Return to your dwelling. We'll come to you in our own time. Innsmouth is about to become the most important place on Earth."

The slabs of rock along the shore spasmed, and water

gushed toward sea and shot in one great wave over Devil Reef. It pounded into the sea. Taumo ran down the pier and past the fish-processing plant.

Pain slashed my belly. The offspring beat my insides. They heaved in one mass, and I fell...

Into the water I went, and pain knifed me, a pain unlike any I'd ever felt.

Koenraad and Maria jumped into the water, and together, they held me; and we swam toward Devil Reef. Colors lit the sky, shot up like fires from the reef. Bubbles burst. Creatures spewed from other dimensions.

Great Dagon trembled and drew his most mighty creatures around him.

And I felt Cthulhu now... *I felt Cthulhu.* Giant tentacles shoved the sea aside. His mighty brain focused only on me.

9

Behind me, the rock slabs pulsed. The bay swirled into eddies that spiraled into the air, snatched the fog, and splattered back down in brown showers. Colors sizzled and slashed from the clouds. Innsmouthians wailed death cries, as their boats splintered and the eddies swallowed them, much as black holes devour all. Villagers lined the mud shore, chanting verses from the *Dagonite Auctoritatem*. I recognized the screeches and the harmonies. They didn't need the book to know the chants. I didn't need the book. These words were in our souls.

The reef burst into waves of heat and color, slices of vibration, the shrills of piping intermixed with beating rhythms and deep moaning. The world opened. The world merged. I rode it all. It was part of me, inside me, and I was inside it.

Swallow me, take me, bring me back into the folds of reality. The human plane, a dull surface, a three-dimensional nothingness tinged with unidirectional time, held meaning. Ants crawled upon its surface. There was no joy here, just fleeting spasms of physically manifested jolts traversing nerves and sizzling across the fibers joining them.

I was joy. I was heat. Koenraad swirled in the other zone, clenching my physical being in his webs, suckered to my true being with his mind. He was not joy. He was anger. He reeked of anger: *Death to Moriarty, he who kidnapped me, attempting to imprison me. Death to Moriarty, he who kidnapped Amelia and Maria, hoping for paltry gold.*

Moriarty meant nothing to me. He was probably back in England in one of his dens, serving serums and Eshockings to the ants. *Step on them, crush them. Rid the Earth of them. Let the Deep Ones flourish.* The Earth would be our portal to true reality, to the other spacetimes. We would settle here, devour the nutrients, replenish, and venture forth.

We slid onto the boulders that faced Devil Reef. The sky split. Ice from other places rained down upon us. Succulent ice, drenched in the spices and sweetness of the other, layer upon layer of crystallized taste fused with orange and gold and green. All entered my skin, pulsed through my veins, and surged into my mind.

Sinking into the other with me, Koenraad relaxed, his mind flushed of Moriarty and hatred. He felt febrile, and depleted. His purpose had been to seed me. His physical essence—his corporeal body—was spent and no longer needed.

Maria's mind intoned a steady stream of offerings from the *Dagonite Auctoritatem*. Her body irrelevant, she merged with the lattices and corners and spasms of time. Energy fields and particles, she expanded and contracted, floated outward, sang with the ice, as it clattered across the rocks of Devil Reef and drilled the water. Beneath, the particles penetrated fish and vegetation, which transformed and merged with us and all that is. Scales became sores, tails withered and dropped off, fins became tentacles. Plants died, while otherworldly seeds sank into the depths and sprouted.

Above Devil Reef, the ice hardened into an awning that stretched over the bay, from the north cliff to the south. Sparkling color and dripping sweet juice, the ice blossomed and bulged and formed magnificent geometries: fractals, spirals, jagged sky-high whorls, heavy protrusions that jutted up, kinked, then pointed out to sea. The reef wrapped vegetation and the remains of ordinary animal life around the ice, pressed it, and fused it.

An enormous tentacle rose from the sea directly beyond Devil Reef. It was followed by another tentacle, and then another. They throbbed with intelligence, with power, and all-knowing comprehension. The air thrummed, folded and gave way, and the tentacles curled around the ice-reef awning, suckers facing the sky, tips twitching toward me. The sea opened, and a giant head arose. The eyes were huge and black and flat.

Cthulhu!

I nearly wept at the sight. Koenraad shielded his eyes. Maria swirled around me and into me, particle upon particle. My body convulsed, and as Dagon rose upon Devil Reef, my torso exploded, and all the offspring, the spawn we'd waited for oh so long, surged upward, squirmed, and splashed into the water.

Dagon bared his teeth: each one larger than my body. His green hide glowed, his scales rippled in light. The physical structures—fishlike, froglike—ruptured as he screamed in ecstasy. His scream shattered boats and shacks and half the pier.

Cthulhu's tentacles unfurled and probed the clouds. Ice sheets overhead, ice sheets cracking, the universe opening... Creatures spilled from the beyond onto Devil Reef, where they scooped up my children, held them close, and breathed the life of eternity into them.

The spawn numbered in the hundreds. Some were pure energy, others were formless and made from matter unknown to Earth. Each possessed more power and strength than Koenraad, Maria, and me, combined.

Maria coalesced, a six-year-old form with large green eyes and black hair fringing her ears. I bled upon the rock. I panted. My mind slowed. Koenraad, unconscious, rolled from the boulder into the bay.

10

DR. JOHN WATSON

Four hours after dropping us off in Innsmouth, Hagley returned, as requested. Given how anxious he had been to leave Innsmouth after depositing us there, I had been fretting that he wouldn't show up. We had no other transportation to the Cararo house, and the distance precluded any chance of walking.

"Glad to see you, sir," Holmes said, as we climbed into the vehicle. The driver eyed our filthy coats and trousers. A tall, thin man, Hagley had an easy way about him.

"I guess I'll be tidying up the buggy come morning. No problem, that," he said.

Both Holmes and I reeked of fish and mold. When we had emerged from the wreckage of the *Belle Crown*, we had swum until police rescued us and brought us to shore. They had hosed us down with water, attempting to flush the muck of the Thames off us. This time, I didn't think any amount of hosing would remove the stench from our bodies.

"Now let's get you boys home for hot baths," Hagley said, wrinkling his nose.

"Please," I said. "We'd be most grateful."

"I don't like loitering any more than you do," the man answered, then quickly shut the door and hopped onto his seat, snapped the reins, and whipped the horses to a fast trot.

"At some point, we should talk to Hagley," Holmes said. "I wonder if he drives Dr. Dragoon back and forth between his home and the Cararo residence. I wonder where else he takes the Cararo family. Surely not into Innsmouth, but... what if he does?"

I cradled my injured hand, which throbbed. The bandage would bring Innsmouth filth back to the Cararos' with me. It might infect my hand. I would ask Mary or Fortuna to change the dressing after my bath.

The horses pushed through the Innsmouth muck onto a harder surface, and we pressed into the forest. Denuded trees drooped at our sides. Caws shattered the air. Horse hooves beat the dirt. The reek of fish and excrement clogged my nostrils. I longed to smell anything but Innsmouth— even the stench of Amos Beiler's remains. Holmes and I had dug up his ruined corpse from an unmarked grave in Avebury. I remembered the coils of intestines, the slab of brain we had unearthed. I remembered staggering from the smell. If only I'd known back then...

I burst out laughing.

"What?" Holmes asked. He'd been deep in thought and looked at me, annoyed.

"Amos Beiler. His corpse. Our studies of his remains in our room at the Loggerheads. And me, worrying that the inn would be serving 'Mum's Meat Soup' that night."

"What you'd give for Mrs. Hinds's soup now, eh? I'm afraid we won't be so lucky."

And we weren't lucky, for after a hot bath, the unclotting of Innsmouth gore from my nostrils, and the application of a fresh bandage by Fortuna, my family and I gathered with Holmes for a late dinner of fish heads' broth with fennel. The side dish was a mound of sweetened roe with seaweed.

Fortuna plucked some bread from her pockets and passed it around. "Swiped it from the kitchen earlier," she said, "and I plan to get more tomorrow, a lot more." We swallowed our chunks of bread almost whole. When two maids entered to remove our uneaten meals, Fortuna took Samuel upstairs to his cradle, leaving Mary, Holmes, and me alone in the dining room. Light flickered from the two closest candelabra on the thirty-seat table. The dead fire stifled the remaining Innsmouthian stink that still saturated our flesh. I wasn't the type to douse myself in cologne; nor was Holmes.

Mary urged us to tell her what had transpired in Innsmouth, and we told her about the Taumo family and about Olengran's guards and headquarters. I did not recount my illness in the whale-hide headquarters. I also toned down the guards' threats, their appearance, and their weapons. Hearing a sanitized account of my day, her face blanched, and she started urging me to back down but stopped herself mid-sentence. Mary understood the importance of what we were doing, and this fact became abundantly clear as she in turn told us about her day at the Cararo house.

"Dr. Dragoon is treating Mr. Cararo for a heart ailment, but he's doing so in the billiards room, John, where he has an examination bed."

"What?" I exclaimed. "How do you help an elderly man with a weak heart using billiards? I wonder why Dragoon needs the bed in there."

"John, I don't know. But that's just the tip of the strange activities in this house." Mary leaned toward me, and Holmes scraped his chair closer.

"What else can you tell us about Cararo?" he asked.

"Nothing much, I'm afraid. According to Harry Rinsdale, Mr. Cararo's wealth came from his ancestors' business dealings and relationships with the Innsmouthians. He sent his driver, Hagley, into Boston to find a wife for him. Hagley returned with Hortense, a saloon dancer."

"Saloon dancer. Usually, that means a woman of the night." Holmes pulled out his pipe, tapped it on the table, filled it, and struck a match. He leaned back in his chair and puffed, staring thoughtfully at Mary.

"Exactly, Holmes. I think Mary is telling us that Hortense Cararo is a tawdry sort."

Mary nodded.

"Yes. She married Mr. Cararo for the money, and worse, she's been carrying on with Dr. Dragoon." Mary explained that Hagley had found the Cararo family doctor in the same saloon as Frederick's future wife.

"Dragoon and Hortense were probably *close* in Boston," Holmes said, his eyes narrowing. He rapped his fingers on the table while his other hand held the pipe to his lips. After a few puffs of smoke, he added, "So they came here together, for the old man's fortune, I assume, and they've been bleeding him dry ever since. And what about the children, Mary? Are they Frederick Cararo's or Dr. Dragoon's?"

"Why, I don't know!" she exclaimed. "Frederick wanted heirs, which is why he sent Hagley off to find him a wife—any wife would do, it seems. So I just assumed..."

"Have you seen Jeffrey and Sylvia?" I asked. "Do they resemble either man? More important, are they... are they like other humans, or like the Innsmouth creatures?"

"I've not seen them, no." She shook her head. "I tried to find them, but instead, came across Dragoon injecting Hortense with cocaine—like your solution, Mr. Holmes. They were cooing at each other like lovers." She told us that Mr. Rinsdale had pointed out to her the "nether wing," where the two children supposedly slept. Dragoon's quarters were located in the same wing, she said, "but John, I heard Dragoon and that despicable Hortense chattering about how he drugs both children into oblivion to shut them up. She didn't mind in the slightest. She wants nothing to do with them."

"Her own children. God help us all," I said, shaking my head. I squeezed Mary's hand. "You've been busy. I think you achieved more than Holmes and I did in Innsmouth. There might be a link between the Cararos and this whole

Dagon Cthulhu business. What do you think, Holmes?"

He procured a tray from a side table and returned, knocking out his pipe ashes. Then he took a small case from his jacket pocket, pulled out a cigarette, and lit it. The acrid cigarette smoke floated in the air, mingling with the sweetness from the pipe, and for once, I welcomed it. While I typically hounded Holmes about his love of cigarettes, I wasn't averse to an occasional puff. He offered me the case, and I took three cigarettes, pocketed two, and lit the first. Mary didn't object. Thus far, we had only been here for one day. If we stayed in Innsmouth for too long, we might all end up injecting cocaine, I thought drily. This was clearly not a place that encouraged healthy habits.

"Tell me about the two children, the possible Cararo heirs," Holmes urged, as he pushed the ashtray toward me.

"Mr. Rinsdale tells me that Jeffrey is unusually quiet— he plays with toy soldiers and likes a book about trains, but doesn't communicate with others," Mary said. "He does little else. The nanny does nothing with him, and the poor little boy receives no education or attention. He never leaves his room. Along with hemophilia, he has a mental disease of unknown nature and is not expected to live to maturity, to quote Mr. Rinsdale." Further, she explained, while Sylvia did possess both physical and mental health, her parents cared nothing for her. "She's but six years old, John. So young. The nanny teaches her some lessons, again according to Mr. Rinsdale, but the parents... *alas.*"

"So Frederick Cararo basically has no heir—no male

heir expected to live, that is," Holmes said. "The parents consider their children to be without value and seem incapable of even basic affection. If Mr. Cararo dies, Hortense might inherit everything unless the estate is set aside into trust. But we can surmise that Cararo would not set it aside for Jeffrey or Sylvia?"

I hugged Mary and stroked her hair. I knew how much she loved children, in general, and how she doted on our Samuel. The doctor in me was furious that two children were being drugged and neglected with no hope of release.

"Holmes, we must take action," I said. "We must rescue the children from the Cararos and their doctor. I will have Dragoon's license revoked, if it's the last thing I do."

Snuffing his cigarette, Holmes stared past me and Mary, his focus on the candles that had burned to nubs.

"Let's not get ahead of ourselves," he said. "We can dispense with the doctor easily enough, later on. But let's return to the matter at hand. If Dragoon rather than Frederick Cararo is the father, then we might be able to save the children."

"Why is that?" I exclaimed.

"Because," Holmes said, "Cararo's ancestry must be Innsmouthian, at least in part. He's not mutated in the manner of the villagers we encountered today, Watson, leading me to think that he has more recent human ancestry than the villagers; but still, we know that he shares their blood. It is no coincidence that his family—but no other *human* family—has lived on the edge of Innsmouth for centuries. It is no coincidence that Cararo is so rich—specifically due to the Innsmouth fish head trade. Dragoon, on the other hand, came here from Boston, and as far as we know, there's no evidence linking his family to the Deep Ones."

Mary and I glanced at each other, nodding, both understanding Holmes at the same time. If Cararo was father to the children, they were lost to the world of the creatures we must eliminate from the Earth. But if Dragoon was their biological father, then the children were possibly pure human; abused, yes, and terribly neglected, but with kindness, education, and loving guidance, they could be saved. Even Jeffrey, both physically and mentally afflicted and not expected to reach adulthood, could enjoy a few years of reasonable happiness.

Setting aside the discussion, we decided to adjourn for the night. Wearily, I dragged myself up the stairs to my bedroom. It was only our second night sleeping in the Cararo mansion, and I awakened all night in cold sweats with tuneless shrilling in my mind.

Ch'thgalhn fhtagn urre'h nyogthluh'eeh ngh syh'kyuhyuh! Aauhaoaoa DEMONI aauhaoaoa DEMONI aauhaoaoa DEMONI!

Finally, afraid to fall asleep again lest the keening blur into the nightmares I'd had in London, I lay awake and fidgeted. I focused on Samuel's breathing, Mary's breathing: like two clocks ticking in harmony.

Inhale. Exhale. Inhale. Exhale.

Then: *Screeeeeeeee!*

126

At the unearthly noise, our peace was broken. Mary screamed, leapt from bed, and grabbed Samuel, who was already crying, little red face wet with tears, little fists balled.

Screeeeeeeee!

"Stay here," I said, and in my night shirt, I raced from the bedroom. On the landing over the hexagonal room, the coils in the paintings had unfurled and now lashed the air. Cubes of color exploded, and no amount of blinking erased them. I knew myself to be quite sane. What I saw was actually in front of me. I raced down the curved staircase.

Voices hollered from the vicinity of the dining hall and the billiards-examination room. It was difficult to ascertain *who* was yelling over the incessant *Screeeeeeeee!* noises that shrilled from above me, below me, and seemingly from inside the walls. My ears throbbed, and I sank against the arch leading from the hexagonal room to the main hall. Clapping my hands over my ears, I cringed and tried desperately to block out the shrilling. Muffling my ears didn't help, and still, I heard it: *Screeeeeeeee!* and then, a melody in E-minor took hold. *No*, I thought, *it can't be...* but it was: Michael Nolan's "Little Annie Rooney," distorted into E-minor with discordant trills. This was the song of my nightmares, the bizarre fusion of human and inhuman that I'd first heard after the deadly dimensions opened in Willie Jacobs's tram machine building.

"She's my *syh'kyuhyuh*,
I'm her *urre'h*.

Soon we'll die ne'er to part.
She tried to warn me, tried to explain
Her children were not meant to be plain.
...after the stars are gone...
...after the stars are gone...
Ch'thgalhn fhtagn urre'h nyogthluh'eeh ngh syh'kyuhyuh."

Clinging to the wall, I inched forward, wishing I'd thought to bring my gun. Clad in my dressing gown, which hung to my feet, I would be hampered in any brawl. Eyes open, ears ringing from the words I couldn't have pronounced under threat of death, I tottered from the wall and tried to ascertain the room from which I'd heard the hollering.

A hand grabbed my shoulder from behind and I whirled around.

"Holmes! Oh, thank God you're here!" I cried.

His face ashen, his eyes puffy from lack of sleep, and also dressed in his sleeping gown, he would hardly be a match for whatever we encountered; but at least, there were two of us now rather than one.

"What's wrong with you, Doctor? Be steady, I say."

"Y-you don't hear it?" I whispered.

"Yes, I hear it. The screaming. Dr. Dragoon, Frederick Cararo, and Hortense. From the billiards room."

"Why, Holmes..." I stammered, embarrassed, "I-I hear other things, as well. My ears—"

"You are more susceptible than I am, Watson. You suffered from the neural psychoses, which I did not. Tell yourself firmly that what you hear is not real. Tell yourself," he commanded as I shook my head in bewilderment.

"But I was cured," I said.

"We haven't time for this. Ignore whatever afflicts you. *Follow me.*"

He dashed to the billiards-examination room, and I saw that the door was open.

"She's my *syh'kyuhyuh*,
I'm her *urre'h*.
Screeeeeeeeee!"

I jerked off-balance. I barely managed to stagger to the billiards-examination room, and when finally I got there, I stumbled inside and sank onto the nearest chair.

The room smelled of rich leather and mahogany intermingled with the ashes of the spent fire. Without a coat or blanket, I was already shivering from the freezing night. Innsmouth was colder than London, much colder.

It was a gentleman's room, with overstuffed chairs, side tables, and plenty of ashtrays. From the looks of it, Cararo rarely entertained anyone here. One cue lay upon the billiards table along with the balls, all popped into the triangle that held them prior to a game. The examination bed Mary had told us of was crude: hard wood, thin mattress, soiled sheet. A small black case, large enough to hold a few hypodermic needles or vials of medicine, sat waiting on a side table behind the bed.

My mind flashed to Willie Jacobs on his cot at the Whitechapel Lunatic Asylum. Then I remembered Willie on the floor of the boat, dying, after we'd killer-Eshocked the creatures in the Thames.

"Kill 'em that killed me father," he'd rasped. "Get 'em all, Mr. 'olmes." Those had been his last words.

"Dr. Watson!" It was Dragoon who addressed me, and I lifted my eyes from the small black case and from my memories. Around me, above me, below me: the howling of those from beyond continued unabated. "You must help me talk some sense into Mr. Cararo. Please. You're a doctor. Help me get him onto the bed, where we can administer a sleeping draught."

Holmes, arms shaking from the cold, helped me to my feet and to the billiards table. With my back against the table's edge, I clenched it with both hands.

"Get back!" Frederick Cararo stabbed his cane at the air. "You give me any drugs, and I'll kill you!"

Dragoon held a doctor's bag, which he set upon the examination bed and opened. From it, he removed a syringe. I pushed myself from the billiards table and peeked into Dragoon's bag. As he glared at me, I backed off to my position by the table. I'd seen nothing untoward in the doctor's bag: in particular, no cocaine—unless it was disguised in one of several unmarked bottles.

"One doesn't inject a sleeping draught," Holmes commented. "What is in that syringe?"

"What are you looking for in Dr. Dragoon's bag, Dr.

Watson?" Hortense Cararo interrupted, addressing herself to me. I'd been avoiding her gaze. While her husband wore a heavy robe and nightcap along with slippers, and Dragoon was clad in wool trousers and a jacket, Hortense wore a ruby silk robe that left little to the imagination. Although her teeth chattered and her body shook from the cold, she didn't seem to mind. I supposed that burlesque dancers were accustomed to wearing next to nothing in the Boston winters.

"I thought perhaps Dr. Dragoon had a cocaine supply in his bag," I answered truthfully.

She giggled and smiled flirtatiously at Dragoon.

"He supplies me with whatever *I* want," she said, "but not necessarily from his bag."

"Hortense!" her husband rasped. "Our private lives are to be kept private."

"Where do you keep your cocaine, Mrs. Cararo?" Holmes asked, but Dragoon answered, telling us that if any cocaine was in the house, it would be in the lady's private rooms, not that it was any of our business.

"Do you want to indulge with me, Mr. Holmes?" Hortense cooed. "We know from Dr. Watson's accounts of your adventures that you enjoy the needle from time to time, yes?"

The shrilling from walls, ceiling, and floors subsided, and thankful, I sank back into the chair near the door. All I wanted was my wife, my bed, and a good night's sleep.

"Let's do it." Hortense sidled up to Dragoon, rubbing her

body against his. He shivered, not from the cold but from something else. He eased her away.

"Not now, sweetness. He's in no mood."

"You drug me like the others, and I'll send you both into the streets!" The elderly Cararo tottered, dropped his cane, and fell to the floor. Huffing for air, he clutched his chest.

"Maybe he's dying," his wife said, then glanced at Holmes and added, "the poor, dear man. We have two doctors in the room! Do something!"

Dragoon knelt to inject Cararo with whatever was in his needle. Feeling compelled to intervene, I rushed to the old man's side and knocked Dragoon's arm away. The needle fell to the carpet.

I demanded a stethoscope, and I placed my ear upon Cararo's chest and by his lips. Air hissed in and out of his mouth. His heart sounded steady, his pulse felt strong.

Together, Holmes and I lifted the old man and helped him to a chair. We gestured at his wife to back off, and as for Dragoon, we commanded him to stay clear of his patient.

"You don't know what you're meddling in, Holmes!" Dragoon yelled, all pretense of manners and compassion gone. "My patient is insane. He's not at all well. You don't know. How would you?"

"Sir, you might want to remain calm." Holmes spoke to Frederick Cararo, ignoring Dr. Dragoon.

"I'll give it all to 'em, that's what I'll do!" Cararo bellowed. "Dagon and great Cthulhu, they come, they're here! All my life I've waited, and finally, they've returned!"

"Shut your mouth," Hortense hissed, balling her hands into fists and edging toward her husband. Holmes rose and held her back, extending his arms to keep both the wife and her lover from gaining access to Cararo.

"How dare you," she hissed at Holmes, but he didn't waver.

"Mr. Cararo," he said, "would you allow us to get you some help? Dr. Watson and I can take you to Boston ourselves and check you into the finest hospital. I fear that you might be in danger here. Please, I urge you to consider my offer."

But instead, Cararo pulled himself to a sitting position and raged at us. He snatched up his cane and jabbed it at his wife, at Dragoon, and even at Holmes and me. His eyes glazed. The vein throbbing over his drooling lips, he denounced all of us in the most vile terms, then abruptly switched topic.

"The hatchlings flood the sea," he rasped, "and mighty Dagon gains his army. Yog-Sothoth has opened the gate. Hospitals won't matter. Silks and satins won't matter. My family has ties here. They will rule, not the likes of you!"

"But what about our children?" Hortense whined. "Don't you care what happens to them?"

Dr. Dragoon, highly agitated, plucked his needle from the carpet and tucked it into his bag. He straightened his wool jacket.

"You have lost your wits, old fellow," he told his patient, then, mustering up his fake-warm doctor's voice, added, "please let us take care of your affairs before it's too late. There *are* two children to think about, sir. Your heirs."

"Heirs? Those two?" Cararo burst out laughing. He yanked a bell from the pocket of his robe and rang it. "One's feeble-minded, the other's a girl. I have no heir! My money and all that I have will go to Dagon and Cthulhu!"

"Your children," I said sternly, "are human beings. Your son, I am sure, deserves more care than he gets here. As for your daughter, you should be ashamed, sir. Have you no heart?"

Holmes and I glared roundly at the bunch of them: Cararo, Hortense, Dragoon.

"I have rung for Mr. Hagley," the old man snorted, "who will take me to Innsmouth, where I will be among friends. The rest of you are hereby on your own. I bid you adieu." With a flourish of his hand and an upraised chin, he gestured at us to leave his presence.

Holmes and I were only too happy to leave the madman to himself. Hortense and Dragoon clung to one another as they departed.

"Not to worry, my sweet," the doctor crooned. "He's old. He's lost his wits. It's nothing new. It happens."

"But we'll lose all, and I've given that withered, decrepit, old monster my finest years," she wailed. "He's taken my body." She shuddered. "Everything!"

"Give him the night. In the light of day, he'll see things differently."

Holmes shook his head, and as we reached the upper floor where our bedrooms waited, he told me to get some rest.

"Don't let any absurd nightmares interfere. You're going

to need your wits about you, Watson. I fear that Frederick Cararo is heading down a wretched path. The wife and Dragoon will toss us out of here if we don't help them, or pretend to help them. They're a bad lot, those two."

"And the children?" I said softly.

"We will do what we can. We have much to attend to, Doctor. We have yet to meet with Olengran. We have yet to close our world to Dagon and his fellow creatures. We have yet to permanently shut down the deadly dimensions. Then there's the matter that brought us here. *Cthulhu*." His body quaking with cold, he opened the door to his bedroom. "With Cararo's sudden outburst about Dagon and Cthulhu, I know that we're running out of time, Watson. His outburst surely coincided with something that has happened, something we don't know about. Tomorrow, good doctor. For now—" He pointed to my bedroom, but one door away from his, and I nodded and stumbled off to a deep sleep.

11

After a few hours, I awakened, my mind fixated on the drugs that Dragoon might have been administering to Frederick Cararo and his children. Clearly, the doctor didn't provide sleeping draughts. One possibility was paraldehyde, a sedative and hypnotic injected into the deranged for approximately the past ten years in England. Side effects included tissue necrosis and nerve damage. Injections were painful. Another possibility was chloral hydrate, also a sedative and hypnotic, sometimes used for recreational purposes. Those who frequented Moriarty's dens or the opium haunts of England might dabble with chloral hydrate, but doctors also prescribed it.

As a sick sun straggled from behind black clouds, the household awakened. We bustled downstairs to the dining room. Fortuna gave me her word that she would befriend the cooks and make sure we all had enough bread to sustain us. She would also beg for anything else she found in the kitchen; any vegetables, fruits, cheeses, baked items. We had little hope that she would find much.

Breakfast was the same as before: the cake-like American muffins, herring in strange sauces, strong coffee. The Pinkertons all had hangovers and apologized profusely for their absence during the night's disturbance. Harry Rinsdale, in particular, promised us that he would hereafter ban alcohol and poker from the Pinkertons' evening rituals. The red-haired Terrance McCole glared at Rinsdale and muttered that "this is an unfair punishment."

"What do you expect us to do all day, sit outside a baby's boudoir and talk about nappies?" Knuckles Smith grumbled.

"Babies don't have boudoirs, idiot," McCole said.

"It doesn't matter," Smith answered. "We can't be expected to do nothing all day. And at night: what then? This has to be one of the worst assignments I've had. We're detectives, Terrance, not babysitters."

Holmes slammed his fist on the table.

"Gentlemen," he said firmly, "your avocations have no relevance. The only thing that matters is that you protect the Watson family at all times. You are to keep watch over Samuel, Mary, and Fortuna twenty-four hours a day. And if you hear anything out of the ordinary in this house, you must immediately check it out. And bring your guns. Do you understand? For if not, I will report you to the government authorities, who will report you to the head of the Pinkertons. You will be dismissed, I am certain, and replaced with more suitable protection."

Rinsdale choked on a shred of herring and spat it out. He dabbed at his mouth with a napkin. With both McCole and Smith rising in protest, Rinsdale waved them back to their seats. He addressed Holmes.

"I give you my word, sir, that this will not happen again. Am I right, boys?" He stared at his two underlings, who looked miserable but nodded.

"Sorry, boss," the Knuckles fellow grumbled. "It won't happen again. But can we play cards? No beer or whiskey, I swear. Just let us play cards."

Holmes nodded at Rinsdale, who agreed to the request. The head detective added that "if all goes well, boys, I'll see to it that your next assignments are more interesting. In the meantime, if it's danger you crave, I suspect you'll have plenty of that here."

By now, we'd all finished with the morning's fare, and Holmes was keen to head back to Innsmouth and crack into Olengran's headquarters.

"There is no way those guards will let us into the inner sanctum," I said. After yesterday's infiltration of the place, I saw no point in trying again.

"With more time, I'll find a way," Holmes replied. "Mary, my dear, would you be kind enough to leave the Doctor and me with the Pinkertons? We have business to discuss. I don't want to upset you in any way."

"I can hear anything you have to say," she said. But she gestured at Fortuna, and she, the nanny, and Samuel headed into the hall for what I assumed would be another hellish day at the Cararos'. My poor family. They were like prisoners here.

Shortly after they left the dining room, Hortense Cararo slinked in with Dr. Dragoon. She was either drunk or drugged, or both. He propped her up with an arm around her waist. She encircled his waist with both of her arms. I felt my cheeks grow warm. My god, the lack of manners and the nerve of these people.

Dragoon gently maneuvered her into a chair next to me. I smelled no alcohol on her, yet her manner was woozy: she slumped in the chair, and I had to help Dragoon lift her shoulders and straighten her position. She giggled, her eyes hazy. The limp brown hair was a tangled mess on her shoulders. A red satin gown clung to her body. Falling to her ankles, it was nonetheless slit on either side to the tops of her thighs. Odd for such a garment, it was long-sleeved with fake-leopard cuffs encircling her wrists. Additional strips of fake fur formed a plunging neckline. From what I could tell, the lady of the house wore nothing beneath her gown. I tore my eyes away, thankful that Mary and Fortuna had already left the dining room.

Dragoon sat next to her and across from Holmes, snatched up a muffin, and placed it on a gold-edged plate for Hortense. She wrinkled her nose. He spooned herring onto his own plate from a silver tureen with bas-relief octopi swirling around its upper edge.

Holmes lit his pipe and stared at them through narrowed eyes.

"Where is your husband, madam?" he asked.

She giggled, and Dragoon placed a hand on her arm.

"Mr. Cararo has left us," the doctor said.

"As in...?" My heart leapt. Had they murdered the old man?

"Oh, no, Dr. Watson," Dragoon laughed. "He's not dead, not that we know, that is. He *left* us. You were there, gentlemen, when he rang for Mr. Hagley."

"But where did Mr. Hagley take him?" Holmes inquired. "Into Innsmouth, as Mr. Cararo threatened?"

"Well, I suppose so," Dragoon murmured. He lowered his voice and cupped his hands over his mouth. "We really must find him, Mr. Holmes. His very life is at risk out *there*. Mrs. Cararo and the children..."

Hortense's eyes shut and she slumped over, her head landing on my shoulder. I nudged her back to a sitting position. Her head lolled. Gurgling, she snapped her eyes open again.

Holmes ignored her. He didn't reply directly to what Dragoon had said. We both knew that the pair before us cared nothing about Frederick Cararo, Jeffrey, or Sylvia. They cared only about themselves. They wanted the Cararo fortune.

"Where might Mr. Cararo go in Innsmouth?" Holmes asked. "Does he have any close friends there, the type to take in a man in the dead of night?"

At that, Dragoon laughed again.

"He has *family* in Innsmouth."

"What? *Who?*" Holmes cried. When the doctor didn't answer, he asked again, this time more forcefully: "*Who?*"

"You will find my husband?" Hortense gurgled.

"If I know where he is, then yes, Dr. Watson and I will attempt to bring him home."

"Should we bring a Pinkerton?" I suggested. "Mr. Rinsdale, do you care to accompany us?"

"Hell no!" the man said. "I'm not going into Innsmouth. I was hired to stay here and guard your family, sir, and that's what I'm going to do."

"Hortense and I will accompany you," Dragoon said. "I want to make sure the old man is... safe."

"He fled from you, sir. Do you think it wise that you and Mrs. Cararo accompany us?"

"I will have it no other way," the man answered firmly. "I am his doctor. I know what's best for him. And Hortense is his wife. You, sir, with no ill respect, are new to these parts, and you are a stranger."

Holmes and I had decided to play along with Dragoon and Hortense. It was essential to keep Frederick Cararo at the estate. Otherwise, the doctor and wife might throw us out, and where else could we possibly stay near Innsmouth?

We had no choice but to agree to Dragoon's suggestion. Holmes did so with the grace of a gentleman, and disgusted as I was, I followed suit.

We offered ten dollars to Hagley if he would agree to make another journey into Innsmouth.

"The old man's gonna kill me if I take you there," he said. "I'll lose my job."

"I'm gonna kill you if you don't take me to Mr. Cararo,"

Dragoon replied. "And I'll make sure that Mrs. Cararo fires you *before* I kill you."

Holmes shrugged.

"I've driven buggies before, Mr. Hagley. It's not difficult. You don't have to take us yourself. Just tell us where you deposited Mr. Cararo."

We huddled in heavy coats beneath black clouds that threatened to explode with rain at any moment. Already, a mist obscured the road in front of the house. It clawed at my skin, pricked me beneath my rain cloak, jacket, trousers, and gloves. What the deuce was in the air? Perhaps the foul atmosphere carried pollutants that irritated the skin. Perhaps I was overthinking and worrying needlessly that the tiny otherworld creatures were clawing at me again. As I scratched my arms, Hagley told us that Mr. Cararo was staying in a shack two alleys over from the Taumo residence.

"Relative of Taumo," he said. "They're all relatives of Taumo in Innsmouth—well, almost all of 'em…"

"What's the name of the family where he's staying?" Holmes demanded, as he hoisted himself onto the driver's seat. I clambered into the buggy along with Dragoon and Hortense. The doctor sat in the middle, and I was thankful for the wafts of cologne that emanated from him. I was also glad not to be crammed next to Hortense, whose dizziness had begun to pass. Both scratched at their arms and necks. Noticing my discomfort, Dragoon told me to get used to it.

"It's in the air," he said, "the brown fog. It won't hurt you. You just scrub it off and make do. If you're lucky, you'll be out of here soon enough and back in London."

"And you?" I asked. "Where will you go, Dr. Dragoon?"

With a puzzled expression, he squeezed Hortense Cararo's hand.

"Why, I'll still be here, Dr. Watson. My home is here. My patients are here. I would never think of leaving them."

Not bothering to respond, I thought grimly that, as soon as Dragoon and Hortense disposed of her husband and she inherited everything, they would leave not only Innsmouth, but the country.

Mr. Hagley supplied a more precise location of Mr. Cararo's whereabouts to Holmes. He muttered a name that sounded something like *C'lk'grhw'erm'ye*. Then Hagley shut the door, and Holmes snapped the reins. The horses trotted into the mist.

PART TWO

THE ARKHAM SANITARIUM

12

The mist grew thicker as we emerged from the forest and neared the village. The buggy slid on the icy ground, and Holmes slowed the horses.

"This isn't a good sign," Dragoon told me. "The black cloud that's descended over Innsmouth, rolling in from the sea, as it always does, portends the orgies and caterwauling—"

"...the orgies," Hortense murmured.

"They go crazy here, become mindless," Dragoon continued. "You don't want to be anywhere near the mud beach or in the village at all when they start—" He broke off and shook his head.

Neighing and snorting with distress, the horses shied along an alley. I heard Holmes's reins snap as he commanded them to move forward. From the distant coastline came shrieking and wailing much louder and more discordant than my nightmares.

She's my *syh'kyuhyuh*,
I'm her *urre'h*.

Soon we'll die ne'er to part.

She tried to warn me, tried to explain

Her children were not meant to be plain.

...after the stars are gone...

...after the stars are gone...

Ch'thgalhn fhtagn urre'h nyogthluh'eeh ngh syh'kyuhyuh.

Hortense bolted upright, reached across Dragoon's lap, and clutched at me.

"I'm sorry, Dr. Watson, but what did you say?" Her voice was shrill. "Not *that* song, not *that*!"

I'd thought the tune was in my head, percolating up due to the screeching of the villagers. Were they singing the tune? I focused, but their voices skittered in all directions, the syllables forming sounds unlike any language I'd encountered during my travels. Feeling like a fool, I asked Dr. Dragoon if I'd spoken, actually said the words aloud.

"You said nothing," Dragoon assured me. "She's—" his eyes slid sideways at Hortense "—not quite all *here*. She's suffered a lot. Married an insane old man. Lived in that house. Her children. *Oh.* The *children*." He shook his head. "The strains she endures, Doctor, I don't know how she manages."

I'm sure you do, I thought. I must have uttered the words of my nightmare, for how else would Mrs. Cararo have heard them? The villagers' screeches were not of this world.

We jerked to a halt, wheels creaking. Holmes jumped from the front of the buggy and secured the horses, consoling them. I wondered what he had tied them to, for any structure in Innsmouth was rotting and liable to fall with the slightest tug from the weakest of horses.

The door swung open. The outline of Holmes's face, long and thin, was etched as if from charcoal on a black canvas. I staggered out of the vehicle, Holmes holding me steady, and then he helped Dragoon and Hortense. Blinking rapidly, I peered into the murk, trying to get my bearings. The screeching and clucking grated on my ears. Holmes clamped his hat securely over his own ears, tying strings beneath his chin. Hortense wrapped her arms around Dragoon, with her head on his shoulder. *It might be a blessing that she has remained drugged*, I thought, *for how else could one bear living in this environment for so many years?* As for Dragoon, his face and body shook: jittery, frightened.

Holmes had tied the horses to a plank of wood jutting from one of the shacks that lined the alley. Ice beneath our feet, we moved slowly, holding onto each other. We passed a hut shaped like one of the American "muffins" we'd seen at breakfast, though this had mold slathered down the sides and smeared across the top. As always, the stench assailed me, permeating my senses, seeping into the core of my being. If one gathered all the rotting corpses buried beneath the earth, if one gathered all the garbage and filth and feces: still it would not match the stench of Innsmouth. It was as if the earth had opened and disgorged its insides in one putrid upheaval, as a volcano disgorges lava. The resulting vomit was Innsmouth.

Holmes kicked open the door to the muffin-shaped hut, and mold fell from above us and splattered into slimy blotches upon the ground. I stepped from ice to mold to a hard dirt floor. On the opposite side of the round room, a single candle burned. Piles of fish heads and bones were heaped on the floor. Sitting with his back to the fish debris and his legs stretched out, Frederick Cararo picked his teeth with a fingernail and surveyed us. His eyes lit upon Hortense and slithered up and down her body, then set upon Dragoon, at whom he sneered.

Slime dripped from the ceiling. Splotches broke free and fell like dead fish, ricocheting from my head and arms.

"*C'lk'grhw'erm'ye.*" Frederick Cararo addressed his wife. "We share blood, my dear. There's no longer any reason to hide it. Dagon has risen from Devil Reef. Cthulhu is here. The spawn grow and thrive. Our wait is over."

"You're insane!" she spat. "You need to come home, Frederick, where we can take care of you. You can't stay *here*!"

"Sir." Dr. Dragoon slid free of Hortense and yanked at Cararo's upper arms, trying to force him up. The old man resisted, but was no match for the doctor. I hurried to Dragoon's aid, and between us, we forced Cararo up. Then, linking his arms over our shoulders, we dragged him to the door.

"What are you doing here, sir?" Holmes asked. "Have you come to Innsmouth to be with your kin? Have you come for the festivities upon the beach? Are you part of the Dagonite order?"

"Idiot!" the old man bellowed. "Of course, I'm part of it! I own Innsmouth, and beneath me are Taumo and his kind. The only one above me or anyone else here is Olengran."

What is Olengran's function? I thought. *Why do they need him if Dagon and Cthulhu have "risen," as Cararo insists?*

"Just shut up." Hortense let out a stream of curses at her husband. No more flirting. No more fake sweetness. Hortense was showing her true self: a hard woman who never took *no* for an answer. "Get your ass in the buggy, Frederick. You're going home. I mean it." Her forehead creased into a deep frown. Her eyes were steel.

Too frail to fight us, her husband had no choice in the matter, and Holmes and I deposited both of the Cararos and their doctor in the vehicle and slammed the door. It was too cramped for another passenger, so I sat up front with Holmes, wedging myself on a corner of the driver's seat.

"I don't like to leave them alone with him," I muttered. "And I have been wondering why they are so keen to fetch him home. If they just let Cararo stay here, he'll most certainly die, and then they inherit all. Why do they bother, Holmes?"

He turned the horses from the coast and the caterwauling, and drove toward the forest.

"Money," he said. "Think about it, Watson. They need to control the old man. If he's alone in Innsmouth, even for one day, what happens if he changes his will and leaves everything to Taumo or Olengran? If he's at home, they watch over him, make sure he doesn't change his will."

Nodding, I understood Holmes's point. It had always been about money. Hortense had married for it. Dragoon had come with her to feed off Cararo through his relationship with the old man's wife.

"Why didn't the two of them kill him off long ago?" I asked. "Why wait?"

"Suspicious death." Holmes steered us into the forest, where the tarnished air was but a ghost of the Innsmouth stench. "They had everything they wanted. Cararo already has a heart condition, and he's so old, Watson: the poor sap won't last long. Hortense would inherit everything. Why risk *murdering* Cararo when they had no need? Even now, they won't murder him outright, not with us here. No, Watson, I do not think we need to fear leaving them alone with him in the buggy.

"The Pinkertons, much as they hate being here, would view Cararo's outright murder as suspicious. I believe the police would come to these parts and do the same. Also, we don't know the full nature of Hortense's and Dragoon's pasts. Of what we know about Hortense, she worked with shady people in shady places. I would put nothing past her. As for Dragoon, I think we can both agree that no respectable doctor would live here."

"With the uprising of the esoteric gangs, all this Dagon and Cthulhu worship orgy nonsense," I commented, "perhaps Dragoon and Hortense think it's time to start injecting Cararo with drugs to speed up his demise. He's throwing himself into the freakish worship that's gripped the village. He's threatening to leave his estate to Dagon."

"Such a death would not appear suspicious," Holmes agreed. "And Dragoon could have hastened a heart attack any time in the last few years."

"Until now," I said, "there has been no reason to act in haste. That type enjoys toying with their victims. Cararo must know about their relationship—they don't seem to be capable of hiding it. Perhaps it even intensified their pleasure to watch the old man squirm."

"Dr. Watson, you surprise me!"

"I've known many women, Holmes. But not in that manner, of course," I hastily added. "I've heard from women about their desires. As a doctor."

Someone banged a fist against the front of the buggy, and Holmes stopped the horses short, telling me to hold the reins while he found out what our passengers wanted.

"Head to Arkham!" Dr. Dragoon cried. "It's time to put him in the asylum! He's stark raving mad, I tell you!"

"Harrumph. I'm no more insane than you. Release me. Get your hands off!"

"Perhaps Dr. Dragoon is correct, Mr. Cararo. Your health might be best served at a hospital. Your heart, for one thing," Holmes said.

Yes, I thought, *I agree with Holmes. In a hospital, Mr. Cararo would be protected from Hortense and Dragoon. At home, they'll jab a needle into his arm and provoke heart collapse.*

"I won't go! No! Take me back to C'lk'grhw'erm'ye, or take me home!"

"Please, darling..." came the ooze of Hortense's cajoling.

"Frederick, you lost your mental faculties some time ago," Dragoon said in his fake-kind doctor's voice. "We're friends, so I didn't want to have you committed to the asylum. Had you been any other of my patients, by God, I would have insisted upon the services of a good hospital long ago."

The vehicle rocked back and forth, as the horses pawed at the dirt, snorted, and reared. I could hear people struggling behind me, and peeking over my shoulder, saw Holmes lean into the buggy, yelling at the others to break apart and show some decorum.

Finally, Holmes returned, and I squeezed my body to the edge of the driver's seat and handed him the reins. His face was flushed, his eyes flashing.

"A wretched bunch, Watson. I had to pin down Cararo while Dragoon gave him a sedative. Let's hope Arkham Sanitarium takes him in—Dragoon has given me directions to the place. I have no doubt that Dragoon and Hortense will inject Cararo with drugs frequently now and in higher doses to hasten his death. Given the old man's ravings, an asylum might be best, and frankly, I don't think the wife and the private doctor will sign him into an ordinary hospital. They *want* him declared insane. I suppose that will prevent him from changing his will, but it is better than being killed, all the same."

For a moment, we stared at each other, remembering the dreadful day when we had taken Willie Jacobs to the

Whitechapel Lunatic Asylum. I had never heard anything, good or otherwise, about Arkham Sanitarium.

I slept during the journey from Innsmouth to Arkham. It was nightfall when we arrived. Holmes left me with our human cargo and soon returned with two men in soiled white coats. They directed us to the back of a large, decrepit mansion, twice the size of the Cararo house and teetering on the brink of collapse. The Arkham Sanitarium ached from the suffering imprisoned within its flaking gray façade. A miserable moon decayed over limp trees, disease mottling their trunks, branches clawing at us beseechingly. One of the white-coated men took charge of the horses, relieving poor Holmes of his burden. I could tell that my friend was weary. It had been a long, hard ride, and a difficult day that had not yet ended. We were far from our lodgings, and after committing Mr. Cararo to the care of the asylum—assuming we succeeded in doing so—we faced another long journey to the house.

Dragoon and I held the drugged and sleeping Frederick Cararo between us, and we dragged him across the scabby weeds.

Hortense, wearing heels, demanded that the orderly who was not looking after the horses carry her into the building. She had unbuttoned her coat, and noticing her thigh-high gown, he grinned and obliged. She was whispering into his ear and giggling, when Dragoon abruptly turned and castigated her.

"We're here on behalf of your husband, Mrs. Cararo. As your family doctor, I suggest that you keep that in mind." He pointed a finger at the orderly. "And you, sir, I'll have your job if you dally with this woman, the wife of a respected man of high standing."

At that, the orderly snickered.

"You dare to laugh?" Dragoon said sternly. "You don't believe my threats? I can assure you that I have the authority to make good on them."

A rear door stood open with two additional orderlies awaiting us. Both held candles to light our path through the dim windowless corridors of the asylum. A dingy cot on metal wheels drooped by the wall. As we stepped into Arkham Sanitarium, a woman screamed as if on cue, and I shuddered.

The fellow carrying Frederick Cararo's unfaithful wife set her down. Shreds of light played across his face, then disappeared as the men holding the candles turned to lead the way. In that brief blink of light, I saw that his face was disjointed as if from too many pub brawls. The nose had several kinks, and with a split straight down the center, the nostrils pointed in opposite directions. Unshaven hair sprouted from pitted skin; the strands squirmed like worms, and I saw with horror that they were thick and gray. I have to say that I was relieved when the men holding the candles turned, and I no longer had to look upon the orderly's visage.

"Respected men of high standing never come to these

parts," he said. "Few come to Arkham for any reason."

We set Frederick Cararo on the cot, and the orderlies took over, pushing him on broken wheels over a broken floor. Hortense was forced to walk on her own, and complaining, she trailed behind us.

Holmes's stick tapped our way forward. The two of us linked arms so we wouldn't fall in the gloom.

"What is the nature of Arkham, then?" he asked the wormy orderly. "Are its citizens related to those of Innsmouth?"

"Ha! Funny question, that," the man said. "We are known for the Miskatonic River and the delicious fish therein. Good for eating, if you're out of Innsmouthian catch. Other things live in the river, such as those that dwell at Devil Reef. The town is ancient, maybe more so than Innsmouth. The people who service Miskatonic University—maids, cooks, servants, you get my meaning, sir—could just as well live in Innsmouth, yea. But our kin be here, and I don't know with a certainty that marriage is common between them and us."

"Why is that?" I asked, trying to sound casual.

Again, he laughed at what he clearly considered my naiveté.

"Breeding requires certain *parts*, sir. We don't share those same parts with the Innsmouthians."

Beside me, Holmes's body tensed. I couldn't see his face in the darkness. The candles were far ahead of us, in front of the cot, and with the orderlies blocking the feeble glow, it was like swimming deep beneath the sea, where the sun is unable to probe far enough down to cast light.

"But you have a university here, near the sanitarium?" I asked. "Do you train your doctors there?"

"Miskatonic University," the wormy one answered, "does not train doctors, no, sir. Funny questions you ask. The locals study there, those with more brains than the rest of us. Necromancy. Alchemy. The rites of the Deep Ones. The ways of the *Dagonite Auctoritatem.*"

Dragoon's voice boomed from beyond the cot.

"Gentlemen, enough questions. If the sanitarium has a bed for Mr. Cararo, let's consider ourselves lucky. This is the closest hospital to Innsmouth. Cararo's insane. He thinks himself a creature from the great beyond, with ancestors harking back to an influx from the South Seas. He must be formally committed. I should have done this years ago."

From behind us, Hortense grunted.

"Damn fool old louse, that's what he is." She emitted a flood of curses. "That I let that decayed flesh *touch* me... disgusting! Disgusting... that those *cankers*—those hideous *children*!— were born from my loins... disgusting! *Disgusting!*"

"Let's not mince words," Holmes muttered, while I boiled with fury. That a mother would refer to her own children as hideous cankers, why, it took all my self-control not to lash out at her. Yet I remained silent. Nothing anyone said would matter to Hortense Cararo.

We swung down another corridor, then the rolling cot crashed through metal doors into a musty room with unpainted stone walls, dripping with moisture, the floor no better. The orderlies lit candles on the wall using the ones they held, then they left us, telling us to sit tight and wait for "the Judge."

"They certainly have different titles here in America," I noted. "Doctors are never called judges in England."

"The head of the asylum isn't a doctor," Dragoon pointed out, much to my surprise. "I don't like the man terribly well, but he'll do my bidding."

"And how do you know this person?" Holmes inquired.

"You might say we had dealings back in Boston," came Dragoon's answer. Hortense laughed; her body drooped over the cot where her husband snored.

"What kind of dealings?" Holmes pressed.

"Just *dealings*. Like I said, we got along okay. The Honorable Alfred Troutenbuck was forced to resign from the Massachusetts Supreme Judicial Court for reasons best kept from the public ear."

"You know the reasons?"

"Sure," Dragoon said. "It was no big deal for these parts, I can tell you. Happens all the time. Troutenbuck, a graduate of both Dartmouth and Harvard Law, presided over the Boston trial of some of the Taumo clan. This was years ago, maybe a decade."

"About the time you and Hortense left Boston for Innsmouth," I noted.

"Sure, but the two aren't connected. Cararo sent Hagley for *us*. Troutenbuck helped Hortense and me out of some scraps back in Boston, that's all. We paid handsomely for his help. But he came to Arkham Sanitarium as its director

159

after he..." Dragoon paused. "Can't you guess, gentlemen?"

"Did he suffer from neural psychoses: hallucinations, hearing things?" I asked.

"Was he mutated in some way?" Holmes asked gently.

"I'll say!" Hortense shrieked. "I'll say he mutated! Those Taumos got to him, that Olengran!" She burst out laughing. "He had a roll with some of the locals. Bad, bad idea!"

Frederick Cararo snorted, blinked, and awakened, stared at the drooling walls.

"W-where am I? *Arkham?* You dared to bring me *here?*"

Dragoon and Hortense hovered over him, trying to ease him back down, but he pushed them aside and sat with his legs dangling off the side of the cot. At that moment, the metal doors clattered, and a white-coated, bleary-eyed man entered. His badge identified him as the Honorable Alfred Troutenbuck.

"Gentlemen." He nodded at Holmes and me, and then at Dr. Dragoon. "I know you," he said to the latter. "What brings you to my domain?" Gazing at Frederick Cararo, he added, "A patient?"

Holmes and I stared at each other, then returned our attention to Troutenbuck, who was as odd a creature as anyone I'd met or seen in Innsmouth. His bloated head throbbed: rapidly, then slowly, then with no apparent pattern. He was bald—unless I counted the wriggling worms fringing the back of his head, with one poking out of his forehead and dangling to the tip of his nose. He shoved that one aside, but it immediately squiggled over his eye and back upon his nose. His mouth was a lipless slit. Beneath the white coat, I couldn't imagine... nor did I want to try... but I was able to ascertain that Troutenbuck had three arms and a cluster of legs. Feet suckers squelched across the damp stones. Toe fringes sprouted from stumps, started slithering up my legs; I swatted them off and tottered back. My skin crawled.

"I demand to go home," Frederick Cararo rasped. "These people are trying to lock me up. For their good, not mine."

"May I introduce myself?" Holmes interjected, telling the director both his name and my own. "We're here on behalf of the American government, staying with Mr. Cararo."

"I see. Hired hands, eh?" Troutenbuck surveyed Cararo, and seemingly for show, asked him a couple of simple questions—who was the President, and what was his own name—which Cararo had no difficulty in answering. "He's fine," Troutenbuck announced. "What gives here?"

"Good heavens, man, what kind of examination was that?" I said. "His heart is weak. We fear for his well-being, and in his present mental state he may well suffer an attack."

"Whatever ails his heart does not require the care of the Arkham Sanitarium," the other said.

"But he's lost his wits," Hortense crooned, sidling up to Troutenbuck.

"You know me," Dragoon added. "I'm his private doctor. He's insane."

"Yes, I do know you, Dr. Dragoon," the asylum director said. "Or is it Mr. Dragoon now? Didn't you lose your license after that sordid affair in Innsmouth? I remember you well. Of course. You are not one of us."

"You know me well enough," Dragoon pressed, ignoring the reference to the loss of his medical license, "to understand that I wouldn't be here if the matter weren't of an urgent nature. I've been this man's private doctor for a decade. He needs your help, Justice Troutenbuck."

"Are you aware how much Mr. Frederick Cararo donates to this sanitarium?" Troutenbuck said. He helped Cararo off the cot and smoothed down the elder's coat. One of his three hands slithered out of a long sleeve, and fingertip frills danced along Cararo's arm. The old man smiled broadly and clasped the frills, then released them. Troutenbuck's mouth slip cracked open; his version of a smile, I guessed, as I simultaneously realized that the two were friends. Cararo gave money to keep the Arkham Sanitarium open. There was no way Troutenbuck would have the man committed against his own will.

"Gentlemen," the asylum director told us, "take Frederick Cararo back to his home, to his loving wife and children, who need him more than we do here in Arkham. This man is no more insane than Mr. Sherlock Holmes or Dr. John Watson. As for you, Mr. Dragoon, go back to your own kind. Boston, New York."

He would not listen to our protests, and it proved impossible to speak to him without Hortense or Dragoon present. Fearing the worst, we were forced to leave the Arkham Sanitarium and return to Cararo's mansion, where Holmes and I would tell the Pinkertons to keep Dragoon away from Frederick Cararo and to watch over the man at all times. They were not the most competent lot, Holmes pointed out drily, and they reminded him of the London police who had allowed Mary and Samuel to slip past their watch upon my apartment. I spent the entire journey back to Innsmouth bouncing on the wedge of the driver's seat, worrying that harm would befall my Mary and Samuel. The Pinkertons hadn't done a great job protecting my family, and adding Cararo to their duties would only make matters worse.

13
PROFESSOR MORIARTY

Screaming, clanging, and explosions punctuated the night. Even without the noise, I would have found it difficult to sleep on the dirt floor surrounded by heaps of animal and fish remains. Taumo's extended family, my hosts, disappeared in the middle of the night—at what point, I didn't know; I heard them screeching and clacking as they burst from the shack to join the hysteria in the alley. *Were these nightmares?* I rolled over, my back aching, wondering what was real and what was hallucination. By the time a wisp of sun infiltrated the early morning sky, which clasped the village like the hood of death, the alley was quiet.

Despite my surroundings, one item of good cheer stayed with me. Taumo's relatives had assured me that Amelia and Maria were safe with their kin in another dwelling similar to their own. The location was easy to remember— an alley in one direction, then an alley in another. And, much to my surprise, they had informed me that the other two men from England—Sherlock Holmes and Dr. Watson, no doubt—had been seen arriving in Innsmouth with two women and a baby. Watson, that fool, must have brought his wife, Mary, and their son, Samuel. As to the identity of the second woman, I assumed her to be a servant.

My back stiff, my legs aching, I sat with my head on my knees, cradling my forehead, while waves of dizziness flushed over me. Sweat dribbled down my face. I forced my eyes open and lifted my head. A few yards away—across the room from me—bubbled a pot of overcooked stew that stank of fish and meat. My stomach rumbled. The desire for food, any food, overcame the emetic odor. Crawling over bones, I inched to the cooking pit, which radiated the red of fire's death. A pot hung from a metal hook. I peeked over the rim. Meat chunks, probably rodent, swam in a sick stew of suckers, tendrils, and shells. I shrank back, my hunger abated.

I have to get out of here. I need air, badly.

Bolting from the open door, I faced the empty alley, where rats skittered past a scrawny cat too feeble to stand. The cat's tongue lolled. It would not live till noon.

From the distance, I heard the villagers, their voices a cacophony of shrill warbles and booming cascades. What the deuce was going on?

The empty shacks failed to blot out the sky over Devil Reef, where colors crackled in an awning between the cliffs. Ice spewed from the colors and pelted the bay, which I couldn't yet see; but I heard the bombardment upon the boulders, and it sounded like a thousand bullets hitting steel. Speaking of bullets...

I thrust my hands into my coat pockets and felt both of my guns and the knife. I was quick with both guns and knives, and equally quick with my fists.

Another wash of hunger swept over me, and fury filled my head, the type of fury I could never contain; once it gripped me, *beware*. This was the fury that killed men. It took a lot to drive me to the edge. My typical cool intellect had no control over the fury.

But now...

Days without proper food and drink had sapped me. There was something about Innsmouth that killed the weak and made the strong sick. The soiled air permeated the lungs, seeped into the body.

My fury eased, dizziness washing it away. I stumbled toward the bay. I couldn't go much longer without food.

I reached the beach, and beyond, the rock slabs. Yes, I'd been *correct* about the ice, which clattered and then skittered across the boulders and the rock. Yet I'd also been *wrong* about the ice, for it wasn't *ice* in any form I understood. The colors were richly hued and not of this world. They split and merged into other strange colors, and the ice itself—the ice whirled upward, forming intricate shapes, all etched in weird patterns. Spirals rose, then broke from the awning and plunged into the sea, hit the water like spears. Sleek stalks rose from the water, opened into flowering shapes, yawned up, then cringed and fell back to the sea. In the awning itself, vegetation and fish and sea animals struggled for release, though most had been pressed to death by

166

the ice, their blood staining the otherworldly colors and dripping, dripping onto Devil Reef. The pier broke off at the rock slabs; it no longer sank into the bay, securing the tiny boats filled with fish filth. The boats had disappeared, probably destroyed by the waves and the bay's *energy*, an energy that I would claim to be alive if I didn't know better. *Energy isn't alive*, I thought. *It has no consciousness, no intellect, no ability to conceive a plan and enforce it.* But this energy *felt* different. It crawled up my spine and scraped my nerves. It terrified me.

Dropping to the mud, I crawled into the midst of the villagers. I don't know what I sought: food, sanity, escape? Around me flailed tentacles, arms, legs, frilled appendages of unknown use. Around me sores bulged, broke open, and claws snapped the sky, teeth ground into the flesh of others. I saw things that to this day haunt my nightmares. *The grinding of orgies, the cannibalism, the deformities.* The noise crushed me.

To my left by the bay, the misshapen building rocked to an unknown beat. I stared, mesmerized by the rocking, and fell back with my arms and legs outstretched. A face appeared over my head, eight sunken eyes glazed, nose holes widening then shriveling into soiled skin, multiple mouths leering at me, dozens of teeth bared, each sharp enough to kill me in one strike to my neck or chest. Something burrowed into the mud next to me. Something scraped my arms, my waist, my thighs. The beast face shifted from view. Above me, tentacles intertwined and writhed, and the drool of beasts poured down and green slime splattered across me, saturating my clothes and slicking my face. I spat, trying to clean the filth from my lips, but my efforts only served to dilute the drool and slime; and it dripped into my mouth. It burned my tongue, yet slid down my throat and somehow... *oddly*, it tamped the acid in my stomach. It filled me. I licked it from around my mouth, I yearned for it. My neck strained, my head lifted, my mouth opened wide. I drank it in.

Satiated, I disentangled myself from the villagers and slopped over them to the rock slabs, which clattered and threatened to break into the sea. It was hard to maintain my balance, but I had to reach Olengran's building. The sooner I left Innsmouth, the better, for this place would kill me. I dared not count on Fitzgerald infecting Olengran with smallpox. The disease would take time to kill the Dagonite leader. I didn't have the luxury of time. I would blast my way into the building, kill Olengran, retrieve Amelia and Maria from Taumo's relatives, then travel on the next boat out of here and return to London. I would leave Sherlock Holmes and Dr. Watson in Innsmouth. If I was lucky, they wouldn't make it home.

In fact, luck had nothing to do with their fates. I was much stronger than both of them together. I might make it out of Innsmouth, but those two, a pair of weaklings saddled with a wife and a baby? There was no way they would ever escape.

Whirlpools frothed and spiraled throughout the bay. The water roared in the centers of the whirlpools, spiked upwards, and spewed rocks and plants and fish corpses into the sky. Directly beyond Devil Reef, a gigantic tentacle rose and jabbed the ice awning. The rock under my feet ripped up, then thundered back into place. I fell, and on hands and knees, stared in shock as suckers the size of an Innsmouth shack puckered and secured themselves to the awning. On the mud beach, the villagers piped, whined, and wailed. Strange words, *strange…*

Ufatu maehha faeatai tuatta iu iu rahi roa cthulhu rahi atu daghon da'agon f'hthul'rahi roa. Ma'a marae himene poerava moana moana.

The ice canopy cracked and splintered, raining icicles and hail into the bay. Waves broke over the whirlpools and thrashed the boulders. I dove off the rock in the nick of time, just as the water thundered down. My arm aching from the fall, I scrambled to my feet and clutched the wall of Olengran's building, which wobbled. I held onto that slime mess as if my life depended on it, which I presumed it did.

Meanwhile, the waves flooded the mud, and with a fierce undertow, swept Innsmouthians, both dead and alive, across the rubble of rock and into the bay. Whirlpools sucked down the creatures and spat them back up in sprays that rained down into the giant waves. The tentacle curled, its tip high over Devil Reef, the suckers clenching and unclenching. A bulbous head rose, and flat, black eyes stared at Innsmouth as if seeing nothing. These were the eyes of a killer, one with absolutely no feeling or remorse, one that killed without meaning. I employed men who possessed these attributes, though my killers were motivated by money. In the case of the thing before me, I was sure money was not in play. This creature killed its worshipers with neither reason nor mercy.

Olengran's guard, the one I'd seen talking to Fitzgerald the other day, raced from the front of the building, dove into a wave as it slammed into the blubber wall and splashed back into the bay in a giant spray. Following the first guard, more creatures dove from the building, tossing their rifles aside. Kinked in multiple hinges, they unfolded their bodies and hurled themselves into the furious sea. In a moment of clarity, I realized that Olengran remained inside: *unguarded*.

Clinging to the wall, I crept along the side of the building toward the pounding surf. Very dangerous, I knew, for a wave could whip down and suck me out to sea. My fate would be the same as the Innsmouthians', corpses slivered to pieces, debris resting for eternity beneath a million tons of water.

Fury rising again, I saw no way to access the building. Death was certain. Reversing course, I inched back to the rear of the building, intending to return to the edge of Innsmouth, back where the village oozed its filth into the surrounding forest. I slogged through mud up an alley past shacks that I knew would now stand empty. I wondered how many of Taumo's extended family would remain. I wondered if Taumo and his wife and children would live through this day. I didn't care.

Pausing by a mound of garbage and bones, I enjoyed the tingle of a mounting thrill as an image flashed through my mind. *Sherlock Holmes dead and swept to sea. John Watson rotting beside him on the sea floor, a giant tentacle squeezed around them both, pulverizing their bodies to dust.*

Ah, yes! It wasn't a far-reaching thought. It was quite possible. It might already have happened.

I was panting from the thrill of it.

Pushing myself off rotting shack siding that clattered by the garbage mound, I peered up the alley toward my destination, the forest.

That's when I saw him.

He came out of nowhere.

As if my nerves weren't already unsteady, as if I wasn't having a difficult enough time keeping a firm determination to cope, to survive, to conquer...

Now: *this?*

The air cracked open and disgorged Koenraad Thwaite. He was invisible one second, visible the next. He broke forth, landed on toe suckers, his froggy body crouched and ready to spring. His neck flaps shook. His presence filled the air with a high-pitched shrill that rang out over the pounding of the waves and the screams of the creatures, as they released themselves to the thing at sea. *Those creatures,* I thought in another moment of sheer clarity, *aren't afraid of death. They welcome it. They give themselves willingly to that monster beyond Devil Reef. These are screams of ecstasy.*

Koenraad also screamed words of ecstasy, but I didn't understand them. I felt them; inside my head, I felt the words and knew their meaning. Amelia Scarcliffe had given birth. The spawn rode the sea. Dagon had risen, and with Him came Great Cthulhu.

Then Koenraad saw me, and his ecstasy turned one hundred and eighty degrees into its opposite: *rage*. He pounced on me. Suckers pinned me to the mud, mighty fists battered my face.

Under his body, which must have weighed thrice my own, I squirmed but could not break free. The hammering of my face hurt, but I was accustomed to the pain of a fist fight. Eventually, I would fall unconscious beneath the blows. Koenraad would kill me.

Yes—his words filled my head—*you will die for what you've done, Moriarty. You kidnapped Maria, held my beloved Amelia captive, even attempted to imprison me. I have sired my spawn, and my life nears its end. Humans mean nothing to me: Earthworms and ants!*

Confused, I fought back. *Why kill me if I mean nothing to you?*

His rage obliterated my thoughts. He didn't understand me. He stopped beating my face, and instead, put two paws around my neck.

We reclaim what's ours. All on Earth lose meaning. Rejoice, human, that you are sent to sea to dwell with Great Cthulhu.

His grip on my neck was so tight that I struggled to swallow and to breathe. Growing faint, I forced words into my brain. *Who is Dagon? Who is Cthulhu? Who is Olengran? What is all of this? Why kill your worshipers?*

Why kill humans? If I was going to die in this manner, I wanted to understand the reason.

His thoughts were becoming more disconnected from language as the shrieking around us grew louder. *No reason for your death. No reason for worshipers' deaths. Great Cthulhu, most powerful. Dagon, Yog-Sothoth, Nyarlathotep, and I: we exist throughout universe in all planes and dimensions, everywhere. This is our birthplace. No care if humans here. Ants. But you, Moriarty, you are special.*

So you do feel revenge? I countered.

His paws tightened around my neck. *No revenge!* he screamed into my brain, followed by incomprehensible syllables.

I didn't believe him. This was revenge, pure and simple. He'd broken the creed of his own kind, and he'd told me himself: He felt something for Amelia Scarcliffe. She had just given birth to his offspring. If his only reason for existing was to reproduce, then his life was spent.

He fell back from me. I gasped, my neck suddenly free, sucking air into my lungs. He lay at my feet in his tattered black robe, his neck flaps vibrating. I pulled a gun from my coat pocket. I held it to his ridged forehead. He deserved death. He had made my life a misery.

My brain filled with his memories. They trickled into me like a drying stream:

Breed, breed, breed. It saturated the air like the buzz of crickets. The moment was exquisite. The third oath of the Order of Dagon, to spawn a child with a Deep One.

Koenraad, Deep One, I searched for centuries for Amelia Scarcliffe, she of required ancestry. Koenraad, supreme almighty of the Order of Dagon and of the slab of open waters at Half Moon Bay, the one descended from Captain Obed Marsh. I have brought forth Dagon; I have opened the door. This is the beginning of the return of Dagon and Great Cthulhu and the Others, who have ruled from the dawn of time.

Koenraad's rage sputtered.

I slipped the gun back into my pocket. It was useless. Nature would terminate him. I would save the bullet. Also, I reflected, had the frog-thing any strength left, he could flit back to wherever he came from; my bullet would be worthless.

Struggling up, I stared down at Koenraad. The power of these creatures was immense. How could I ever gain control of Amelia and Maria? That thing out at sea would crush me before I had time to take a breath. Perhaps I was wasting my time on the Dagon gang, its gold-cranking machine, its hold on the London underworld. Yet if I relinquished control of everything, where would I be but dead? Just as Sherlock Holmes lived to solve crimes, I lived to commit them. I knew it was a disease, this lust I had for power and wealth, for *control*. But wasn't it equally true that Holmes's lust to solve crimes—at all costs to himself and those around him—was also a disease? Both of us were obsessed.

I would pursue and kill Olengran. I would do anything to regain control of the London underworld.

The mud trembled beneath my feet. Koenraad's words burned into my brain:

We are finite.

They are infinite.

We are mortal.

They are forever.

His name will be the last word on my lips.

Koenraad's lips parted. His last word was a whisper.

"Dagon."

I grimaced with disgust, that a male would live only to reproduce, that his death would be so meaningless to him: it filled me with loathing. Koenraad deserved to die. He wasn't a man. He was a beast from some unknown hell. He was pathetic.

Amelia, his mate, dwelled but one alley from where I stood. She and Maria must never learn that I had been present when Koenraad died. Their power far exceeded this weakling's feebleness. God help me should they come after me.

Not that I believed in God.

The forest called to me. Rest, a cool breeze, meat I could grill over an open flame, some fresh water to quench my thirst and wash the Innsmouthian filth out of my mouth. I would sleep on a blanket of pine needles tonight, freezing but safe from these damnable creatures.

14
DR. JOHN WATSON

After our journey from the Arkham Sanitarium back to the Cararo estate, I told Mary in a few brief words about our visit and interview with Troutenbuck, and then fell into a deep sleep, unencumbered by nightmares and trills ripping my eardrums. When my eyes fluttered open, it might have been the wee hours, so feeble was the light, but Mary told me it was noon.

"Samuel?" I muttered.

"He's fine," she assured me. "Fortuna and I have been playing with him in the dining room since ten. He's due for a feed and a nap."

"The Pinkertons?" I inquired, twisting from beneath the warm blankets and placing my feet on the rug. I pulled on my robe to reduce the sting of cold air. "Where are our three detectives?—a term I certainly use lightly in this case."

Her eyes twinkled. I noticed that she no longer wore her usual London attire. Her dress was plain and threadbare, meant for labor rather than adornment. A simple ribbon held her blonde hair in a bun on the back of her head.

"Mr. Holmes instructed Harry Rinsdale to watch over Frederick Cararo twenty-four hours a day, to never leave the old man's side. The other two are outside our door right now, as usual."

"Yes." I nodded while heading toward the hall, anxious to wash and don trousers and a shirt. I'd slept much too late. "I don't trust Dr. Dragoon at all. Or Hortense. They're both quite capable of murdering Cararo. Something irregular happened in Boston a decade ago, before Hagley brought the two here, something involving the Honorable Alfred Troutenbuck.

"We may never learn what Hortense and Dragoon did back in Boston. Troutenbuck presided over a criminal trial involving the Taumos. He left his position, most likely in disgrace, and, seriously disfigured—" I shuddered at the memory "—went to Arkham. Dragoon lost his medical license. So I don't have to ask the authorities to revoke it." I chuckled. "One thing I don't have to worry about. Not much, but I'll take any progress."

"But John, I have been thinking this over. If Troutenbuck and Dragoon are old associates, or former criminals in arms, then why wouldn't Troutenbuck accept Frederick Cararo into the asylum, as Dragoon requested? Why turn down an old friend?"

"Obvious, Mary," I answered, feeling vaguely like Sherlock Holmes when he forced me to reach conclusions that he had already determined.

"Because they weren't friends," she said.

"Exactly," I said. "Cararo gives money to the asylum. He's more a friend than Dragoon, who told us himself that he paid off Troutenbuck to dismiss criminal charges against him. Possibly, Hortense was involved in the crimes, as well. They might have involved prostitution, extortion, blackmail, or perhaps something worse. Paying off a disgraced justice, who ends up running an asylum, is not the basis for a friendship. Quite the opposite, I'd say. Dragoon is an ugly reminder of a past Troutenbuck wants to forget."

With that, we parted, as she went downstairs to talk to the staff about a meal for me, and I headed off for the day's ablutions. Terrance McCole and Moe Knuckles Smith sat on either side of the bedroom door, McCole reading a local rag while Knuckles shuffled cards.

Before long, we were all in the dining room again. Fortuna had indeed procured bread for us, along with tinned apples and pickled vegetables.

"She's made friends with the cook," Mary explained, "who was able to sneak her some tinned goods along with the loaves."

Holmes finished his meal, and clearly satisfied, leaned back in his chair, legs crossed, smoking his pipe with a faint smile on his lips. As I stuffed myself, he supplied the day's agenda.

"We've lost the morning," he said. "I'd like to talk to the children. I'm not sure we have time for another trip into Innsmouth to attempt a meeting with Olengran. I believe something has happened in Innsmouth, Watson, of great magnitude. I believe that Olengran is no longer as prominent a figure to these Dagonites as he was prior to the so-called risings of Dagon and Cthulhu."

"What? Why put so much effort into seeing Olengran if you—" I sputtered around a sip of bitter coffee.

"It's not what I think of Olengran's utility, Doctor. I refer only to the villagers. Olengran was their only direct conduit to Dagon. He must have unique powers. Remember what Frederick Cararo told us," Holmes said.

My mind flickered back to the billiards-examination room and Cararo's ravings yesterday. *I'll give it all to 'em, that's what I'll do!* he had screamed. *Dagon and great Cthulhu, they come, they're here! The hatchlings flood the sea, and mighty Dagon gains his army. Yog-Sothoth has opened the gate. My money and all that I have will go to Dagon and Cthulhu.*

I admit that I was puzzled. I remained quiet, savoring the sweetness of spiced apples and waiting for Holmes to explain.

"If Olengran was one of these infinite beings, he wouldn't require guards and ten-foot-thick walls. He's vulnerable. He must be mortal," Holmes finally said, with a look of annoyance at my lassitude. I was too pleased with my plate of food to mind. "Think," he pressed. "Now that both Dagon and Cthulhu are here at Devil Reef, Olengran might be disposable, along with all the other Innsmouthians, Taumo and the like. Olengran, with whatever power he possesses, did not open the gate for Dagon and Cthulhu. Cararo says this Yog-Sothoth opened the gate. What gate might he be referring to, Watson?"

I choked down a bite of bread. Mary placed her hand on mine and nodded at me to answer Holmes. What the deuce? Now they were ganging up on me.

"Simply because I was affected by the neural psychoses, doesn't mean I know about these Dagonites, Holmes. It must surely be the gate to the deadly dimensions," I huffed. "The damnable creatures are flooding upon us, as they did in the Thames and all over London; though I suspect that at Devil Reef, the locus of the Dagon worshipers, the gate releases much worse than we've seen elsewhere." My appetite gone, I tossed my napkin to the table and pushed back my chair. Might as well get on with it. "Have the two of you finished your inquisition? Shall we find Jeffrey and Sylvia? Shall we find a way to go beyond Devil Reef back to the boat and to the Killer Eshockers? Though how we'll get past that reef now…" My voice trailed off.

Mary's face flushed. She grasped my hand again, this time more firmly, and apologized for pressuring me during my meal, the only decent one I'd had since leaving London. My heart immediately softened. I could never be upset with Mary, not for more than a minute. She meant too much to me. She and Samuel were everything. Without them, I knew I'd be nothing, that I'd have no reason to live.

What is the purpose behind the Old Ones? I wondered. *They do not eat us, not that I have seen or heard. They do not force us to build fortresses or grow their food. Do they have a motive beyond mere existence?* To think that the Old Ones, Dagon, Cthulhu, and the rest of the creatures might have no reason to live beyond mere existence baffled me. Unlike wild animals that lived as prey and predator, seemingly without conscience, the Old Ones possessed powerful *intellect*. Amelia, Maria, Henry Fitzgerald, the worshipers, the Innsmouthians, Taumo and his wife: many of the Dagonites had intelligence akin to normal people. They were tainted with physical mutations and odd ways. Some clearly had abilities that Holmes and I—and all other people I had ever met—lacked. But, and this point was critical, I thought, the pure Old Ones—all the beasts cracking from the sky, as well as those from the Deep, such as Dagon and Cthulhu—lacked conscience, morals, ethics, love. They felt... *what? Nothing?*

"The day lags." Holmes broke into my thoughts. "Come along, Doctor, let us find the children. I know the situation is baffling. Nothing is straightforward. Logic feels distorted. One can't trust one's own senses. I am... *floundering*."

It was a huge admission for Sherlock Holmes.

"I'm sure all will be clear, soon enough," I said, hoping to lift his spirits.

We locked eyes, and I knew that neither of us believed it.

Mary led us through the hexagonal room and down what she said was the nether hall, where Jeffrey and Sylvia had rooms.

"Dr. Dragoon's quarters are supposedly here, as well," she said. "But you see, there is a short hall to the left." She pointed. "I believe that the children and Dragoon are in the three rooms in this main corridor because I've already been down the short hall. It is there that I witnessed Dr. Dragoon inject Hortense Cararo with the seven-percent solution in her sleeping quarters."

Holmes insisted that he wanted to see Hortense's rooms; "briefly," he said, "in case I observe something of note. Then we'll talk to the children, which might take a lot longer." Mary and I agreed, and the three of us swung left down the short hall, trying to be as quiet as we could. The oak floorboards groaned beneath our weight. When I pressed my hand to the wood-paneled wall, it groaned as well. Holmes put a finger to his lips, as if any of us could help the creaking of the floor and walls.

Two statues stood between the rooms. One represented Frederick Cararo, clad in the military uniform of an officer, with a sword at his side. The other represented his wife, wearing the garb of *her* former occupation. Quickly, I averted my eyes, noticing that Holmes did the same.

Mary waved at the first room, which was a vivid pink that reminded me of orchid gardens we'd once visited. Holmes flinched as he peered into the room, which cast a pink glow upon his skin. He ducked inside while I remained in the hall with Mary. After rattling through drawers and poking at perfumes and satin gowns hung in an ornate cabinet, he returned.

"Evidence of drugs. Powder. A needle case. Nothing else of note. No weapons, for example. No *Dagonite Auctoritatem*. No love letters from Cthulhu."

Rolling my eyes, I pulled him forward, and after skirting the statues, we paused in front of Hortense's second room. Mary twisted the knob and peeked inside, then opened the door, and we all entered.

Hortense lay on a tufted chaise of pink satin. Her head on a plush pillow fringed in lace, she was either unconscious or asleep. Her legs were crossed at the ankles, naked to the thighs. With Mary present, I made sure not to look at the rose corset and garters. Instead, watching Mary's reaction out of the corners of my eyes, I checked Hortense's pulse at her neck.

"Alive," I whispered. "A slow heartbeat." A wisp of air emanated from the woman's lips. "Breathing. She's drugged. Look at her arms, Holmes. You know what those punctures mean." I spoke sternly.

"Dragoon injects her. Mary's told us that already. Yes." He turned away and rummaged around the room as before, squatting on the floor, peering at fibers, opening drawers and noting their contents. "Well, well. Nothing but cosmetics, crude magazines, chocolates, and a series of medical bottles. What does that tell you?"

"That she doesn't have much on her mind," Mary commented. "It's sad, really."

"Drugs and Dragoon. What a life," I agreed, as we returned to the hall and made our way back to the main corridor and to the nether hall, where the children and Dragoon supposedly slept.

"She does have Jeffrey and Sylvia," Mary said. "She could

have more of a life, something semi-decent. She *chooses* a life of moral depravity."

"Choice may not come into it. You don't know a person's past and how it affects their present," Holmes told her. "She might have been born to an addict. She might have been thrown out at birth. She might have taken to the streets as a child. I have known such people, and plenty of them."

Holmes was correct. He and I had seen our share of addicts in Whitechapel, those who slept in the streets by Moriarty's Eshocker dens. We'd encountered many hard men born to hard lives.

But we'd also seen our share of good people, who had been born to poverty—such as Willie Jacobs and Timmy Dorsey, Jr. Jacobs was as fine a man as I'd ever known, and Timmy had helped us battle Professor Moriarty. The Baker Street irregulars, lads on the street, were a good lot, as well.

"There is always hope, Mr. Holmes," Mary said. "Although she's an addict, Hortense could at least have the decency to care for her children. She chooses not to care. She chooses to cavort with Dr. Dragoon."

"True," Holmes conceded, but then added, "yet for some, the drugs take over, leaving addicts no longer in control of their own minds. I need only remind you both of the neural psychoses inflicted by the creatures. People all over London lost their senses. Dr. Watson himself was afflicted."

"Really, Holmes!" I protested. "I still loved my wife and child. I still cared about people. I was always in control of my own mind."

"Were you, Doctor? The visions, nightmares, auditory hallucinations? My friend, I don't mean to speak ill of you. I agree that you resisted mightily, and in the end, were quite yourself." At that, I calmed. "And yet," he continued, "not all were as lucky as you. I need only remind you of those in the Whitechapel Lunatic Asylum, hapless victims, all of them, of strange maladies."

"Perhaps Hortense is an example of mental infirmity," Mary said. "Perhaps she neglects and abuses her children due to these same strange maladies."

"Perhaps," I said, "but I think whatever ails her is far more severe."

We had reached the first room in the nether hall, when voices rang out from the third room, the one farthest from us. A booming voice, belonging to Dr. Dragoon, declared that "Cararo must be committed! I demand it!" Several other voices, all male, rose in argument.

"I won't have it!" This was the Honorable Alfred Troutenbuck. What the devil was he doing here?

"But Dragoon speaks the truth!" another man cried over a flurry of voices. "All this talk about Cthulhu and Dagon and Yog-Sothoth—the man must be committed, for his own good, as well as for the sake of his children. I cannot bear to think that poor innocents might see their father raging in such a ludicrous manner!"

"I've known Frederick Cararo for years," Troutenbuck said. "He's a fine man in full possession of his faculties. I see no evidence of insanity. If we were to commit him to the asylum, we would be forced to commit half of Boston. The man is elderly, and that does not constitute a crime, nor reason for commitment to a sanitarium."

Holmes, Mary, and I clustered together by the second room, and Holmes twisted the knob without opening the door. Should the door to the *third* room suddenly open, should a man fly raging into the hall, we could either bolt into the second room or pretend to be leaving it. But either way, the men arguing about Cararo's fate would discover us and realize that we had been listening to them.

Worried for her safety, I motioned at Mary to leave, but she would have none of it. She shook her head, and rather than retreat, inched closer to the room where the men screamed.

Counting approximately ten voices, maybe a dozen, I concluded that Dragoon had convened a board of some sort in an attempt to force them into declaring Cararo insane. Further, pondering what type of board this might be, I concluded that it must be related to the Arkham Sanitarium, for why else would its director be present?

I don't know how long the three of us stood there, listening to the arguments, but they seemed to go on forever. Time always feels longer when one worries about being discovered eavesdropping and subjected to the wrath of madmen. I'd been in enough tight corners and scrapes in life to know the feeling well: racing heart, shallow breath, nerves taut.

Holmes's back was flat against the wall, but he appeared

unperturbed. His brows furrowed in concentration, as he focused on the argument.

"I've spoken to Taumo. He insists that Cararo is sane."

"Olengran says the same."

"And how would you know what Olengran says?" Dragoon demanded.

"You're not one of us, Dragoon. We know things that you will never know," the other answered.

"Cararo is loyal to the Order of Dagon," a man said calmly, and all the others grew silent. I didn't recognize the voice, but it was soft, and the man spoke with authority. "He has always given us resources. Money, muscle. He has tentacles of influence throughout Massachusetts, well beyond Innsmouth."

"What does the Order need with money and muscle? Dagon and Cthulhu are at Devil Reef. The Deep Ones don't require human trivialities, Fh'grn'clk." This was another voice that I didn't recognize, calm but high-pitched and brassy.

"Klighhh'trp, we are of the Order of Dagon. We are still here, are we not?" I recognized the calm voice, the one with authority, of the one known as Fh'grn'clk. "We still run the Arkham Sanitarium. Our families still live in our homes. We still take care of them. The Deep Ones might not care about trivialities like money and influence, but we do."

Mary cupped her hands and whispered into my ear.

"It must be the board of the Arkham Sanitarium. They refuse to commit Frederick Cararo or declare him insane because he gives them all his money."

"And he gives them influence across Massachusetts," I whispered back. "Power with the government, perhaps."

"If you declare him *sane*," Dr. Dragoon insisted, "Hortense and I will appeal to the governor of Massachusetts. He will take our case seriously. Tell them, Klighhh'trp. You know."

The asylum board burst out laughing. I heard the clicks, trills, and clucking of those possessing features of the beyond.

"Dr. Dragoon speaks the truth," Klighhh'trp shrilled, and the laughter in the room dampened, as the others heard him out. "I've been on this board for fifty years. I've been in the Order for much longer. Since birth. Times have changed. The Order no longer needs what ordinary humans offer. Frederick Cararo ceases to be relevant to our cause. Why attract the attention of the governor of Massachusetts to Innsmouth? What good will that do? They've hated us from the beginning. They've shut us off from the rest of the world, which is fine with us, of course." Here, he broke off and chuckled.

"I have heard," Troutenbuck interjected, "that we are not *quite* shut off from the rest of the world. Innsmouth has visitors from afar, not only the detectives prying into our affairs, but others, as well. Two new visitors, I am told, journeyed from England and are in Innsmouth. They go by the Earth names of Amelia and Maria."

"But who are they, and can they cause trouble for us?" Klighhh'trp asked.

This time, it was Troutenbuck who chuckled.

"Hardly. My friends tell me that they are of our kind."

A chill ran through me. I would never forget the screams of the deformed Dagonites as Holmes, Willie Jacobs, and I had boarded the *Puritani* to battle the creatures upon the Thames. "Glory to Amelia and Maria, mothers of Dagon! Amelia, mother of the hordes that come from the sea!" I glanced at Holmes, whose face had gone white.

"Two more of our kind in Innsmouth," Klighhh'trp shrilled, "is no threat to us. That they came from England is peculiar. However, it is the humans that concern us. We don't want them here now that the Deep Ones have finally returned to our shores. I say, declare Frederick Cararo insane, put him in the Arkham Sanitarium, and let human time take its toll on his old body."

"Deadlocked again," Fh'grn'clk moaned. "You are the only one, Klighhh'trp, who votes with Dr. Dragoon on this matter."

"You've not heard the last of this," Dragoon said bitterly. "I *will* have my way."

"Gentlemen, we're done here," Troutenbuck declared. "I have a hospital to run."

Holmes motioned at Mary and me, gently nudged open the door next to us, and we slipped into the second room. Just in time, for as Holmes shut us into the room, we heard the adjacent door burst open. The board of the Arkham Sanitarium had adjourned. We waited for the footsteps to recede into the distance, for the voices and clucking to peter out, before moving or speaking.

We were in a cramped room, where a boy lay chained

to a steel-post bed. He was oblivious both to his chains and to us. Like his mother, Jeffrey Cararo dwelled in the nightmares of drugged slumber. The sweet dustiness of mildew floated above the pungency of urine. My eyes burned, and my nose started itching. On the floor, a broken toy soldier hung over the side of a tattered children's book about trains. Light trembled through a small window over the bed. The fireplace dead, the room was as cold as the outdoors, and I shivered, as did Holmes and Mary.

Mary had already moved to the child's side. Holmes and I stared at each other, both listening to Dragoon and Klighhh'trp, who whispered right outside the door. It was a heated conversation.

"I've done what I can," Klighhh'trp said. "I can't keep the board deadlocked any longer. Troutenbuck will have me removed."

"Does he have the power to do that?" Dragoon asked.

"I'm afraid so," the other answered. "He controls everything at the asylum, including the board. I will have to vote as he wishes. Cararo will be declared sane within the week."

"Quickly, untie him," Holmes said. "You get one wrist, Watson, I'll get the other."

Mary moved back, giving us room.

"I can't believe what they've done to this poor little boy," she said, sniffling back tears. "Who treats a child like this?"

"Evil people," Holmes said. "You were right, Mary, about

Hortense. There is no justification for abusing Jeffrey like this."

"And there's Sylvia, too..." Mary shook her head, dismayed. "Do they chain her up like this too, I wonder?"

The steel chains were but loosely secured, and I easily dislodged them from Jeffrey's wrists. As I had done with his mother, I checked his pulse and breathing.

"He's alive, but barely," I muttered as I straightened up, tucking my stethoscope into a pocket. "Are they *trying* to kill him?"

"I doubt it." Holmes peeled a thin blanket back from the boy's chest. "They just don't care. Come. Let's get the poor fellow into the light, where you can examine him better. We must awaken him, feed him. This won't do. No, this won't do at all." His gray eyes were sharp, his features stern.

"I'm almost afraid to touch him," I said. "He's so frail, Holmes. Look at the bruises on his flesh. His elbows are swollen and must hurt when he's awake. Look at the dried blood over his upper lip. The boy has nosebleeds that nobody tends to."

Holmes removed the blanket from the rest of Jeffrey's body. Before us lay a skeletal figure, naked but for damp undershorts, his flesh mottled with hemophilic bruising and blue from the cold, his knees and ankles as swelled as his elbows. He stirred slightly as Holmes tucked an arm beneath his shoulders and lifted him to a sitting position.

"This boy is eight yet looks five. They must have been starving him since birth. Mary, can you find a robe, anything? And if you can, find clean underthings for the boy, would you?" I asked. While Mary dug through a splintered set of drawers, I placed a hand on the boy's cheek. "Jeffrey, can you hear me? You're safe. We're here to help you."

He groaned, and his eyelids fluttered open once, then closed again. Cradled in Holmes's arms, his body sagged, his head fell to his chest. I lifted his head with both of my hands.

"Jeffrey, wake up. I am Dr. John Watson, and I'm going to take care of you. This is my friend, Mr. Sherlock Holmes, and my wife is here, Mary. We have a boy of our own. We'll make sure you're safe, I promise."

Mary pulled undershorts and another garment from the drawers and hurried to my side.

"The warmest thing I could find. There wasn't much. I'm so angry, John, I could scream." When I glanced at her, afraid that she might let loose, which would have been most unlike her, she added, "but don't worry, I won't. This just makes me furious! Hortense wears silks and satin gowns, and that Dragoon, he swaggers around this place reeking of perfumes, with perfect hair and nails. Cararo is no better. Clad like a king, treating people like slaves. We must save these children, John, I insist!"

"We will," I said, taking the undershorts and the other garment from her while Holmes sat on the bed and tried to coax the boy awake.

Jeffrey moaned from blue lips. His nostrils were almost sealed shut from the dried blood. The image of Willie Jacobs's death flashed into my mind. Afflicted with phossy jaw and nervous tics, he'd clawed and batted at his nostrils until *they* had bled. In Willie's case, the blood had dried and scabbed. He'd picked at the scabs until his nostrils had bloated into two misshapen scars on his phossy-diseased face.

I would not let Jeffrey Cararo suffer a similar fate: the torture of an asylum followed quickly by death. I knew of no treatment for hemophilia that worked, but I was determined to do what I could for the boy.

The garment that Mary had found was a pair of flannel trousers riddled with holes gnawed by insects and rodents. I slid Jeffrey's legs into clean undershorts, followed by the trousers. He was so feeble that it took nothing for me to pull the clothing up to his waist. He stirred again, but did not awaken. I secured the trousers around his waist with a piece of string, tying it over his concave stomach. Mary returned from the drawers with a shirt as thin as the blanket, and Holmes and I clad the boy's upper body. I was not surprised to discover that the shirt had no buttons.

"I'll carry the boy, while you look for the girl," Holmes told me.

"Done," I agreed, "and let's hope she's in better shape than her brother."

"Mr. Rinsdale told me that Sylvia is not affected by the same illnesses as her brother," Mary said.

"Has Rinsdale actually seen the child?"

"I believe so," she said, "but I honestly don't know. Of the three Pinkertons, Mr. Rinsdale is the only one who seems to care about what's happening in the house. Yet like the other two detectives, Mr. Rinsdale would rather be anywhere but Innsmouth. His information might be hearsay or from gossiping with a maid."

"We'll learn the truth soon enough," Holmes said. "It's always best to observe things—and people—for oneself."

With Holmes carrying Jeffrey, we walked down the now-deserted hall to the first room, where we found Sylvia.

She lay on the floor in a pool of urine. Six years old, her scrawny, malnourished body looked, at most, four. Also drugged heavily, her eyes opened and went wide with terror when she saw us, and she struggled to move her limbs. Her eyes rolled. Her mouth opened to scream, but no sound came out. Instead, she gagged.

I rushed over, propped her up, and clapped her back until she stopped gagging. She sputtered a few times, then started crying.

"Does anything hurt? Are you injured?"

Instead of speaking, she continued to cry. Her face went red and her mouth opened wide and emitted a stream of ear-piercing shrieks.

"Calm down," I said, and repeated what I'd told Jeffrey moments before, that we were here to help. We were friends. We were parents. I was a doctor. And so forth. Nothing helped. Sylvia's shrieking intensified.

Mary clapped a hand over the girl's mouth.

"Shhh, Sylvia, you must be quiet, or *they* will come," she admonished.

The girl stared at Mary. The shrieking splintered into a muffled moan, then ceased.

"*They...*" Sylvia whispered, shivering face streaked in tears. "You mean... Mother and Dragoon?"

"Yes." Mary took the girl in her arms and hugged her while stroking the tears from her cheeks. "We don't want that, do we? We don't want *them* to come."

"No, no, *no!*" The lips trembled, the tears welled.

"No crying," Mary said softly, "and no screaming. You're a big girl, Sylvia. I know you can do it. Steady, sweetheart. Be strong." She cradled Sylvia, rocked her as if the girl was a baby. Sylvia responded by snuggling close to Mary, her body curled into a fetal position. Life in this house had thrust the girl into a state of constant terror and trauma. She looked as if she had been starved, beaten, and drugged since infancy. I wondered how she would ever recover.

This time, it was my wife who gave the orders, directing me to find clean clothes for Sylvia. Holmes, still holding Jeffrey, sat on a metal bed no different from the one in the boy's room. Steel chains dangled from the bed posts. A thin blanket lay rumpled at the foot.

"These are prison cells," I sputtered while pulling a dress and undershorts from broken drawers that matched Jeffrey's set. "No heat, no food, and the chains... Holmes, the *chains!*"

Holmes had never desired children of his own. He didn't even want the bother of marriage or the company of a woman. But he had a heart.

"Why would anyone give birth to children only to abuse them?" I said. "What is the point?"

"For Frederick Cararo, unborn children represented potential heirs," Holmes said, as if I had actually expected an answer to my rhetorical questions. "For Hortense, they represented inherited wealth that would not be denied her, and for Dragoon, they represented the same. The children were financial instruments."

"John, *look*." Mary's head lifted from peering at Sylvia.

"What is it?" Holmes asked, as I stooped next to Mary, the girl's dress and undershorts in my hand.

"Sylvia has medical problems," I said simply and gestured at Holmes to remain silent. I didn't want to upset the girl further. Holmes would see things for himself, and soon enough.

She was anything but "normal." Harry Rinsdale hadn't known what she was, for Harry Rinsdale had never seen the child undressed.

Beneath Sylvia's upper two legs, two lower legs sprouted and ended in mid-thigh stumps. Black bristles coated her back. A strange symbol marked her right shoulder. The symbol reminded me of the etchings on the bone spheres we'd found by the crushed remains of corpses in Jacobs's tram machine building, Amos Beiler's barn, and in the French tunnels run by Marceau Poisson.

"The Order of Dagon. She's of Innsmouthian ancestry, Holmes," I said, and the hideous song burbled up and started looping over and over again in my mind.

She tried to warn me, tried to explain
Her children were not meant to be plain.

...after the stars are gone...
...after the stars are gone...

When one looked up at the sky of Innsmouth, it was like peering into the deepest of wells. I'd not seen a single star since arriving in Innsmouth, nor had I ever seen such an atramentous sky, not even during the worst storms in the darkest nights of London.

15

Depositing Jeffrey and Sylvia on Holmes's bed, we directed Terrance McCole and Knuckles Smith to split up, with one man guarding Fortuna and Samuel, the other guarding the children.

"Didn't you hear the commotion downstairs?" Holmes asked the detectives. "Why didn't you come and offer help?"

McCole rolled his newspaper and slipped it under his arm. Knuckles swept up his cards and tucked the deck into his pocket. It was the former who answered Holmes.

"With all respect, sir, you ordered us never to leave this room," he said. "You told us, quite severely, as I recall, to guard Samuel and his nursemaid around the clock, so that's what we've been doing."

"There aren't enough of you!" Holmes exclaimed. "Why can't we get more Pinkertons out here? Doesn't the American government understand the nature of the threat out at sea, what's risen at Devil Reef, what these villagers are doing? Don't you people care? If not, what *do* you care about?"

Terrance McCole, with his bright red hair and blue eyes,

typically had fair skin with a flush to it. Now, his skin grew red as a rash. It was he who answered, while Knuckles clasped his hands in front of him.

"Sir, we *do* care! We have wives and children. We all live in fear of Innsmouth, but what can we do? In former times, the government sent the military here. Muskets, rifles, cannons: I tell you, sir, I swear by it, that nothing works against these demons from hell! Sure, we can kill a few Innsmouthians, but to what purpose? We can't kill what's out on the reef, this Dagon. We can't get to Olengran. We can't fathom Cthulhu. I swear, sir, one second the creatures are there, the next they're gone. Vanished into thin air. You tell me, sir, how to kill them, and our police and military will handle it."

"But why can't you get more detectives out here to protect *us*?" I repeated Holmes's question.

"Frankly," McCole said, "we're stretched too thinly. The Pinkertons can do only so much. We cover a wide territory. The police are stretched even more thinly."

"That's not it," I said sternly. "I believe it's more the case that nobody wants anything to do with Innsmouth."

"You don't know the past of this place, sir. You don't know how many men have died here, fighting those demons. That's why our government finally requested your help. Your government tells ours that Mr. Sherlock Holmes is our only hope."

"I'm sorry. I meant no offense, and I do appreciate your confidence in my abilities. Frankly, I'm not sure if I'm up to the task, but if necessary, I'll die trying to rid the Earth of these monsters," Holmes said, apparently concluding, as I had, that there was no point railing against the only men brave enough to come near Innsmouth to help us. I'd rarely heard him speak in such a defeated tone, and it disturbed me. "I did ask you to watch over Dr. Watson's family," he continued, "you're right about that. But now you must split up. Jeffrey and Sylvia could die under your watch. You must protect them at all times, too."

"And we're guarding Mr. Cararo," Knuckles muttered. "You have Harry up there watching over him night and day."

"True enough," Holmes acknowledged. "Tell me, sir, exactly where is Mr. Cararo's bedroom?"

"There's a third level to this house, accessed by a staircase down the nether hall on this level," Smith answered. "It's a winding staircase, narrow and old, used by servants."

"Frederick Cararo uses a narrow, old, winding staircase to go to and from his quarters?" I asked, dismayed.

"He insists, sir," Smith said. "Says it's his house, and he'll do what he wants. Prefers his privacy, he says."

The ceiling to the hexagonal room was over our heads and the second floor, and one could skirt a narrow walkway around the hexagonal shape. Wood panels, perfectly polished, formed the walls. Seeing no halls or doors, I asked Smith to point out the nether hall.

He pointed to a location on the hexagon that would have matched the location of the nether hall on the main floor.

"Push there," he said. "Middle wood panel. Be exact

about it, and the wall will swing open."

"Mr. Cararo *really* doesn't want people disturbing him," Terrance McCole stressed. "He flies into furies. Only go up there if you must."

After the detectives moved the chairs apart such that one was in front of Holmes's room and the other in front of mine, we obtained a basin of water, soap, and towels. Holmes, Mary, and I returned to Holmes's room, guarded by Knuckles.

"So Harry Rinsdale has been in a far wing of the upper level of this house, guarding Frederick Cararo," Holmes commented. "He probably didn't hear anything, probably has no clue that the board of the Arkham Sanitarium was meeting here. That explains why he didn't rush downstairs upon hearing the commotion."

"And," Mary noted, "as with Mr. McCole and Mr. Smith, you gave explicit instructions to Harry Rinsdale, that he should not leave Mr. Cararo's side."

"Indeed I did," Holmes agreed.

We were busy for some time attending to Jeffrey and Sylvia: we washed them, fed them with supplies procured from Fortuna, and laid them down side by side on Holmes's bed. They were listless, especially Jeffrey, but we were able to rouse them enough to get some food into their bellies. I knew that both were likely to remain woozy from Dragoon's drugs for a long time. Their bodies must have been thoroughly polluted by a lifetime of such injections. I suspected that Dragoon had started drugging them shortly after they were born.

After a quick supper, the three of us decided that we had done enough for one day. Holmes again confided in me that he was floundering, unable to find a path that would rid us of the monsters.

"We're making no progress," he complained. "I have no more clues about how to close this case than I had when we arrived in Innsmouth."

"But you told me that you had thought of a way we could get inside Olengran's building," I said, trying to sound encouraging.

Mary snuggled with Samuel and tucked him beneath his blanket. Holmes spread thick blankets on the floor and settled down, still attired in his day clothes. He pulled several additional blankets over his body. Mary, clearly uncomfortable sleeping with Holmes on our floor, slid into bed wearing her day attire, and resigned to my fate, I did the same.

Holmes rolled to his side, his eyes half shut. The fire dimmed to a glow.

"Olengran no longer matters as much to the Innsmouthians, in that this Yog-Sothoth has opened the way for Dagon and Cthulhu. Yet Olengran clearly controls a power of great magnitude. Even with Dagon and Cthulhu out at Devil Reef, the Innsmouthians keep Olengran under lock and key. Remember, he is mortal," Holmes murmured, thinking aloud. "For those of us who share in his mortality... there may be no other way to reach Dagon and Cthulhu. Yes, we need to gain access to Olengran's private quarters. I believe we will find answers within."

Still murmuring, he dozed off, and then fell silent but for the rise and fall of his breath. The fire crackled. Samuel burbled nonsense. Mary rolled toward me and looped an arm around my waist, her hand upon my chest. Threads of light twitched across the ceiling. In the crepuscular murk, my thoughts dimmed. I tumbled into a troubled sleep.

BANG!

Mary and I jumped up, as did Holmes, who rubbed his eyes and scrabbled to his feet.

BANG!

Metal clanked, someone howled, voices jabbered.

"No! Don't! No!" came a muffled voice from downstairs.

Holmes and I raced into the hall, where we found Fortuna in her night dress and cap.

"Stay with the baby," Holmes cried, "and stay with Mary!"

"But what—?" she asked. "What is it?"

"I don't know!" Holmes said. "Just go to the room. Now, go!"

She scurried into the bedroom and crouched by Mary, who was rocking Samuel in her arms, trying to soothe his crying. Thankfully, Mary did not follow me this time. She stayed where it was safe, with Samuel and Fortuna, in the bedroom.

Knuckles had clearly been asleep at his post by our door. Bleary-eyed, shaking himself awake, he jumped from his chair. Farther down the hall by Holmes's bedroom, where Jeffrey and Sylvia slept, Terrance McCole was in a similar state: rousing himself, half-rising to his feet, bewildered.

"I demand... No!" The muffled voice from below *died*. Crack! Crack! Crack!

"You *are* good at that," Hortense Cararo said from somewhere in the hall below.

"S-sorry, sir," McCole spoke on behalf of Knuckles as well as himself. "When we were together, we traded shifts. Apart, I guess we dozed off at the same time."

"You're not that far apart!" Holmes said. "Stay awake now and keep watch!" He streaked downstairs with me on his heels.

Behind me, Knuckles cried out, and I turned. Harry Rinsdale appeared from the opening in the hexagonal wall, which whisked shut.

"Boss! There's trouble!" Knuckles said, and Rinsdale gestured at his underling to follow him. I realized that Rinsdale, like the other Pinkertons, had fallen asleep on the job. I glared at him, and he muttered that a man had to "sleep once in awhile." Holmes didn't notice that the Pinkertons were trailing us. He had already reached the main floor.

The commotion came from the billiards-examination room. I caught up with Holmes there, and we dashed in to find Hortense cooing at Dragoon, who leaned over the billiards table and casually struck a ball with his cue. Hortense stiffened as she saw us, but Dragoon glanced our way and returned his attention to the table. Crack, crack. Two more balls spun into the corner pockets.

"What do you gentlemen want at this time of night?" Dragoon shifted the cue to his left hand. He reached for chalk and rubbed it on the tip of the stick. "Are you interested in a game of billiards? I'm taking bets, if you want."

Was the man insane?

Strapped to the examination bed, Frederick Cararo had passed out. Naked from the waist up, his withered flesh was pocked and riddled with pustules. His ashen face and blue lips trembled. Despite the cold, sweat soaked his white hair. A hypodermic needle jutted from his arm, a bloody rag holding it in place.

"What goes on here?" Holmes demanded.

Hortense, in her usual slinky attire, giggled. Without a robe or long sleeves covering her flesh, I could clearly see the needle marks: they wriggled up her arms like ants. Her eyes glazed, she wobbled and clutched at Dragoon to keep from falling. He nudged her off, busy with his chalking, and Holmes helped her to a side chair. She clung to Holmes, gurgling things that made my skin crawl. He ignored her crude remarks and insisted that she needed medical help, that at least she should get hold of her senses.

"Look at your husband," he said sternly, pointing at Cararo. "What are you doing to him? Watson, take care of that man, would you?"

I was already at Frederick Cararo's side, gently pulling the needle from his arm. It dripped, and I dared not get the unknown liquid on my skin. I set the needle aside. Cararo was out cold, his breath ragged. I dared not try to revive him by patting his cheeks and otherwise jostling him. The pustules concerned me. They might be contagious.

Rinsdale fell into a chair near the examination bed. Holding his head in his hands, he slumped over, his eyes shut. Still wearing his day clothes, his rancid odor mingled with the reek of Frederick Cararo's decaying flesh. Knuckles guarded the entrance—as if anyone would want to come into *this* room—or perhaps, I thought, he was ensuring that neither Hortense nor Dragoon escaped. I didn't care if they left forever, and I am sure Holmes felt the same.

"Boss, you okay?" Smith asked, and I realized that he had followed us to protect the exhausted Harry Rinsdale, who nodded but noted that Cararo was definitely *not* okay. He told his underling to keep Dragoon away from the examination bed, at which the evil doctor laughed.

"You're all fools," Dragoon said, as Hortense burst into another round of giggles.

I needed water and cloths to clean Cararo's pustules. I peered at them more closely, then in terror drew back. Some were open sores, but most were scattered—the size of peas—beneath his skin.

"Holmes," I gasped, "move away!"

"What is it, Watson?"

"Smallpox!" I cried. Holmes and I stepped away rapidly. "Move back," I told the Pinkertons. "He's dangerous."

But neither man listened to me. Rinsdale was too exhausted to stand up. He slumped lower in his chair, head bent, barely awake. Knuckles tried to pull Rinsdale from the chair, and, failing, stood firmly by his boss's side and shook his head.

"My first priority is to protect Mr. Rinsdale and Mr. Cararo," he said.

"Fool!" I cried. "Those pustules—don't touch them! I've seen this sort of thing before, in hospitals, under strict isolation. They're hard. Some have already scabbed. Look, Holmes, there, on his stomach, where the scabs are flaking off. This is an advanced stage. How could we not have seen evidence of this earlier?"

Dr. Dragoon shrugged, twirled his billiard cue and set it on the table. He sauntered over to the liquor cabinet.

"Around these parts, diseases affect people differently. Around these parts, people aren't always what you think they are. Some have... shall we say, *conflicted* ancestry?"

"H-he is a freak," Hortense gurgled. "I've always known, since the first time..." she quivered.

"What was he doing down here in the middle of the night?" I demanded. "How long has he been infected with the pox?"

"Well, those are two distinctly separate questions." Dragoon flashed me a smile. Nothing unnerved this fellow. He had no conscience, no soul.

"He probably wanted a snack," Hortense said. "He can be very insistent. He demands what he wants."

"And what were you doing down here in the middle of the night, Mrs. Cararo, along with Dr. Dragoon?" Holmes asked.

"I also needed something tasty to get me through the night," she said, erupting into hysterical laughter.

"And the pox?" I repeated. "How long?"

"Don't know," Dragoon said. "Must be recent, but like I said, he's not totally human. He's of the others. Innsmouthians." The doctor poured himself a drink, threw back his head, and downed it, then poured himself a second. "Hortense and I came downstairs for a game of billiards, as we often do, and we found the old man half-naked and raging in the hall."

From the chair by the examination bed, Rinsdale groaned. His only job had been to keep guard over Cararo so Dragoon couldn't get to the old man and hurt him. *The London police and Scotland Yard*, I thought, *often plodding and frustrating, possess a professionalism unknown to these detectives.* I'd heard of the Pinkerton agency, and they had a first-class reputation. These three must have been aberrations, the only men who would take Innsmouth posts. The others were smart enough to reject the positions, even under threat of losing their jobs.

"Are you in the habit of strapping Mr. Cararo to this bed, sir, while you inject him with... *what*?" Holmes demanded.

Again, Dragoon shrugged. He sipped his drink, then answered as if what we were witnessing was a trivial matter.

"I often give Cararo his sedatives on the bed while I keep my game up. No bother, no big deal, and why not? What would you do, Dr. Watson, with an old man with a heart condition who rages in the halls at night?"

Why wasn't Dragoon afraid of the smallpox? I wondered. He had strapped Cararo to the bed, touched the infected skin. How often had Dragoon exposed himself to the disease?

From across the room, Harry Rinsdale rose, still only half-awake.

"We've been guarding this house for a while now. I've seen Frederick Cararo take a bath. I've seen him disrobe for bed. I would have noticed skin like... *like this*! He wasn't like this before today."

"You'd best get away from the examination bed, sir," I warned again.

But I was too late.

He was twirling his mustache when it happened. One twirl, and then...

Frederick Cararo's body swelled, his head bloated to twice its normal size. Pustules littering his chest broke through his skin and exploded, shooting bloody pulp into the air, where it splattered across Harry Rinsdale and Moe Smith. The latter wrenched his boss off the chair and started dragging him away from Cararo. More pustules popped, shooting pellets the size of giant hail at the heads of the two detectives. Cringing, Smith released Rinsdale and tried to shield his head with his arms. Rinsdale tripped and fell down. The pellets continued flying up, ricocheted off the ceiling, and drilled holes into Rinsdale's clothes and face. Smith reeled under the bombardment, blood dripping from the holes on his hands, which dropped to his sides. He reeled, then fell, as the pellets pulverized his scalp into mush.

Holmes and I pressed ourselves back against the liquor cabinet. Holmes held one arm across my torso, keeping me from racing to the rescue... which I had no intention of doing. All I wanted to do was race from the room. But there was no time, because at the moment I thought to dash off, Frederick Cararo screamed, and his chest opened—*split right down the middle as if by a scalpel!* Organs and pulp shot to the ceiling and splattered back down on his body. Choking on his own intestines, he moaned his dying words, which I recognized as Dagonite gibberish.

"Eeesh-beanjzh-ig-gooolmoreunjghtzaicklefrosh g'vlag!"

Hortense shrieked and clapped a hand over her mouth, staggered back. Dragoon dropped his glass, and it shattered on the floor. He grabbed Hortense by both shoulders and drew her close, and she cringed in his embrace, hiding her eyes, weeping.

Frederick Cararo's limbs broke free of the restraints. Pustules pulsed across his bloated face and down his neck. His eyes exploded, then what was left of his chest. Gore shot up and rained down. Harry Rinsdale lay panting upon the floor, riddled with pellet holes. Knuckles Smith lurched to his feet, swayed in place, then wobbled over to Dragoon and Hortense. He pried them apart, and as Hortense fell across the billiards table, two fists pummeled Dragoon's face, first one cheek, then the other. Dragoon teetered, one hand going to his face, which flooded with shock; then he quickly recovered, his face grew mean, and his right fist lashed out and landed a feeble punch to Smith's jaw. Smith didn't even flinch. His meaty arm drew back, and his mighty knuckles slammed into Dragoon's stomach.

The blow hit Dragoon hard, and Holmes and I leapt out of the way as he fell against the liquor cabinet, knocking all the bottles to the floor. Had Smith not been hit by the smallpox pellets—mutated into giant balls—had his brains not turned to mush, Dragoon would have been a dead man. But Smith's head no longer resembled a head. Crushed to bits, it was a mess of brains and blood and bones. Dragoon clenched a fist. And down went the man of muscle and grit, down he went to the floor, falling head first and crashing by Dragoon's feet.

The doctor forced himself up and peeled Hortense from the billiards table. Bloody and bruised, he helped her limp to the door, to which Holmes and I had also retreated, aghast and unable to tear ourselves from the scene.

"Disgusting man!" Hortense spat. "That he ever touched me!"

"Long ago," Dragoon muttered, "not after the children..." His voice trailed off.

Their words barely registered.

Like Amos Beiler and Theodore Jacobs, Frederick Cararo had fallen prey to whatever came from *beyond*. Tentacles sprouted from his remains and writhed in the air, and from their tips sprayed a grayish slime. Bones exploded out of the pulpy mess, shooting up and clattering against the ceiling and the floor. The slime glued Rinsdale to the floor. He wriggled beneath it, but it covered his head as well as his body, and within moments, his lungs rattled, he choked, and fell silent; and his wriggling ceased.

Frederick Cararo, Harry Rinsdale, and Knuckles Smith were dead. The Innsmouth curse had killed them.

After that night, life in the house changed. Mr. Hagley forced the staff to clean the corpses and their remains from the billiards room. They were not a happy lot. They demanded that he drive them to Boston in the buggy, but he refused until they had done as he demanded and also buried Cararo, Rinsdale, and Smith in the garden at the back of the property. Worried that the staff would contract smallpox, I urged them to seek emergency medical help as soon as they arrived in Boston. Hagley bundled them up and drove them in groups to the city. He repeated the trip until nobody remained in the house to cook, clean, or fix anything.

We made sure to give Hagley money for food and supplies each time he made the journey. Holmes also sent a note, via Hagley, for delivery to the Boston police, requesting assistance and asking for any criminal records relating to Hortense and Dragoon.

Days passed. I wondered if Hagley would return after depositing the final load of staffers in the city. If I had been the driver, I would have stayed far, far away from this place. But he did return, telling me that he'd spent his life here and had neither family nor friends.

"I might as well live out my remaining time here," he said in his easygoing manner. "Who would want the likes of me, sir? I'll live and die here, and when I'm gone, shovel me into a hole out back. Mark it plain and simple."

"With a cross?" I said, wondering where I would find a coffin should something happen to Mr. Hagley.

"No cross," he said. "We don't do crosses in Innsmouth."

I was afraid to ask, but—

"What then?" I said, unable to resist the urge to know what he meant.

Using a quill and parchment, he inked a few symbols. His eyes were steady as he handed me the parchment.

My chest tightened.

"These are the arcane symbols from *beyond*," I said, staring at him.

"I am Innsmouthian," he said softly. "Why else would I have lived here all these years?"

"Yes," I murmured, "yes, I see."

But I didn't see, for Hagley looked as human as any person I'd ever known. He bore no marks of the creatures: no tentacles, no toe frills or suckers. He had one head with two eyes, one nose, and one mouth. He had two arms and two legs. Yet the symbols he wanted on his grave were the same as those etched on the spherical bones found by the corpses of Amos Beiler and Theodore Jacobs.

Of course, Frederick Cararo's body had mutated immediately before *his* death. Modern science supplied no answers about how a person could bear the hidden marks of ancestry.

"Any word from the Boston police?" Holmes asked. "You delivered my note, I assume?"

Hagley nodded, his eyes downcast.

"They refuse to send officers here. No policeman has ever returned safely from Innsmouth. They told me that they'd look into criminal records about Hortense and Dragoon, but good luck waiting for that to happen, Mr. Holmes."

"Right," Holmes said simply. "To learn about those two and any criminal past they possess, I would have to visit Boston and insist that the police allow me to research their files. I don't know that it matters sufficiently to divert my attention from the case at hand. Much more important is my mission here: eliminate the scourge of Old Ones and Deep Ones, seal those dimensional rifts, and put an end to the threat posed by these creatures."

With Hagley off fixing and washing the buggy after his long trips, the rest of us convened in the dining room. Fortuna appeared exhausted to me, and I worried about her health. She was haggard and thin, nervous. She nibbled a few crumbs. With Samuel snoozing in Mary's arms, Fortuna continually crossed herself and muttered prayers.

Hortense and Dragoon tried to convince Holmes that they had known about the smallpox.

"I knew he had smallpox," Hortense lied to Holmes, as she picked at herring on a gold saucer. Dragoon had been drugging her even more than usual since Cararo's death. "This is why I refused to sleep with Frederick, Mr. Holmes. This is why we kept Frederick on the upper floor by himself, far from everyone else. My husband didn't want privacy. He wanted me. But I couldn't be near him. He was infectious."

Her voice stilted, she looked at Dragoon for prompting as she faltered during her little speech.

Holmes ate heartily and urged me to do the same. I forced myself to eat several thick slices of bread with jam. My friend paused mid-chew and addressed Dr. Dragoon.

"You, sir, have already told us that you were unaware that Mr. Cararo had smallpox. Both you and Mrs. Cararo took all your meals with her husband. You stayed in this house with him. And no precautions were taken for the health of the staff, nor for your guests."

"She's not well," Dragoon commented. He dabbed an embroidered cloth on his lips. He stirred coffee with a gold spoon. "She's been through quite a shock, gentlemen, as you fully know."

"As we all have," Mary interjected, rising with Samuel. "It doesn't excuse her lies or behavior."

"Whatever you say," Dragoon retorted, answering like a schoolboy.

Holmes and I pushed back our chairs, and we left with Mary and Samuel. Fortuna hung on my arm.

"They didn't mention smallpox when trying to get the hospital to admit him," Mary said. "Clearly, they didn't know about the smallpox, nor do they seem remotely concerned that they might be infected."

"Hortense is too drugged to be concerned about anything," Holmes said drily. "Dragoon has probably protected himself with inoculations. I doubt he cares about Hortense despite their years together. He's too cold to care."

"Probably wants her inheritance. Once she formally has all, her life will be at risk," I added.

"But did they knowingly kill her husband?" Mary asked. "Within days, the Arkham Sanitarium board was planning to declare Mr. Cararo sane. He had planned to change his will and leave everything to the Dagonites."

"Perhaps Dragoon injected Cararo with something lethal rather than a sedative," Holmes mused. "It would have been simple to administer a fatal dose of morphine or cocaine. The only way to ensure Hortense's inheritance was to murder her husband."

"And the smallpox?" I said.

"We cannot know when Cararo contracted the disease. Perhaps, as Dragoon further suggested, the disease affects those with Innsmouthian blood in a manner we don't know."

"There seems to have been no incubation period. Normally, smallpox takes weeks to develop, grow, form pustules, scab, and so forth. Cararo had no symptoms yesterday, according to Rinsdale, and what happened to his pustules was unlike anything I've ever seen, Holmes."

With both Harry Rinsdale and Moe Smith dead, Terrance McCole had fled the mansion along with the staff.

"I'll work at petty labor, in saloons or factories, I don't care. Anything but the Pinkerton agency!" McCole had declared. "I've had enough of all of this. You're on your own, Mr. Holmes!"

The Pinkertons had been little use in protecting us, but they had been better than nothing. Now, as we returned to our bedroom, Mary and Fortuna begged—as they had done repeatedly during the past days—that we all return to London.

"Samuel's at risk here. And we have to bring Jeffrey and Sylvia with us," Mary insisted.

It was Holmes who answered my wife. His voice was gentle but firm.

"Watson and I can't go anywhere—not yet, Mary," he said. "We can't get you past Devil Reef. Those monsters will kill us if we step foot on the pier. I have no way to get word to the *Elysium* to come for us."

"We can all go into Boston and take a boat from there," Fortuna said. "Please, Mr. Holmes, before it's too late and we die! Think of the baby!"

"Please, John," Mary pleaded.

"Watson?" Holmes was leaving the decision to me.

Unknown to Mary, Holmes and I had debated at length whether to send my family back to London without us.

"Mary, there's certainly no way out of the Innsmouth port, and the waters around Boston might be extremely dangerous, what with those creatures appearing everywhere off the coast. I couldn't live with myself if I let you, Samuel, and Fortuna cross those waters. You're safer here than at sea."

"Oh, John, whatever will we do?" she wailed.

It hurt me to see her nerve break like that. Mary was typically so strong and calm. It had been enough to watch Fortuna weaken this past week, and now, Mary...

"Mr. Hagley should take you all to Boston. You will be

safer there than here, until Holmes and I have finished our business. Then we will come to you," I said.

"Yes," she said slowly, "go to Boston without you..." She pondered it for a few moments, then said, "But I can't do that, John. We were apart before, in London, and it didn't serve us well. Samuel and I need to be with you. I feel safer with you than on my own. These monsters could be all over Boston, just as they were all over London."

"The house is cleansed, for the moment, of disease," I said, "but I don't want Samuel anywhere near a possible smallpox contamination. He's so young. Mary, Boston is an unknown, but—"

"We'll stay in our room," she said firmly, "until you can go with us. Mr. Holmes, please promise me that you and John will leave quickly. Nothing is worth risking our baby. We must get out of Innsmouth and return to London."

"Not that London is free of the monsters," Fortuna whispered.

"John, whatever will we do?" Mary wailed again.

I had no idea what to tell her. Holmes's eyes held little resolve, and I knew that he was as worried as I was about our predicament.

PART THREE

EXPLOSIVE DEATH

16
PROFESSOR MORIARTY

Forcing myself to eat raw slop from shells and drink putrid water, I tried to think of the fare as steak and wine. It didn't work. Nausea and hunger burned my stomach. I had a new appreciation for my London clientele, who would give their souls for Old Ones Serum and Eshocking in my dens. Their daily lives were much like my current one in Innsmouth. Consequently, they would do anything to escape into fantasy worlds, delusions, and deathlike slumber.

I had tried sleeping in the forest, and I had tried hunting for my food. Unfortunately, there were no wild animals left in these parts, for the Innsmouthians had devoured everything remotely near their village. I had hunted for hours, and I *know* how to hunt, yet the forest had produced nothing but skeletons, every bone licked clean of meat. Neither had I slept as I'd hoped, for there was no overhead shelter in the woods. *At least in a shack, I'll be protected from the elements*, I had thought. *Further, why sleep in the open, where a monster can easily kill me?* My nerves rattled, I had slinked back into the village, where I felt safer under Taumo's protection.

A spot by the wall in an Eshocker den would have been more comfortable than the place I curled up for the night—with a dozen of Taumo's relatives on a dirt floor in a one-room shack by the fish factory. Tentacles pressed me to the floor and twitched over my body all night. Mold dripped from the ceiling and splattered onto my face, mixing with the slobber and sweat dribbling from the beasts.

At some point, the tentacles released me, and the writhing, twittering, bleating mass of fat, sweat, meat, and bones heaved up, disentangling into separate beings. Rubbing my eyes, I massaged my legs, both of which had fallen asleep and tingled. Back aching, I turned on my side. Villagers awakened, and shrills rose from the shacks crushed together all around me. The thrum of hooting, screeching, clanking, and yowling sounded from the beach. Taumo's relatives dragged themselves out of the shack and away from me. I heard them in the alley, shuffling and squelching toward the beach, their voices escalating to frenzied screeches.

I crawled outside and stood, steadying myself and blinking. Creatures slithered past, others hopped on toe suckers. Fat and bone dangled from mouths, oftentimes several mouths on the same face. Teeth protruded from shoulders, arms, backs, and haunches. Gills twitched. Hand frills danced in the air, curling and then plugging the mouths, as the beasts sucked something from them.

I trailed behind the villagers, my body stroked by a thousand frills, sniffed by a thousand tubules, and licked by a thousand tongues. The mass of beasts propelled me through the alleys and to the shoreline.

"*Cthulhu! Cthulhu!*" the villagers shrieked.

"*Dagon! Dagon!*" they screamed.

A monster rose like a gigantic, winged octopus from beyond Devil Reef—and the villagers shouted again: "Cthulhu!" Its tentacles curled into the clouds, and suckers, each larger than my body, clenched and unclenched in the air. Great wings were folded on its back. I couldn't imagine the wingspan: the width of the entire village of Innsmouth? The head alone blocked any exit from the bay. Its body remained beneath the water, and I trembled to think how large it must be. Another monster—*Dagon*, the villagers' shrieks told me—with an enormous frog face splashed in the water by Devil Reef, occasionally leaping and hovering in the air via its webbed wings. Melanoid clouds clung to the sky, a black pit to the heavens. Dagon's wings cast shadows within shadows. Black mud became blacker. Slate rocks clanked and wheezed. The Innsmouthian limbs tangled and writhed like a million eels. The screeches and clacking shook the buildings, and several collapsed to rubble.

If I could only find a vehicle, some mode of transportation out of here, I'd leave Innsmouth and make for Boston. I'd return to London, and leave the Dagonites and their gold to Dagon and Cthulhu. At this point, I would be content to control petty thievery, prostitution, drugs, and the like. I would consider myself lucky to get out of Innsmouth before contracting a deadly disease. It would be a miracle if I retained my hearing; the noise was worse than the food, water, air, and accommodation.

Hiding in the alley near Olengran's headquarters, I waited for a chance to burst in and confront him. I would no longer wait for Fitzgerald to infect Olengran with smallpox. The incubation period was too long, and when I had concocted my plan months ago, I had thought Innsmouth was probably like Whitechapel: a cesspool of degenerates, rot, and filth. I had not understood that a descent into Innsmouth was a descent into Hades. Orpheus and the Bacchantes— dancing wildly while yammering about divine fury, and in some interpretations, torturing Orpheus to death—swept through my mind. Orpheus had knowingly traveled to the underworld to save his love, Eurydice. I had traveled to Innsmouth without realizing it *was* the underworld, and certainly, my motivations did *not* involve love; unless one counted the love of gold.

Sherlock Holmes and Watson were in Innsmouth, as well. Like me, had they heard the stories of Innsmouth but dismissed them as the hysteria of delusional idiots? Even the worst stories I had heard from the most idiotic people, I thought bitterly, hadn't prepared me for the reality. It was unlikely that Holmes and Watson had understood Innsmouth any better than I before coming here. I had yet to glimpse them anywhere in the village or upon the shore.

Crouching behind a heap of bones—*a dead dog,* I realized with a start—I had a poor view of Olengran's fortress. Flies buzzed and fed off the carcass. Straining my eyes to focus more clearly within the cocoon of darkness, the spasms of shadows within shadows, I crept past the dog and squatted by the corner of the alley. The view was slightly clearer here, but my position was more dangerous.

Occasionally, a guard emerged with a rifle, stalked around the perimeter, then disappeared back inside. Whenever he approached, I ducked behind the dog and flattened myself to the ground. Twice my height, the guard smelled more rancid than the dog carcass and all the Innsmouthians cavorting and bleating in the mud. His huge head jiggled on a neck as long as one of my arms but half the width of my wrist. Strips of cloth coiled around his body, which ratcheted up and down as if composed of a dozen joints.

No sign of Fitzgerald. No sign of Holmes.

Time slithered into endless hours. In the madness and the darkness, time lost meaning.

Jabbering, buzzing, and clanking rose to a crescendo and held steady. Death wails burst—the air filled with them, and my mouth filled with the *taste* of death: rust, iron, and acid. *Unearthly,* I thought. *I'm losing my wits. I'm seeing what can't be real. I'm hearing what can't be real. I'm tasting what can't be real. And time no longer exists.*

Why didn't Dagon fly to shore and over the hordes? Why did Cthulhu wait beyond Devil Reef with his tentacles curled to the clouds? Why didn't the monsters crush

Innsmouth, and from there, crawl, fly, or plow across America, killing everyone and everything? They waited for something... *but what*?

Worse, I thought, were there *more* of them? How many monsters had yet to emerge from the sea and sky, from what the London newspapers called the deadly dimensions?

A crouched figure limped around the side of Olengran's building. It must have come *from* the building, and hope jolted me back to the here and now. What was it... *what*?

Moving slowly, it came toward me, and I shrank back, peeking over the carcass. *It* was female. Short, injured, but clearly female. Two legs, two arms, wearing a sacklike dress. I couldn't ascertain her age or facial features. She slipped past me, headed up the alley past the dead dog.

Yes, she has two eyes, one nose, and one mouth. Hair tucked beneath a cap. Possibly human, possibly not.

I followed her to a hovel halfway up a muddy incline. Her dwelling, a hut in the general shape of an American-style muffin, tottered on a lump of moldering earth more suited to housing the dead than the living. She crawled through an opening in the mud-bone-seaweed walls. I'd seen a lot of these muffin-shaped huts in Innsmouth. The poorest of the poor lived in them.

Crawling up the graveyard mud, I wriggled to the opening. Inside, a candle sputtered. She saw me by its light and sprang back, as she tossed a spent match aside.

"Who are you?" she hissed.

I ducked low, for if I straightened up, my head would

have hit the mud-bone-seaweed ceiling. And I wanted to approach her cautiously and gain her trust. Here was an unknown person, who apparently had access to Olengran's domain. I needed this woman.

"I am Professor James Moriarty." I ran a hand through my thinning hair, slicking it back. My coat was filthy and my hat long gone in the wind by the bay, so it was hard to *look* like a gentleman; but truly, one's social dominance is all in one's demeanor, is it not? I smiled, then said, "I have recently come here to help with matters of Innsmouth. My specialty is mathematics—" a term I assumed the woman would not understand; and from her quizzical look, I knew that my assumption was correct "—but I am also highly educated in other matters. I am a man of *means*, Miss...?"

"Move near the candle," she hissed, waving an arm, and I did as told, moving closer to the anemic strand that passed as light so she could study me.

"*Human*," she pronounced, as if observing a rare insect under a microscope. "From where?"

"London, England," I answered.

"No sense," she said.

"Far away, my dear, and I'm exhausted from my journey." A long pause.

"What do you want from Goldi?" she finally asked.

"So your name is Goldi. Is this due to your hair or your skin, my dear? Or to your sparkling personality?"

"No sense," she said again, her head cocked.

In a quick flourish, I plucked the cap from her head. She

SHERLOCK HOLMES VS. CTHULHU

gasped and shrank back again; but I handed her the cap and gestured at her hair.

"Beautiful," I said in the tone of voice I typically used to seduce women into my bed. "You are... *lovely*."

The hair, if one could call it that, was a sand-colored mop of tangled snakes, each the size of my little finger. But she brightened, somehow determining from the tone of my voice that I found her appealing.

"No sense," but this time, she added, "I like the *human*."

She's relaxing, I thought. *She's no longer as tense, no longer by the wall. She's moved closer, she's peering at me.* I smiled more broadly, although my stomach reeled at the sight of her. Clearly, my new friend was *not* human. *Not as deformed as most in these parts, however*, I told myself. I would steel myself. No matter how disgusting the task, I would do whatever must be done to get what I wanted.

And so I engaged in conversation with Goldi, and I endeavored to draw her out without giving away too much information about myself, embellishing and lying, as necessary. She settled on the floor about a foot away from me.

Her wits dimmer than the light, she would be an easy target. Her exposed deformities consisted of the *hair*—and also the gills fluttering upon her neck and the scales on her arms and legs. I learned that her family had died in service to Taumo, when a big wave struck Innsmouth years ago. The fish trade had been hit hard. Outsiders had tried to muscle the business from Taumo.

"Father, brother. Died."

"Fighting?" I asked, and she nodded.

"They were protecting us from outsiders. *You* are an outsider."

"No." I shook my head, keeping the smile on my face. "Not outsider. Not me." I jabbed my chest. "I'm a friend of Goldi."

"Goldi *needs* a friend." She scrabbled across the one-room hut, snatching up bones and gnawing them, drinking from a jar and offering me the green liquid, which I declined.

I plied her with cigarettes, which she apparently enjoyed a great deal, puffing through several rapidly; so I gave her all that I had, including the fancy case. The smoke filled the tiny room and suffocated the stench of Innsmouth. Her face glowed with pleasure.

"Friend of Goldi, do you have *more*?" She desired gifts, and I couldn't blame her. Yet I had nothing else to offer. No necklaces, no baubles of any kind. No chocolates. No flowers. Just my innate charm and some cigarettes. But she was a simpleton, and a lonely one, at that.

The seduction was so easy, it bored me. Had she been deformed but intelligent, or had she been physically unremarkable but a simpleton, it would have been much more fun. Thankfully, I did not have to consummate the matter. Had we reached that point, I doubt that my determination would have held.

I spent the night with Goldi, curled beside her, and it was the soundest sleep I'd had since arriving in Innsmouth. I felt safe with Goldi—safe from the infernal mass of bodies and tentacles and dripping ooze. She apparently felt comfortable with me, too, snuggling beside me as a human female might do. By dawn, Goldi was under my spell and would do anything I requested. I promised her whatever she desired.

"I have all that I need. I have Olengran," she said.

"Olengran feeds you?" I asked.

"Olengran. Yes." She nodded, her eyes glowing, and in that moment, I realized that even had I *wanted* to seduce Goldi fully, I would have failed, for Goldi was beholden only to Olengran. She worshiped Olengran. He was a god to her. I was but a human.

I tried to pry it out of her: what was so special about Olengran, what was his purpose; and what was her role?

"Olengran mighty Cthulhu Dagon serve," came her answer in broken English. "Olengran power. Goldi, clean."

"You *are* clean?"

She shook her head.

"You clean *for* him?" I asked, to which she nodded vigorously.

"Olengran. Goldi, clean," she said.

So she was Olengran's maid. She came and went as she pleased. She had *access*, and my mind reeled with the possibilities.

Leaving the hut, we tottered through the mud. The crowd had thinned... or died... and many slept in mounds along the shoreline. The rock slabs were littered with creatures, strewn like slumbering seals flopped into mounds and slopping into the water. Waves spewed over the boulders farther out, where the pier used to stretch. The eddies had disappeared, as had both Cthulhu and Dagon.

"Wait." She motioned me to the ground by the whale-hide wall, where I stared at the waves and the strange shapes of Devil Reef, and then she went to look for the guard. Within minutes, she returned, nodding to me that it was safe to approach, and we entered the building together. I stepped around the sleeping guard with the giant head, still clutching his rifle, and followed Goldi into the building, straight into a tiny closet littered with sacks, rags, and buckets that reeked of decay and blood. Noticeably missing were other tools of her trade, such as mops, soap, towels, and sheets.

I fingered the vial of smallpox in my pocket. Distracting Goldi required no effort.

We chattered and hugged, and I cuddled with her in that closet, all the while dribbling smallpox on the sacks and rags. While caressing her gills and tucking hair strands the size of garter snakes beneath her cap, I sang the praises of Olengran.

"You have Innsmouth blood," she crooned. "You are not an outsider."

"Yes," I lied, "like you, my blood must contain that of the Order of Dagon. Recent, as you are more fully formed than I." A faint blush bloomed on her cheeks. "My changes are minimal," I continued. "Perhaps after I mate, my offspring will be as you are, Goldi, my dear one." I was laying it on thickly, but she was agreeable to all that I supplied. Yet on the topic of mating and offspring, she remained firm. Her only reason for being was to serve Olengran. It was not her place to produce spawn.

"That is for others. That is *done*," she said matter-of-factly.

Eventually, she broke free from me, gathered buckets and as many rags as she could carry, and told me that she must attend to Olengran's needs.

"I soothe his flesh. He likes ocean water. Don't worry, I bring you food," she promised, slopping into an outer room with stools that shook on the floor, which resembled a layer of thick fat.

If only I could light a cigarette and smoke, as we had the night before in her hut, I could obliterate some of the stench of this place. But I had given all my cigarettes to Goldi, and smoke would draw attention from the guard. I had to bear it: *like being in the whale's stomach while the acids churn*, I thought.

It is worth it.

Goldi was—at this very moment—transporting smallpox into Olengran's private sleeping chamber. As soon as she returned, I would be done with her. I would get out of here, and fast, and let the smallpox work its wonders. Goldi would be a dim memory, at best.

I was also done with Professor Henry Fitzgerald, who could rot and die in Innsmouth for all I cared. My men had overpowered the police and hustled Fitzgerald out of his London prison. Then I had followed Fitzgerald, who, as I had hoped, brought me straight to Amelia and Maria. When the three embarked for Innsmouth to, as they put it, "bring forth Great Cthulhu and Mighty Dagon," I had bought my own ticket here. I had been unable to resist. All that ranting about dominating the world, subduing all the people, and so forth: along with the gold, it was the stuff of my dreams.

Tucking the smallpox vial into a pocket of my trousers, I settled back against a pile of rags. I propped up my knees and clasped my arms around them. Gently, I rocked, waiting.

Come on, Goldi, do your work, get back here, get me out of here. How long does it take to soak Olengran with water? She had planned to obtain food for both of us. Perhaps this was the reason for the delay. Or perhaps I was over-anxious, and time had stalled, as it had yesterday.

My coat, which had cost a small fortune in London, was caked in muck. It reeked. I required new suits upon my return to the city.

Bored, I examined the floors, walls, and ceiling: all constructed of whale blubber and hide. I could jump up and down in here, if I dared; but I dared not move much, lest the guard discover me.

Come on, Goldi...

My nerves on edge, I longed to break from the closet and return to the alleys. Just when I thought Innsmouth could get no worse, it proved itself up to the challenge, and as always in this accursed village, I ended up in a place worse than the last.

Something banged in the room outside the closet, making me jump. The guard rattled, clanked, and shrieked. He spewed syllables in high-pitched squeals and keening, in bellows and booms.

"Ufatu maehha faeatai tuatta iu iu rahi roa cthulhu rahi

atu daghon da'agon f'hthul'rahi roa. Aauhaoaoa demoni aauhaoaoa demoni aauhaoaoa demoni."

Another voice rose over the din. This one was yet shriller, louder, and when it boomed, the building shook violently. The door to the maid's closet flew open, revealing me. My heart hammered. I squeezed behind the debris and supplies in the closet to hide from sight. Nobody was outside the door. Nobody had opened it. The shaking of the building had wrenched it open.

Directly across the room from where I huddled, another door burst open. A huge beast bulged through the open doorway and billowed into the main room, squashing the stools.

The guard with the giant head dropped his rifle and pressed himself against the door leading outside. He grunted and gibbered nonsense, while the beast's flesh oozed forth, unleashing hidden claws from dozens of fatty orbs that made up its outer surface. The bloating continued, as orb upon orb popped from the flanks of the thing, and claws dug at the blubbery walls and gouged them with long, bloody grooves.

And then the guard trilled something I *did* understand.

"Olengran! Olengran!" He screamed the monster's name over and over again, chanting and bobbing.

At last, I thought, *so this is Olengran...*

Olengran shimmered before me, a translucent series of globules floating in and out of view. He filled the room, then shrank, only to bulge forth again. The claws grasped something—a book made of the same material as the walls, the whale hide. He shrieked syllables, claws tugging one page over the other, eyestalks dangling from the orbs and goggling at whatever was in the volume.

Surely, it wasn't Shakespeare. No, there was only one book that would matter to one such as Olengran.

He shrieks from the Dagonite Auctoritatem, I thought, *but why?* I remembered hearing about the wretched volume from those who worked for me in England. Amelia and Maria had memorized the spells, or knew them from birth: I didn't know which, nor did I care; it had only mattered to me that the two could chant the unutterable and open the way to riches and power.

The thing that was Olengran popped more orbs from its trunk, orbs that bulged toward the outer door. The guard squeezed outside, screaming nonsense, and barely kept his life, as Olengran oozed orb upon orb through the outer door. With each shove of a sphere, the hinges broke further and the entire structure shook yet more violently. As the last of him trailed from his abode, I slipped across the slime he had left in his wake and staggered from the building, where the waves pounded the rock and the villagers flailed and trilled.

"*Ufatu maehha faeatai tuatta iu iu rahi roa cthulhu rahi atu daghon da'agon f'hthul'rahi roa!*" Olengran thundered.

"*Aauhaoaoa demoni aauhaoaoa demoni aauhaoaoa demoni!*" the villagers cried.

From Devil Reef, spheres bubbled up, pushing against the clouds, and the sky burst, and out tumbled monsters of all dimensions and colors. Teeth glittered, wings unfolded, jaws snarled and snapped, and a howling rose that would have killed Satan, had the Devil been real and there—but I believed in neither God *nor* Devil. Yet if ever there was anything more hellish than this, I would defy anyone to convince me.

Dagon's frog head rose over Devil Reef, then his webbed wings thrashed the sky twice, and his body lifted into the fray of monsters dropping from the wounded sky. In one long dive, he swooped onto the boulders near Olengran's building. *So close, he is so close!* My heart thundered in my ears. Cthulhu emerged from the sea, and the waters receded, collecting strength, and then surged into killer waves that thrashed the shore and flushed the screaming Innsmouthians to sea, where they smashed against the boulders.

The villagers, who had worked to bring these monsters into our world, were dying for their loyalty. They smashed in green-slime heaps of bone, claw, flesh, and frills against the spikes of Devil Reef. A few straggled back, seeking refuge in the alleys. Replacing them on the beach were the beasts from beyond: squirming, wriggling things; floating tendrils, barely seen; enormous grotesqueries with bulging limbs and heads and multiple torsos in all directions.

They came.

Olengran's orbs reproduced into a hundred, a thousand, maybe ten thousand. Shimmering, translucent, they slathered the rock and the mud, merging with those that wriggled, floated, and bulged. His mouths, now numbering in the hundreds, screeched those horrible syllables from the *Dagonite Auctoritatem* he still held in his claws.

The guard had grabbed his rifle, and he tugged at Olengran. If not for the guard's sheer size and strength, Olengran would instantly have crushed him. To my shock, Olengran's orbs began sinking to the rock, flattening from spheres into ellipses. His shimmer faded to a dull gloss. Once flattened, the globules coalesced.

Perhaps the smallpox had worked its magic, and quickly. Infection would create a different reaction in a creature such as Olengran than in one such as myself. Whatever he was, Olengran had weakened.

Would he die?

I could only hope so, for this had been my purpose.

Olengran and his *Dagonite Auctoritatem*... had they opened the sky and released the monsters; had they unleashed Dagon and Cthulhu to smite the Innsmouthians? Was this Olengran's duty, to unleash all this power upon the Earth?

He had been waiting for the time to be right. Amelia and Maria were in Innsmouth. Koenraad *had* been here. Dagon and Cthulhu had already shown themselves.

As the guard rolled the deflated mass of Olengran back into his private room, I wondered about Olengran's copy of the *Dagonite Auctoritatem*. Surely, the monster would have memorized the words, but he had read directly from the book. He hadn't dared miss a syllable, I concluded. As for the smallpox, I felt certain that I had infected Olengran, whose body had gone berserk and swelled into monstrous proportions, forcing him to emerge from the confines of the whale-belly dwelling.

I also realized that, in the mayhem and during my escape from the building, I must have dropped the smallpox vial. No matter; it held but one or two drops of the liquid, and my work here was done. Olengran had been transformed into a mutated and much more potent monster, only to weaken, and I hoped, to die. Sadly, I could not divine my next step. I was no closer to conquering the Dagonites than I had been before infecting Olengran.

This place was beyond my skills. Again, I reflected, I would have to be content to earn my living with drugs, burglaries, prostitution, and other traditional methods. I would leave the monsters to America.

Exhausted, hungry, I was ready to go home. With any luck, the monsters would kill Sherlock Holmes and that foolish pest, John Watson. They would die on the rocks along with the other vermin.

17
AMELIA SCARCLIFFE

Our minds locked as one, Maria and I drifted with the currents, immersed in Dagon's water. I rode the eddies, letting the essence of the Others float over my skin, twine in my hair netting, in my toe and hand webs. My suckers clasped coral and rock, I shut my eyes, and I was one with all. Maria was farther out, past the reef, where Cthulhu waited. Her corporeal self twisted into the alternate forms of the Others: translucent orbs, filaments, dust, and particles.

Ecstasy, her thoughts filtered into mine. *Dagon has come and has claimed your spawn. Great Cthulhu readies Himself for the final word. Those of Earth die and wash out to sea. Those of Beyond flood the sea and crawl upon the shores.*

My time as Amelia ends, and ecstasy it is, indeed. I felt her mind respond, agree, grow warm with the knowledge of all. Bubbles gurgled around me, on me, and in me. Interdimensional spaces yawned, colors beckoned. I had no real name; neither did Maria. We existed. That was all that mattered: that our kind existed, flourished, and simply *was*.

Maria tensed. The currents of water shifted, tightened around me.

What is it? I asked, mind to mind.

Taumo, she answered. *He comes. The air jitters from his agitation.*

Popping my toe suckers from the rock, I bobbed to the surface, and saw him there: half-*us*, half-*them*, Taumo on the ruined pier, standing with Taumo-mate. In the breeze, his rag robe clung to his body. He held the baby-bo in one arm, his finger frills stroking its face. The baby-bo was more *us* than Taumo; unlike its father, the child had no discernible form and was a gelatinous blob with multiple heads and tentacles that appeared and disappeared as its mouths howled. Taumo's other arms coiled and uncoiled frantically over his head, while his five eyes scanned the water. His two mouths twitched then opened to screech-clack for us in the old language.

Maria and I rode a wave toward the pier. When the wave smashed over the boulders, we hopped from the water, partially disintegrated into the air currents, and reformed upon the pier. Maria's corporeal form, like mine, had changed since the spawn's release from my belly. Her green eyes no longer blinked; now they were flat and circled in black. Her hair had transformed into scales that crept down her face and over chin barbels. Her arms had mutated into dozens of dorsal, pectoral, and caudal fins. Her gills pulsed with the beat of Dagon's essence, as did my own: one everywhere throughout times, space, and dimensions.

If Taumo and his mate were surprised by our appearances, they didn't show it. *Innsmouthian*. I admit that I felt some pride in it, that even with their half-*us*, half-*them* blood, the Innsmouthians *understood*, which made them one with us.

In the ancient language, Taumo said, "Olengran has served your kind since time began. Loyally, he waited through the eons. Now he grows weak. He is infected with a disease from the outsiders and will die if you don't help."

"What are we to do?" Maria asked, but in her mind, she reflected, *Why should we care?*

"Olengran has served his purpose. You know that. Those not of pure blood eventually die." I addressed Taumo-mate. "Most of those who lived with you in the village have been swept to sea and crushed to dust. Those where we lived are dead. Don't you expect death? Don't you welcome it?"

The mother snatched the baby-bo from Taumo. Her eyes went wild. Her finger and toe frills wriggled in the air. Her stomach arm bolted out and curled around her infant, which chirped the words of the Deep Ones.

"Please help us," the mother pleaded. "My baby, he is more like you than any who came before him. Surely, my baby is pure enough to save!"

"It's not a question of saving or not saving," Maria explained. "It's a question of essence. If the child is pure, he will survive the cataclysm, and he will join us in the realms beyond this one. If the child is more outsider than we are, he will be flushed to the sea floor with others of your kind."

Taumo-mate was incapable of crying. I felt her heart quiver with fear, I felt her mind scream for help. But her eyes, not being of the outsiders, could not weep for what she must know was the imminent death of her baby.

Even after centuries of worship, these Innsmouthians with their half-human blood resist Dagon and Cthulhu. Such is the nature of humanity. It never accepts the inevitable. Maria's thoughts were tinged with surprise and not a small measure of bitterness.

Taumo's snake arms smacked the pier, knocking splintered planks into the waves. He and his mate jumped back several feet, then several feet more. She clenched the child to her feeding hump. Maria and I floated in the air around the Taumo family, circling them before landing on the pier.

"Have you no regard for Koenraad?" Taumo demanded. "Do you feel *nothing*?"

At this, I laughed, letting my gills flutter freely, emitting raucous clanking and ringing noises associated with my thoughts.

"Like me," I said, "Koenraad was an instrument of the Old Ones and of Cthulhu. We exist. We don't. It does not matter. Yes, we feel, but not in the way of humans or those of you with half-human inclinations."

"Then what? What *do* you feel?" Taumo-mate exclaimed. "If not love or hate, then what desires do you possess? Are your lives really that empty?"

Maria bristled, and I sensed via her mind that she was struggling not to kill the Taumo family and toss them to their deaths. Her thoughts came in a torrent.

We feel frustration with your kind. We feel loyalty to each other and to our way. We feel the ecstasy of freedom, of the sea and currents, of the nectars that await us in the other dimensions.

I held her back from unleashing her fury upon the Innsmouthians.

I wondered if those of the Order of Dagon had ever understood Olengran's true nature. "Are you aware of why Olengran is important?" I asked Taumo. "Do you know why Dagon has kept Olengran at Devil Reef throughout the ages?"

"Of course I know," Taumo stated firmly. "I am the leader of Innsmouth. I am the leader of the most vital sect of the Order of Dagon, reporting only to Olengran. Now, my people are gone, dead at sea. I have always understood the rules of the Order, the ways of the universe."

"And?" I prompted.

It was Taumo-mate who answered me.

"Olengran existed such that he could utter the incantations from the *Dagonite Auctoritatem* that would open the way for Yog-Sothoth. The stars aligned. The spawn devoured all. Olengran called to Yog-Sothoth, and through him, to Dagon and Cthulhu."

"But why Olengran? Why didn't you utter the incantations?" I asked Taumo.

"You know!" he cried. "Why do you torture us with these questions? Olengran's tongue is special. Olengran speaks the special words. Nobody else can utter them." His voice lowered, and I suspected that he was now resigned to his family's fate.

"We cannot save Olengran," I told him. "You have just given me the reason."

"You cannot utter the incantations to save him," Taumo said. "You haven't the power."

"Nor does anyone, including Cthulhu," Maria said. "The world is as it is, endless and without any purpose, Taumo. There is only one meaning to life, and that is life itself. You exist for a speck of time. Enjoy the moment in which you breathe, the morsel of food, the quenching of your thirst, the warmth of your mate. There is nothing else. For Deep Ones, time is infinite, but our purpose is the same."

I gestured at the village and the beach. Skulls, piles of pulverized flesh, and scattered tentacles, tails, and feet littered what used to be Innsmouth's center of worship, work, and play. This place would never be the same. Few villagers remained.

"Do you think Olengran's guards are still alive, or his maid?" I asked, and Taumo and his mate both shook their heads sadly, *no*.

As if on cue, a tall figure slinked out of the building where Olengran had waited patiently all these years. It wasn't Olengran, nor was it a guard or a maid.

It was Professor Henry Fitzgerald.

What's he doing here by Olengran's building? Maria and I both thought simultaneously, and as one, we left the Taumos on the pier and raced across the rock slabs to the weathered whale-hide headquarters of the Order of Dagon.

There is no longer any use for him, Maria thought.

Agreed, I thought. *He looks weak, and he has the disease. Witness the pustules. He hasn't long to live.*

Fitzgerald dropped and rolled to his side. We stood over him. He saw us, registered the sight with dismay, for we no longer looked quite like Amelia Scarcliffe and Maria Fitzgerald.

"You?" he stammered, pointing at Maria. "Are you Maria, my daughter? What has happened to you? How can this be?"

She flicked her gills and stared away from him and across the bay to Devil Reef. As she answered him, I received another shock, staring in disbelief as Professor James Moriarty lurched from a nearby alley. Now, this was a true surprise. I had no idea that Moriarty was in Innsmouth.

"I never *was* your daughter," Maria said, "and for lack of any name you might understand, my name—this Maria Fitzgerald nonsense—is a token."

"Whose daughter, then? *Whose?*" Fitzgerald cried, just as Maria noticed Moriarty approach, limping, haggard, and with a beard at least a week old.

Maria's fish lips hissed, and I hissed with her. Moriarty had kidnapped our corporeal bodies, had imprisoned Koenraad, albeit briefly. Did I feel human emotions, such as hate and revenge? No. Both Maria and I had mutated well beyond the taint of human form since I had disgorged my spawn. But humans were born to die, and this one—Moriarty—would not have an easy death. We would see to it.

Maria shook off her surprise at seeing Moriarty.

"My powers have always been immense. I'm of Deep Ones blood. I've known for a very long time that you couldn't possibly be my father," she told Fitzgerald, who stood now, tottering and blinking rapidly. It was as if he hadn't heard her—had instead forced himself up to confront Moriarty... or possibly to defend himself from the professor.

As it turned out, the first reason was correct, for Fitzgerald plunged at Moriarty, beating the other's face with his weak fists.

"You followed me here! You don't belong here! You infected me, you piece of filth, and now I'm dying; and by God, I'm taking you with me!" Fitzgerald raged.

Moriarty, as bedraggled and weak as Fitzgerald, put up a meager defense, battering the other man with equally weak blows.

"Get off, you idiot. You're dying, yes." Moriarty pushed at Fitzgerald's shoulders, then grabbed his wrists. "I don't care if you die, and you won't take me with you. It's impossible. I'm immune."

"You're not immune to *this*!" Fitzgerald broke free, and he smashed his right fist into Moriarty's stomach, following with a heavy blow to Moriarty's skull. Moriarty doubled over, sank to his knees, but clasped Fitzgerald's calves and brought him down to the rock, where they rolled and wrestled across the remains of villagers.

"Cthulhu demands your death!" Fitzgerald screamed at one point, and Maria collapsed in a fit of laughter.

"Laugh at this," Fitzgerald yelled at her. "It was Moriarty who killed your precious Koenraad!"

...as if Maria and I cared...

Moriarty straddled Fitzgerald, sitting on the man's stomach, and squeezed Fitzgerald's neck.

"We all have it, ha ha ha, all of us," Fitzgerald sputtered.

"Die, just die!" Moriarty yelled, his fury rising, his strength returning for one last round. "I'm sick of you, Fitzgerald, and all your trouble!"

"The smallpox will undo you, Moriarty," the other babbled as his face went blue, his eyes bulged, and he gasped his final breaths. "Olengran got the pox. But he didn't get it from me, as you planned. And you won't get any gold from what you've done! There are powers here far beyond you!"

Moriarty's fists tightened.

"Shut up!" he screamed.

"Olengran got the pox from Frederick Cararo." Fitzgerald started gagging on his own drool. His limbs thrashed, then shook at his sides. He no longer struggled. He accepted his fate.

As he should. Human, Maria and I both thought.

Moriarty squeezed Fitzgerald's throat even more tightly, then released it.

"What was that?" he said. "Tell me, or I'll make sure you suffer for as long as I can keep you here upon the rock."

Fitzgerald gurgled, tried to force out words, but didn't succeed.

"Tell me!" Moriarty demanded.

"Cararo," Fitzgerald choked out, "got the pox from me, the night he stayed in Innsmouth. I came to see him, asked Cararo for help with Olengran. The... the pox reacts quickly in Innsmouthians, it's immediate, bloats them, explodes them."

Moriarty released Fitzgerald's neck and sat back, panting.

"I... don't... care," he said with a groan. "I don't care about Olengran, about smallpox, about the gold of Whitechapel. Nothing is worth what I've endured in Innsmouth."

Humans thrived on drama. They were all pathetic, thinking themselves important, as if they mattered.

Fools.

Maria and I splashed into the bay and plunged to the sea floor, where the water was cool, the vegetation lush, and the food plentiful.

18
DR. JOHN WATSON

While Mr. Hagley brought the buggy to the front of the Cararo house, Holmes and I waited impatiently: he tapping his walking stick against the stone walkway and staring into the forest. As for me, I lit a cigarette, flicked ashes, and frowned at my surroundings. When Hagley had first brought us here, we'd all been relieved and grateful for fresh air, pine trees and oaks, and wide lawns. But for the octopus-shaped knocker on the Gothic door, the house had appeared welcoming.

Now, we wanted nothing more than to leave and never return. I would get my family out of Innsmouth if I died doing it. Remembering Frederick Cararo's demise only last night, I trembled. God help me if Mary or Samuel died like Cararo: mutating into a monster, then exploding. I wouldn't wish the deaths of Harry Rinsdale and Knuckles Smith on anyone, either—suffocating under the bloody remains of a former client, or smashed to bits by Cararo's killer smallpox pellets.

The clatter of hooves wrenched me from the memories. I

glanced at Holmes. He looked briefly at me, then lowered his
eyes. I'd never seen Holmes downcast, at a loss. We'd never
battled anyone we couldn't outsmart and capture, but those
were all human murderers, thieves, and scoundrels. With
an intelligence surpassing any that I've ever encountered,
Sherlock Holmes had yet to determine how to defeat the
monsters from beyond. How do you battle creatures that
pour from cracks in the sky? How do you battle giant
monsters that rise from the sea? It was hard enough coping
with the likes of Hortense Cararo and Dragoon and the
mutated Innsmouthians. And the curse of the Deep Ones
had spread further: it was in Arkham, as well, from the
looks of the freakish creatures running the sanitarium.

"Mr. Holmes, are you and Dr. Watson ready to depart for
Innsmouth?" Hagley stood by the buggy, holding the door
open for us. He had been on the road for days, transporting
the staff to Boston.

"Mr. Hagley," Holmes answered, not getting into the
buggy, "do you know anything about what they are hiding
inside Olengran's private quarters? By your own admission,
you have Deep Ones' blood, and you've spent your life here.
Surely, you know something useful."

"Nobody knows, sir. Nobody has ever been allowed
inside the place."

"No gossip?" Holmes prodded.

"Nothing. If nobody's allowed inside, who is there to
gossip?"

I remembered what Holmes had told me. "Even with

Dagon and Cthulhu out at Devil Reef, the Innsmouthians keep Olengran under lock and key. Remember, he is mortal. For those of us who share in his mortality... there may be no other way to get to Dagon and Cthulhu. Yes, we need to gain access to Olengran's private quarters. I believe the answer lies within."

Hagley gestured at us to get into the buggy, but Holmes shook his head.

"Not yet. Tell me, sir, how you came to find Dr. Dragoon and Hortense in Boston. Tell me about Troutenbuck and Taumo—how are they involved? Why did Troutenbuck lose his job helping Taumo? I'm desperate for answers, sir, and can conclude nothing without facts. Once I have facts, perhaps I can weave them into a solution."

I urged Hagley to tell Holmes anything and everything he knew that might help our cause. Being a quiet man, tainted slightly with the blood of Deep Ones but not taking sides between humans and Innsmouthians, Hagley seemed not to care one way or the other about the fate of anyone or anything. His employer's gruesome death hadn't upset him.

"My way of looking at life, gentlemen," he commented, "is that it's simply a precursor to death. We all die at the right time, when the stars align. Life and death mean nothing." When I asked if anything made him happy or angry, he said, "A full stomach makes me happy, and an empty stomach does the opposite. Think of the trees and the weeds, Dr. Watson. They're alive, and they don't care about anything. Why should we?"

"We are conscious creatures."

"Ants are conscious, Doctor, as are birds and beasts of all kinds, yet they don't care about anything. Why should we?"

"I would state," I responded, "that they are not *self*-aware."

"But of course they are. They eat, they reproduce and tend to their young, they build homes, they pursue and kill prey. Then they die."

Frustrated, I dropped the discussion, remembering my earlier reflections about the purpose of the Old Ones and of those such as Dagon and Cthulhu. Being conscious differed from having a conscience. Killing for a reason differed from killing without purpose or awareness.

"Tell me what you know about Dragoon and Hortense," Holmes pressed. "Anything, sir, that you can tell me... it might prove useful."

"I'll tell you what little I know," Hagley said, "and then I insist that we leave for Innsmouth. I *am* tired and need rest." After a pause, he continued, "I found Dragoon and Hortense in a Boston saloon, where he made his money hustling billiards and pimping women. Hortense was his lover and made her money the old-fashioned way."

"Indeed," I murmured. "And how did a fellow like Troutenbuck become involved with them, Mr. Hagley?"

"Well, Taumo, along with a few other family members, was dragged into court because they'd muscled other fish traders so they could control all the Boston fish distribution. Worth a fortune, of course."

"And Troutenbuck was the judge in the case," Holmes

said. "Did Troutenbuck grant Taumo and his clan the rights to control the Boston fish trade?"

"Yes, sir, he did. Taumo handled the Innsmouthian fish trade for every major establishment in Boston."

Holmes climbed onto the buggy seat, and I followed, keeping quiet and letting him pursue his line of questioning. His mind was grappling with something. Hope leapt into my heart for the first time since arriving in Innsmouth. Perhaps Holmes would, at last, solve this case.

He closed his eyes, pursed his lips. Perhaps he would reveal the answer to the nightmare, I thought, and I sat rigidly beside him, not letting my body so much as twitch and make the seat groan.

"So," he said slowly, "Dragoon was a pimp, and Hortense a lady of the night. Dragoon knew something unsavory about Troutenbuck, didn't he? From her attitude at the sanitarium, Mr. Hagley, it is simple to conclude that Troutenbuck had in the past used the services of that lady—of Hortense—Dragoon's lover and Mr. Cararo's future wife."

"Indeed, you are correct," Hagley confirmed. "Dr. Dragoon blackmailed Troutenbuck, the judge, to vote in Taumo's favor in the court case, threatening to expose his actions if he did not. For his efforts, Dragoon received ample profits."

"And all the fish money from Boston was funneled into the business of the Order of Dagon," Holmes said, his eyes flickering open and gazing at Hagley. "Lord Ashberton, Henry Fitzgerald, and all the other more minor leaders of the Dagonite gang lived on that money, did they not? And they paid men to do their bidding, to build the structure at Swallowhead Spring, to kill people, and so forth. Am I correct?"

"On all accounts," the driver said. "I must say, Mr. Holmes, that you do put the pieces together in the most astonishing way."

"Holmes, that's marvelous!" I cried, beaming at him.

"Not so fast, Doctor," he said. "This was a simple matter, and we still have larger issues with which to deal. But back to the simple, Mr. Hagley—" Holmes closed his eyes and concentrated again on his thoughts "—This is why Troutenbuck lost his position as a judge. He did as Dragoon demanded, then he bowed out rather than face a public inquiry with the ensuing humiliation. Troutenbuck was able to leave with some respect intact. Taumo found him a new job, that of running the Arkham Sanitarium. But surrounded all day and all night with mutated creatures at the sanitarium, Troutenbuck's body was transformed. The proximity to Deep Ones' blood, his loneliness and desire for companionship, even from Deep Ones... being subjected to their diseases and infections: Troutenbuck mutated."

Hagley nodded eagerly. He was no longer so anxious to leave for Innsmouth. He wanted to hear more of Holmes's deductions. It was as if hearing the truth thrilled him.

"But how, Holmes?" I asked, incredulous. "From a scientific perspective, how does a living creature mutate?"

He shrugged.

"Time will reveal the answers. There is nothing supernatural about any of this. I will believe to the end of my life that science is the backbone of everything. We must remember that the tram machine used phosphorus and lead to create gold. That was a mutation, was it not? Yet one that modern chemistry is not equipped to explain. These other dimensions, whatever they might be, function in ways unlike our own, and they can take phosphorus and lead, and spit out gold. Living creatures mutate, Watson. Our skin changes, our hair, our desires."

"We all mutate!" Hagley exclaimed. "In time, the changes come! The blood brings it forth! Human disease makes the process more rapid. The smallpox mutates us rapidly, kills us. Troutenbuck mutated—*yes!*"

"Sylvia is already transforming," I said slowly. "Jeffrey has never been well. The children have Deep Ones' blood."

"Excellent, Watson," Holmes said. "And which of the parents passed the blood to them? Have you determined it yet?"

I wished that I had remained silent, for now I had to answer another of Holmes's riddles.

"Dragoon is their father, and Hortense is their mother," I guessed, attempting to lead myself to the answer. "Like me and you and a lot of people, Dragoon had inoculated himself against smallpox. But Hortense might have received the inoculations, as well. Drat it, Holmes, tell me!"

"By her own admission," he said, "Hortense avoided her husband. He slept on the third floor of the house, while she slept on the lowest floor. He ran from the house and spent a night in Innsmouth. What happened next? He suddenly showed the later stages of the smallpox infection, as you noted yourself, Dr. Watson. Within hours, his body mutated and burst. The infected mess exploded all over that room, Watson. I expect that Hortense Cararo will mutate and die within the day. You and I are safe. We've recently been inoculated, as have Mary, Samuel, and Fortuna. Besides," he added, "we're human, so we stand no chance of our bodies mutating into monster form and exploding. Dr. Dragoon isn't remotely concerned about getting smallpox. If he had any Deep Ones ancestry, he would be."

"But neither is Hortense concerned," I pointed out. "Of course, Dragoon *drugs* her."

"Exactly," Holmes said. "As Mary has noted, Hortense thinks about nothing but being drugged to sleep and slinking around Dragoon, who is, after all, the one giving her the drugs. If she were clear-minded, Watson, she would be *very* concerned about the smallpox."

Finally, Hagley shut the buggy door, jumped up onto the driver's seat, and snapped the reins. The horses leapt forward, and the vehicle jolted away.

"But how do you know, Holmes, that Dragoon is the father?" I asked.

He smiled.

"Simple, Watson. Perhaps Frederick Cararo was incapable of having children. Perhaps he tried with Hortense but failed, and she ceased sleeping with him. But this is conjecture. Let's look at the facts. Cararo, Innsmouthian and completely committed to his Deep Ones ancestry, was anxious to change his will and disinherit Jeffrey and Sylvia. He wanted to leave his wealth to the Order of Dagon, to Cthulhu, to the only cause he cared about. Why would an Innsmouthian man refuse to pass along his inheritance to his Innsmouthian children? Had the children *been* his, Cararo would have paid attention to them, nurtured them, led them in his ways."

"So he knew the children were not really his," I said.

"As he said himself, he had no heirs," Holmes pointed out. "Since coming to Innsmouth, Hortense and Dragoon have been confined to their own company. They do not mingle with the Innsmouthians, and normal people—humans—do not live here. Dragoon is here only for the Cararo money. He is not of Innsmouthian ancestry. Troutenbuck made that fact clear more than once."

I reflected on the harshness of Troutenbuck's tone, as he'd told Dragoon, *"You are not one of us… go back to your own kind. Boston. New York."*

"Dragoon is not of Innsmouthian blood. Dragoon is human," I concluded.

Holmes nodded.

"Yet Jeffrey and Sylvia *do* have Innsmouthian blood," he said.

"Their mother has Deep Ones ancestry! *Hortense!*" I cried.

"Yes, Watson."

"The smallpox, Holmes?"

He gave no answer. Instead, he stared at the passing trees and breathed deeply, enjoying the fresh air while he could. If the children had been exposed, then along with their mother—and at any moment—they might explode to bits.

In addition to more dead dogs and piles of fish bones and garbage, which I expected to see, Innsmouth had changed. The air thrummed, a low-throated growl. The few villagers who shambled through the alleys failed even to notice us. They fell against the bone-mud walls of shacks, then slumped next to the carcasses and the piles of bones. A cone-shaped creature with six necks ending with assorted suckers, claws, and teeth jiggled near Taumo's shack. Giant larvae swarmed overhead and descended by the thousands to feed on the dead. Black ooze melted over the Taumo home, dripped over the window and door. Tendrils, webbing, eyes, and scales bulged from the ooze, then disappeared, only to reappear in other forms: ridges, protuberances, suckers. As it was transformed, the ooze belched out bubbles that popped, emitting shrill noises like that of a piccolo octaves higher than normal. The air, sweetly thick, coated my nostrils, and I breathed heavily. Holmes did the same, sweat dripping down his forehead despite the still-freezing weather and the ice that pelted us from the clouds.

"Most of the villagers appear to be dead," Holmes said,

looking at the carcasses we passed. "Last time we were here, they were all at the beach, squealing and throwing themselves at the sea. The Order of Dagon was in its final throes, Watson. Their great master had finally shown up."

"Dagon."

"Cthulhu, as well," he said drily. "These monsters around us—" he pointed his walking stick at the cone, the larvae, and the ooze— "are different from the Innsmouthians. They weren't here before."

"But couldn't they be the villagers, only mutated further?" I suggested.

He shook his head.

"No. Look over there, Watson. This *place* changes now, by the day. Innsmouth and Devil Reef are mutating." He pointed again, this time at a shack from which larvae and ooze flowed freely in and out of the roof and the door. Blotches of bright pink and orange seared the air above the shack, fire sizzled along the edges of color, where black waves squelched the flames. I peered toward the shore. The sky over the bay yawned black, a half-circle rimmed with orange, then green, then purple; white and black spears soared from the water and shot into the clouds.

Turning back to the Taumo shack, we approached cautiously. Holmes pulled up his gloves to cover all his flesh. I kept my hands in my pockets, while Holmes knocked once, avoiding the black ooze. We both panted, unable to breathe the sick air.

"Taumo?" Holmes called, knocking again.

Purple burst from the ooze, and orange soared over us and burst into green and pink triangles that burned into my eyes. I had to lower my gaze.

"*Taumo?*" Holmes raised his voice. "It's Sherlock Holmes! Are you in there? I need to talk to you. It's urgent!"

At this, the Innsmouthian burst from the shack, angry. Tentacles flew out and jabbed Holmes's chest, and the detective staggered back. I grabbed his arm and held him upright, as he regained his composure.

"You dared to come again?" Taumo screamed from both of his mouths. "I told you. No Olengran! You must go!" All five eyes glared at Holmes.

"Where is everyone, all your friends?" Holmes asked, shoving the tentacles from him and brushing his coat.

"Cthulhu! We go to Cthulhu! You must leave!"

So great was his loyalty to the Deep Ones, Taumo was willing—*eager!*—to sacrifice his own life along with the lives of his wife and children. Fighting this level of devotion, this irrational behavior, was pointless.

"Fitzgerald is dead. All humans are dead. You will die." Taumo pounced on Holmes. Before I could move, he had coiled his tentacles around the detective's body and was squeezing the life out of him.

"Watson!" Holmes choked out.

I yanked my gun from my pocket and fired one, two, three bullets at Taumo. The creature's flesh took the bullets, sealed the wounds, and if anything, grew a few extra pounds of flab where the bullets had penetrated.

"The spawn is here! You must go!" Taumo screamed. His coils encircled Holmes's body from knees to neck. Holmes's eyes bulged. He couldn't breathe.

"W-Watson…" he sputtered.

"Let him go!" I leapt onto Taumo, latching onto his uppermost torso, and clawed at his eyes. It didn't faze him. I beat his head with my fists.

"We'll leave, I swear!" I finally lied, when I saw it was no use. "No Olengran, I swear!"

At that, Taumo released Holmes, who held his neck, still choking. He careened, and I jumped off Taumo, kicked him for good measure, and pulled Holmes away. Taumo's eyes glazed. He tottered, muttered esoteric phrases, and for a moment, I thought I saw a downcast look upon his face.

Together, Holmes and I made our way through the alley as if heading for the forest rather than the bay. I glanced over my shoulder.

"Taumo's vanished," I said. "He must have gone back inside."

"We'll get into Olengran's without him," Holmes said. "Let's go left here, Watson, and make a dash down the next alley over."

Swatting at the flying larvae, we avoided the shacks over which color and fire crackled, creatures and ooze flooding in and out of the windows.

When we reached the sloped-roof hut built from whale hide and blubber, the door that faced the sea slammed back and forth upon its hinges. The guards were no longer there, and certainly, I saw no scullery maids scurrying about with trays of tea.

The corpses and body parts of the villagers twisted in the eddies and crashed over the boulders. Shreds of the worshipers hung from the dagger-rock of Devil Reef. The sky lay open like a giant wound, discharging the most foul of all life forms: iridescent globules that multiplied and surged into mouths containing both teeth and eyes; snakelike beasts with wings and fish scales. Nightmare upon nightmare spewed from the sky into the bay. Thankfully, Cthulhu and Dagon slumbered in the deep.

With a jolt, I realized that I stood alone on the rock shore. Holmes had dashed into the whale-hide headquarters. Remembering my last experience in the belly of the whale, I hesitated, but in the end—for I could not let him battle the unknown without me—raced after him.

The inner door, ten feet thick, hung open. The walls shook. *The whole place might explode*, I thought wildly. *We have to get out of here!*

I swiveled to yell at Holmes, but he was on the floor, peering through his magnifying lens. He lifted a small vial.

"Watson," he cried, "I have it!"

"What?" I said. "Holmes, let's leave. Come on, Holmes…"

"Someone got here before us," he said. "There's a smudge of dried liquid on the floor by the vial. And the vial itself still contains a few drops. Whatever it is…"

Something pressed against the inner door, making it bulge, then receded again. The building whined and sagged.

I turned away toward the open front door, and saw a wave rising in the bay, taller than the building, a wave carrying limbs and bones and brains. It would hit us at any moment.

Holmes threw me to the floor, and then covered me with his body.

"Keep your head down!" he screamed, just as the wave hit the roof and flooded through the door. Cold water smacked into us. I held my breath, shut my eyes. It was worse than being in the whale's belly. This was being in the belly *while* drowning in the putrid gore of the dead. Holmes and I, with our arms tightly around each other, rode the wave, slammed against one blubber wall, then another, bounced against the blubber ceiling, then to the floor.

We couldn't fight it. The wave was too fierce. We couldn't swim out from under it. We would die here.

A flash of Mary, of Samuel...

The roof convulsed, pushed upward, blasted into the fetid sky. Air—sweet and thick, but *air*—thundered down, fractured the water, splintered it—

"*How?*" I wanted to scream, but was unable to open my mouth lest it fill with the contaminated water.

And the wave washed back out to Devil Reef, carrying half of Olengran's building with it.

Still locked in an embrace that would have shocked Mary, Holmes and I slid across the floor and came up against one of the remaining blubber walls. We stared at the *thing* before us.

Finally, we saw him: *Olengran*.

19

Beneath translucent skin, Olengran's blood beat through a thicket of veins and grooved coils. Littered with eyes, fangs, and slobbering cavities, his amorphous flab slopped toward us, fanning out, tendrils probing for their prey. With slime trickling from the holes drilled all over his flesh, he appeared to be melting; but as quickly as the slime trickled, it gelled and formed new humps of flab. Fangs budded and grew long and sharp. The entire mass of Olengran heaved toward the sky, elongating into a column studded with shimmering spheres.

Holmes and I pressed ourselves against the wall. If it would only cave in, fall, we could make a dash for it. Holmes's eyes could not have been wider. The look of horror on his face terrified me. I had never seen Holmes in this state.

I glanced around the room, seeking an exit route. As quickly as Olengran had elongated, he splattered back down, collapsing into a disk form that flattened and slopped across the floor toward us. Orbs popped from the disk and swelled. His internal coils grew thicker, the blood pounding hard through the veins. A thousand eyes focused on me. A thousand holes slobbered.

"Holmes!" I screamed. "Get us out of here!"

In response, Holmes snapped out of his terrified state, and he stooped and cupped his hands.

"Climb!" he ordered.

Placing one foot in his hands, I grasped the blubber wall, and with mounds of fat in my hands, hoisted myself up. Holmes lifted me higher. My hands grappled upward, found more fat, and squeezed. He pushed my heels, tried to shove me up and over the side of the wall.

I was almost there... *almost...*

...when Holmes screamed, and I lost my grip and fell, landed on my rear with my legs splayed.

Olengran's body bloated in all directions, destroying the remainder of the wall facing the sea. Pustules sprang from his skin, swelled into balloons, and popped. Bloody pulp— the ridged coils and veins—shot from the holes all over him, surging like sea spray on the boulders.

It rained down, saturated me with gore. Also soaked in the rot, Holmes hauled me toward the sea, where the front door had once stood. We slipped across Olengran's slime and flab, stepped upon rock, teetered, and leapt onto the mud beach. Landing on our stomachs, we rolled to our backs, as pellets sprayed out of Olengran and clattered against the rock where we had stood only moments before. The pellets were larger than the hail ejected by Frederick Cararo's corpse.

From a thousand holes, Olengran shrieked nonsense syllables. His voice was more shrill, and punctuated with more guttural clicking, than the mass of writhing Innsmouthians who had worshiped Dagon and Cthulhu upon this very beach.

"*Eeesh-beanjzh-ig-gooolmoreunjghtzaicklefrosh g'vlag!*"

Holmes yanked me out of the mud, and we both ran from the beach into an alley that slinked between two crushed shacks.

"Smallpox!" he screamed. "Watson, the same thing has happened to Olengran that we saw with Frederick Cararo!"

I had already deduced the same. The smallpox had hit Olengran *hard*. He had mutated before our eyes, then exploded.

"But how did the smallpox get into Olengran's sealed fortress?" I said, as we both sank against the wall of one of the shacks and sat panting in the syrupy haze.

"That vial I found, with the drops of liquid," Holmes said. "It had a medical look to it. We might suppose that it contained smallpox. Someone sneaked it into Olengran's room, or possibly, someone splashed it onto something that then was taken into Olengran's room."

"A maid, as you thought when we first arrived?" I pondered aloud.

"I suspect so, yes. I had hoped to gain access using a maid before we became caught up in the Cararos' misfortunes. Someone must have had the same idea."

A giant snakelike beast covered in fur slithered from the ruins of Olengran's fortress. Gripped in two of hundreds of its pincers was an object that I could not identify at this distance. But the snake held *something*. Clicking and gibbering, it wriggled into the sludge with the object.

More creatures joined the snake, shrilling the Dagonite chants. They rolled, scuttled, and flew from the shacks and down the alleys to join the snake in the mud. Holmes and I dared not move from our position. It was horrifying enough to *watch* them slink, flit, and scrabble; I most definitely did not want to draw their attention and then *feel* them upon me.

Like the villagers before them, the spawn that had taken hold of Innsmouth flapped, screamed, wailed, yowled, and beat the mud, intoning the syllables that I thought of as the Deep Ones' language.

What was left of Olengran's building exploded, leaving what looked like the detonated remains of a whale on the rock.

The snake lifted up the object, and a larger beast—amorphous and riddled with eyes and holes, but smaller than Olengran—grabbed hold using a pincer and rolled with the object into the mass of worshipers. The shapeless mass slopped forward, and its wake plastered other spawn to the mud.

Tentacles flailed, waved in harmony toward Devil Reef. Larvae buzzed and clicked hard wings. Globules bobbed, fangs dug into the flesh of others, tendrils entwined into mesh, flab merged, replicated, budded, wrenched apart. The din and the stench hammered my senses. My head whirled.

The shapeless mass rolled closer, and its pincers flicked at the object it held. Pages opened. I saw that the object was a book—a large book with animal-hide covers and leathery pages.

"The *Dagonite Auctoritatem*! From Olengran, Watson!"

Before I could stop him, Holmes jumped up and raced into the crowd.

"Holmes, no!" I called, but much too late, for he was already shoving aside globules and tentacles, leaping before snapping pincers and jaws could grab him, darting around orgies of frenzied spawn before they could wrap their flab around him and choke the life out of him or crush him to death.

He snatched Olengran's copy of the *Dagonite Auctoritatem* from the amorphous monster. Its pincers snapped shut, and finding nothing in its grasp, the creature heaved its massive bulk at Holmes. Fatty orbs splattered into the mud. Holes drilled into flesh widened and then yawned toward Holmes, as if aching to yank him inside the flab.

"Dagon! Dagon! Dagon!" the spawn screeched in unison.

Holmes slapped them aside and raced toward me, clutching the *Dagonite Auctoritatem*. He didn't have to pull me up this time. When he reached me, I was already on my feet, and together, we streaked up the alley.

Luckily, I thought, *if there is anything lucky about this nightmare, Holmes has escaped certain death. Luckily, he's wearing his leather gloves.* I remembered how the Beiler volume had burned my skin. Here, in the dead of winter by the Innsmouth sea, we would have suffered from frostbite had we not been wearing our warmest wools; and without leather gloves, a *Dagonite Auctoritatem* would have stripped all the flesh from Holmes's palms.

A figure darted into a muffin-roofed shack that crumbled on a hill by the ruins of Olengran's fortress. It caught Holmes's attention as well as my own, and we both stopped in our tracks and peered through the murk.

"Who—?" I said. "Another person is here, Holmes."

Tall, thin, balding, clad in a filthy yet expensive coat:

"Professor Moriarty!" Holmes exclaimed.

"Are you sure it's not Fitzgerald?" I said.

"Taumo told us that Fitzgerald is dead," Holmes answered. "No, Watson, it's Moriarty, I am sure of it. After he visited us at 221B Baker Street, pretending to be his own brother, I would know him anywhere. But what is he doing in Innsmouth?" Holmes paused, panted in the heavy air, then said, "He's here for the ultimate power of the Dagonites and this Cthulhu. He's here because he thinks Innsmouth's secrets will lead him to the tram machine gold, to more Eshocker dens, to staggering wealth."

Larvae buzzed overhead and descended. Flab and snakes and tendrils and monsters of all dimensions slithered and clattered up from the beach into the alley where we stood, both gasping for air.

As we hurried up the alley toward the forest, where we hoped Hagley's buggy would be waiting for us, Holmes screamed over the keening of the beasts.

"I should have guessed Moriarty would be behind this!" he cried. "*He* found some servant of Olengran's to give him access to the place; he brought that vial to infect the leader of the Order of Dagon with smallpox!"

"Moriarty will stoop to levels lower than hell to get what he wants," I said.

"But it is thanks to the confusion and death he has caused," Holmes replied, "that I have Olengran's copy of the *Dagonite Auctoritatem*."

Nearing the edge of the village, we both spied Hagley's buggy. I was relieved he was still here, waiting for us.

"I must pay Moriarty a friendly visit when we are back in London," Holmes chuckled, as he tucked himself inside the vehicle, still holding the dreaded volume close to his body. "If he survives his American holiday."

As soon as the horses set off, I closed my eyes and fell into a doze.

But Holmes jostled me with his shoulder, and abruptly my eyes snapped open.

"This *Dagonite Auctoritatem* didn't belong to Olengran," Holmes announced grandly. "Do you know whose copy I hold in my hands?"

My chest tightened.

"For the love of God, Holmes, just tell me," I said.

"I've already given you the main clue." He flashed me a smile. "It did *not* belong to Olengran."

"How do you know that?" I asked.

"Olengran never left his private, heavily guarded room. Nobody entered the room, nobody saw him. Inside that room, he had an ancient book, yet throughout the years, he never used it."

"But how do you know that he never used it?" Now my curiosity was piqued. I had to know the answer to Holmes's riddle.

"Think, Watson."

"I don't know," I said wearily.

"Very well," my friend said, taking pity on me. "We know that the *Dagonite Auctoritatem* exists for only one purpose: to open the rifts of the deadly dimensions and disgorge the creatures from the beyond. Correct?"

I agreed.

"It contains the spells, if you will, the formulae... that let the Old Ones into our world." He shook his head. "I dismay myself at saying these things, yet I believe it to be the only deduction that makes any sense, given what we've observed, Watson."

"But Olengran's copy?" I prodded, shutting my eyes again, waiting for Holmes to let me rest from our excursion into hell.

"Until recently no interdimensional beasts have appeared—those so-called Old Ones that we saw and fought in the Thames," Holmes said. "It follows that Olengran did not use the *Dagonite Auctoritatem* to open the rifts of the deadly dimensions and disgorge the creatures from the beyond."

"He may have tried and failed, meaning he didn't have the required power, even with this copy of the book," I said.

"We shall never know if he tried and failed, Watson, but what we do know is that the rifts did not open until recently. So what has changed? Amelia Scarcliffe and Maria Fitzgerald came to Innsmouth. When the Arkham Sanitarium board met in the Cararo house, Troutenbuck announced that Amelia and Maria had traveled from England to Innsmouth. You do remember?" When I nodded, he continued, "The last time we saw Amelia—when she was outside Moriarty's den in London—she was heavily pregnant."

"Do you think she gave birth in Innsmouth?" I asked.

"It is a guess, and only that," Holmes said, his voice subdued. "The facts, however, tell us that Olengran never used the book to open the rifts, that Maria and a heavily pregnant Amelia arrived, that Innsmouth is now inundated with creatures unlike those we've seen before, and that these new creatures have obliterated the former Innsmouthians, those who were faithful worshipers of the Order of Dagon. It was under these conditions, Watson, that Dagon and Cthulhu rose from the sea by Devil Reef."

So what? I thought. *What does this mean in the scheme of things?*

Without hearing my questions, Holmes answered them.

"For centuries—and if you believe the Innsmouthians, for *eons*—Olengran was in that fortress. He waited for the time to be right, for the stars to align, if you will, and he guarded this specific *Dagonite Auctoritatem*. For whom did he guard this book? Was it Taumo? No. Taumo led the Innsmouth sect of the Order of Dagon. Taumo never used the book, not in all these years. Who was higher in the Order of Dagon than Taumo and even Olengran?"

"Tell me! Who?" I gasped.

"Olengran waited for Dagon to rise from Devil Reef. And that is when everything rolled into motion. The strange new creatures flooding into our world from... beyond, from up there in the sky over Devil Reef. *Watson, he guarded this book for Dagon.*"

20
PROFESSOR MORIARTY

Goldi was a shattered rag doll of bones and battered flesh. The Medusa-coiled hair struggled to maintain its grasp on her bloody raw scalp, and it bobbed in the waves. Her gills vibrated, and she smiled. Her eyes glowed.

I could have scooped her up in my arms, lifted her from the boulders, and brought her back to the confines of her hut, but there was no point. She would not live more than a few minutes longer. It was a mercy, really, to shove her into the bay.

I did it with one foot. The crumbled body easily slipped from the boulders and splashed into the water. She went down, swirled away, with that smile plastered to her face. *Wear it well*, I thought, *your deep-sea smile*.

The villagers had died, they'd gone to sea, just like Goldi. In their place, other monsters shrieked and flailed and swooped through the sky. Cthulhu's tentacles stretched from one side of the bay to the other. His leathery head rested on the fizzing globules and crackling beasts of Devil Reef. Overhead, Dagon flapped his wings, landed on one of Cthulhu's tentacles and grasped it with webbed feet and claws. They were waiting for something, for surely it required no effort for them to destroy Innsmouth and all that lay beyond it.

Diseased clouds ruptured and spat flying monstrosities into air that smelled of nothing from this Earth: rank, syrupy thick and sweet, a mix of sour pickle and corpse filtering through it.

I crawled back up the graveyard mud to Goldi's hut, and then squeezed through the opening in the wall, where I dropped to the floor and curled into a ball.

Emblazoned in my mind was the image of Olengran, the monster who had exploded into the bay, bringing his fortress with him. I had been near the fish plant on the other side of Innsmouth, when I heard the bang, along with the swarms of spawn crawling and buzzing along the alley. They clattered and brayed, spinning wildly in the air, and I fell against a shack, my palms splayed on its bone-slime wall.

Eventually, I had summoned the courage—*I, Professor James Moriarty, who fears nothing... or so I had always thought*—to return to the waterfront, where I had found Goldi. And now, exhaustion overwhelmed me. Did I find the coincidence amusing, that my lust for gold had brought me to Innsmouth, where I now dozed in Goldi's hut? Not really. I do not believe in coincidence, nor in fate. I believe only in intellect and strength as mechanisms to control one's surroundings and one's life. If her name had been Silverton, I would not have lusted for silver. The coincidence existed,

I could not ignore it, but whether it reflected fate, a power beyond my own, was a laughable notion.

Things are what they are, I thought. *I cannot change what I've seen. It happened, and it exists. The monsters are real. They are not fantasies. The creatures that worshiped them were real and not fantasies concocted in a lunatic's brain.*

The drone of the clattering and shrilling lulled me to sleep, and in my dreams, I saw Sherlock Holmes, who laughed at me for being a fool.

"You cannot fight what you see, Moriarty," he said, his eyes glittering, the corners of his mouth twitching into a smile that mocked me. "Give up. Your days as a wealthy man who controls London's underbelly are over. I have given up. I can fight people, but I cannot fight beasts that break out of the sky."

In my dreams, I argued with him. He was wrong to give up, and I would never follow him down that path. I would continue down my own path, all the better because he *had* given up, and he was weak, impotent. A miniature Dr. Watson crawled from the dark and whimpered. On his back, he bore his wife and child.

"And what do we have here?" Sherlock Holmes cried, and his voice was *not* in my dreams.

I popped back into reality. Holmes was slumped next to me in the hut, and with him was Watson, full-sized and very real. I leaned toward the door, thinking about how to get past them.

"I saw you yesterday, in case you're wondering how I found you," Holmes said in a superior tone. "You came to

Innsmouth to satisfy your greed, that is obvious. And it is equally obvious that you regret coming here."

"We intend to leave post-haste," Watson said, as if he cared about me. "You should do the same."

"Spare me your idiocy." I crawled past them. Then I squeezed from the hut opening and stood. I hoped they would not follow me outside; but unsurprisingly, they *did* follow me.

"What do you want, Mr. Holmes?" I demanded.

"Some minor information to fill in the gaps, that is all," he replied. "Unlike the Doctor here, I do not care if you leave Innsmouth. In fact, I think we should all be better off if you stayed."

As if I would give him information...

The nerve of the man, this self-proclaimed scientific detective! It was absurd how exalted and erudite he thought himself.

Had I not outsmarted him every step of the way? It was *I* who had lured Mary and the baby from Watson's home. I could have killed them, just as easily as thinking it. It was *I* who had made a fortune with the Eshocker machines and the Old Ones Serum. Those machines still existed back in London, and I intended to make a second fortune with them. Let Holmes try to stop me. Even though he'd had the police shut down my dens, the technology for those machines existed; and Holmes knew as well as I that once science and technology exist, you cannot turn back the clock and pretend otherwise.

"Give up your quest," he said, "for the tram machine gold and for control of the Dagonites."

"Why do you care? What's it to *you*?" I spat.

The three of us slid down the mud from the hut and made our way up the alley away from the beach and toward the forest. I wanted to get away from them.

"You cannot possibly reap any riches or reward from any of this." Holmes's gesture took in the whole of Innsmouth.

"I don't want any of this," I answered. "Do you think me mad?"

He eyed me, still plodding toward the forest, and it was a minute or two before he spoke again.

"So you have given up your desire to control the deadly dimensions and all that breaks forth from them?" he finally said.

"I never give up, Holmes," I said. "You misunderstand."

"Pray tell." His walking stick tapped the side of a shack.

"Here's what I tell you, and then you will leave me alone, or face my gun and my fists."

At this, Holmes cast me a bemused glance, as did Watson. They didn't understand me at all. I intended to leave Innsmouth and return to London. These two idiots could have Innsmouth for themselves. Holmes would do my dirty work for me, of that I was certain.

"Henry Fitzgerald and Koenraad Thwaite are both dead," I said. "If you have a way, you can kill Cthulhu and Dagon and all these—" my hands swept with a flourish at the spawn "—inhabitants of Innsmouth. Be my guest. You know how hard I've been working. I came here under the false notion that I was visiting a quaint seaside town, where I might rest. Obviously, my sources provided bad information."

"Of course," Holmes said, as if agreeing with me. "Rest becomes you, Professor. Tell me, did you give the smallpox to Olengran? Was it through a servant?"

"You wish that *you* had done it, don't you?" I laughed. "You also wanted to seduce her, eh? But I got to the maid first. And I infected Henry Fitzgerald, too—Olengran caught the illness from one or other of them. His physiology is so strange, there is no way of knowing which."

"I only wanted information from Olengran," Holmes said.

Undoubtedly you did, I thought. *You will never admit it, will you, Holmes, that I am cleverer than you and always a step ahead?*

Cutting a sharp turn into a side alley, I pointed at the forest. I told Holmes to take Watson with him and leave me alone. They had interrupted my slumber, and I was now off to find another suitable location.

"Did you bring the smallpox from London?" Holmes asked.

"I did!" I proclaimed. "And I succeeded in killing the leader of the Order of Dagon! What have you done, Holmes?"

"And Frederick Cararo, what do you know about *his* illness?" Holmes pressed me.

"I have never met the man. But Fitzgerald said some man, *Cararo*, caught smallpox from him."

Watson averted his gaze. I locked eyes with Sherlock Holmes.

"But you thought too little about the matter," he said.

"Olengran would have been more valuable alive than dead. He could have told us how to repel or perhaps even kill Cthulhu, Dagon, and all the monsters, and how to close the deadly dimensions permanently. You killed Olengran before I had the opportunity to do any of this."

"You admit that I outwitted you!" I cried.

"As I said, you failed to think enough," Holmes answered evenly, "for I am fairly certain that I shall find a way to solve this mystery and put an end to it. I will try one method, and should it fail, I will try another. You will never succeed, Moriarty. I will always outwit you."

With that, he turned from me, and with Watson trailing him, made his way up the alley.

No, I thought, *it is I who have outwitted you, and both of us know it.*

Holmes would not be able to resist killing the monsters, closing the deadly dimensions, and defeating the entire Dagon gang. He had just said so himself. I would get what I wanted—the defeat of the gang and a return to controlling London's criminal underworld—and it was Sherlock Holmes who would give it to me.

The sweetness of it all was richer than the syrupy Innsmouth air.

Defeat me? Outwit me? Holmes has no wits left. I saw Holmes and Watson hop into a buggy and drive off. So there *was* a way out of Innsmouth. I would ask Taumo or one of his clan to get in touch with the driver of that buggy. Surely they would know him. They knew everybody in and around Innsmouth. If my hunch proved correct, the driver would be more than happy to transport me to Boston, and if not, my gun would persuade him.

I set off through the alleys, looking for someone who might help me contact Holmes's driver. My luck had turned. Soon, I would be in London, safe and with a full belly and a soft bed, while Holmes would still be here, thinking himself the savior of mankind.

It took little effort to obtain the information. I had been seen around Innsmouth for a while now. The few villagers who remained alive had seen me with Goldi, knew that Taumo had hidden me away. More than one offered to get word to the driver for me. I was to wait at the shore, they said, and when the vehicle arrived, they would come and find me.

A lot of services, I thought, and I had never paid Taumo anything. He had been much too trusting, and anyone who trusted me was a fool.

Satisfied, I returned to the bay, sat on the rock, and watched light flicker behind a cloud and disappear. In my defense as to what happened next, I will say that I was physically weak and exhausted from starvation and sleep deprivation. I had lost too much weight in a short time, my head swam, and my breathing was forced in that sickening, sweet haze.

A buggy would come for me, yes... but others came, as well. No longer hidden, I was a mouse snagged by a tiger in a closet. The tiger was Amelia Scarcliffe, and with her, she brought her hordes of offspring.

They attacked from behind, not that I could have fought them any better had I seen them coming. By the time I drew my guns, it was too late.

I fired, the bullets bounced off thick hide, and the guns dropped from my hands.

Hundreds of spawn dug their claws into me and lifted me into the sky over the bay. The staccato beat of their wings pounded in my skull. The drooling, the slime, the dead-flat eyes, the tendrils like netting wrapped around my body and head: purgatory had ended, but I regretted nothing. I had led my life, my way. I'd eaten the best food, drunk the best wine, and bedded the finest women. I'd enjoyed every minute. Perhaps in that instant, hanging there above the water, peering through the filaments, gagging on the air, feeling my blood trickle from hundreds of wounds, I realized that I had but one regret in life: coming to Innsmouth. This had been my fatal mistake.

But the rest? I would do it all again.

The eddies swirled, the bones and skulls and freakish monstrosities whipped around and sank in their centers. The boulders beckoned. And beyond...

There at Devil Reef, the gigantic tentacles twitched, the suckers opened and drank of the stink, the octopus-like head with its horrible eyes swiveled and stared at me. One giant mouth opened and emitted trills that burst my eardrum. Pain slashed like lightning through my head. What was left of my ear throbbed. And still, the trilling persisted.

That's when *she* came.

Her gills had enlarged and their color had blossomed into bold hues unknown to this world. No longer pregnant, she was slender, her body shaped like an eel. The toe suckers bulged, rosy, straining to attach themselves. The neck flaps pulsed, and her high-pitched trebles soared with Cthulhu's shrieking, merging into a harmony so shrill that I feared my skull would break.

I remembered Koenraad's dying words.

You will die for what you've done, Moriarty. You kidnapped Maria, held my beloved Amelia captive, even attempted to imprison me. I have sired my spawn, and my life nears its end. Humans mean nothing to me: Earthworms and ants!

And so here she was, Amelia Scarcliffe, with the monsters she had spawned with Koenraad. This was my death. While Koenraad hadn't cared about his own death, I did care about mine.

Yet I was helpless. The knife in my pocket slashed my own thigh, as the creatures and their tendrils squeezed me tightly and yet more tightly.

Choking, I needed air. My eyes saw colors, whirling colors, and nothing else.

And then, as quickly as they'd scooped me up, they dropped me. I fell upon the boulders beyond the pier. My body cracked upon the rock. My eyes flickered open, and color washed upon color, to be replaced by the gauzy view of the bay, of Devil Reef, and of Cthulhu.

The monster did not kill me. It did not eat me. It sat. It reacted as if it had no interest in me or my demise.

My right arm had shattered, and my left leg hurt. Soaking in my own blood, I lay there upon that boulder, pondering my fate.

I had shoved Goldi into the bay, and she was already gone. I would not die this way. The vermin in the sky, and their mother Amelia, did not realize the strength of Professor James Moriarty.

My body screamed with pain, yet I did not scream.

I rolled from the boulder, crashed over rocks and reef, clutched at the pier. The wood disintegrated in my hands. I grabbed again, this time clasping a more solid post, and forced myself onto the planks.

21
AMELIA SCARCLIFFE

Maria and I melted into amorphous form and let our particles drift in the water of Devil Reef. Cthulhu's presence buoyed me. This close, with his head before me and his heavy body consuming the sea, I was one with Him and one with All. Finally, the Old Ones ruled the Earth. *Finally*, and I cared not if I died or lived; and beside me, around me, and within me, neither did Maria. This world was but one option; we could slip into the otherworlds so easily, exist there, return at will—for the dimensions were open.

From his nest at the sea's bottom, Dagon spoke to us. His words thrummed through the water and found their target, just as turtles of this world follow the currents and find their breeding grounds. The water finds All.

Close the rift, Dagon told us, and I felt Maria's particles jolt at this command.

But why, after an eternity, would you seal the dimensions now that we have opened them? she asked. *Why does Cthulhu lie idle?*

You notice, he answered, *that you have both gained in power. You are no longer confined to corporeal form. You think the time is right, that the stars are aligned. But are they?*

At this, my anger flamed. I had fulfilled the third oath of the Order of Dagon. I had given birth, the blood of the Deep Ones crawled over the earth and filled the sky. This *was* the fulfillment of All. The stars *were* aligned.

Close the rift, Dagon commanded again. *You and your offspring will not die as readily as my worshipers died. Yet you have mutated, just as Olengran did before death. The human disease affected the worshipers, affected Olengran, killed all half-humans, all of those not of pure Deep Ones blood.*

Was he saying that Maria and I, or worse, Dagon and Cthulhu themselves, had been infected by the human disease? He was correct that our strength and powers had increased, that our bodies had mutated. It had not occurred to me that it was due to this human smallpox.

Cthulhu cannot rise, Dagon said. *The infection seeps from this world into the other dimensions, where our kind live. Time differs there. It is longer, thinner, more swirled and shaped. In one second of time here, months slip past there, and Old Ones are suffering long and lingering deaths from the infection.*

Maria's particles remained separate, with distance widening between them. Several drifted into the air, through the clouds, and through the rifts into the otherworlds. She urged me to do the same, and I did, sailing my particles into the realms where our kind flitted and danced. Retaining the bulk of myself on Earth—as did Maria—I addressed

Great Dagon. I requested his guidance. I was but a servant to the Old Ones. My existence would continue, elsewhere perhaps, but infinity knows no bounds.

Seal the dimensions from this world. I need my Dagonite Auctoritatem, the one that has been hidden here for eons by Devil Reef. Where is it? Dagon asked. *I left it in Olengran's keeping.*

We didn't know where Olengran's copy had gone. We did our best to chant what we had memorized, what we knew from birth, to do as Dagon requested. But the rifts remained open. Our kind spilled forth from other worlds into this one. I saw that they were as Dagon had described: they had mutated, but not in power and strength; rather, their essence and physical being decayed before me. They flowed from the rift over Devil Reef into the swirling water, where, transformed by the properties of this world, they writhed for life... and failed.

As finally we dispensed with our efforts, Maria and I crystallized into more corporeal shapes, still formless but with mass. Along with the dead careening from the sky, we saw death swept from the shore. The last thing we saw before sending ourselves through the rift into the otherworlds was a sad little family, grasping for each other as the eddies sucked them in and blew them to bits. Long coils for arms, toe and hand frills, and the baby-bo: it was Taumo, the head of Innsmouth's Dagonite worshipers, and his family.

From the other side of the rift, different chemical and physical properties took hold and changed us into our more natural forms. I peered, as only we can from beyond the rift, down at Earth and at Devil Reef.

Dagon and Great Cthulhu thrust their powerful bodies beneath the sea and swam out to the deep. Dagon no longer dwelled at Devil Reef. Cthulhu sank to the bottom of the ocean floor.

22
DR. JOHN WATSON

"I've studied Dagon's copy of the *Auctoritatem*. I'm certain the answer to our problems with the deadly dimensions and the monsters falling to Earth from them is contained in this book, Watson." Tucking the *Auctoritatem* into his traveling case, Holmes peeled off his gloves and sat beside me on the bed I shared with Mary. She was in Fortuna's usual position, sitting in the rocker by Samuel's cradle. The baby gurgled and played with Mary's fingers. Fortuna was busy, packing our cases for travel. It wouldn't take her long. My family was more than anxious to leave Innsmouth.

"Thankfully, everyone will be safe," I said, "before we make use of whatever you deduce from the *Dagonite Auctoritatem*, Holmes."

"First, I must find the truth of the matter," he said with a sideways glance. He pressed tobacco into his pipe, struck a match, and inhaled. His eyes narrowed, then he exhaled, sending curls of smoke throughout the room.

"We are ready," Fortuna announced, pulling on her coat,

which had held up a lot better than either mine or Holmes's. Holmes's was tattered and coated in the filth of Innsmouth. Mine had been wrecked by the monsters of Devil Reef.

"Come along, then." Holmes tamped his pipe and slipped it into his jacket pocket. He slid his coat over his formerly fine tweeds.

"What about Jeffrey and Sylvia?" Mary asked as she stood with Samuel and handed him to Fortuna.

"We cannot bring them," Fortuna said, her eyes warmly upon my wife, who tensed. "Jeffrey is too sick to travel, and both children are... not well."

"They are Innsmouthian," Holmes said. "Mutated. We cannot spread that curse."

"But we promised them," Mary said with resignation in her voice. "John, what do you think?"

We have a boy of our own. We'll make sure you're safe, I promise.

"I gave the boy my word. And yet, what would be safe for these children?" I said. "With Deep Ones blood in them, their mutations mean that they could deform rapidly and... *explode*... like Frederick Cararo and the others. A bit of human disease, smallpox, and they're done for. We cannot bring them with us. It's too dangerous, as Holmes says, to spread that type of disease and to risk the lives of people in Boston, London, or on the boat that takes us home. What if their demise occurs on that boat?"

Nodding but with a sad look upon her face, Mary lifted the baby's bundles while Fortuna grasped the handles of two traveling cases. Holmes already had his case ready, so I lifted my own. "What about the Arkham Sanitarium?" Mary asked, as we closed the bedroom door. None of us would miss this place. We were already halfway down the staircase leading to the hexagonal room. She answered her own question. "Dragoon and Hortense have too much sway at the sanitarium. Jeffrey and Sylvia will be better off with any Innsmouthian family than with Dragoon and Hortense, who will murder them as soon as we're out of sight."

"Most of the villagers are dead," Holmes noted. "I doubt there's much left there other than the monsters flooding out of that slit over the bay."

"Don't forget the larvae and other rapidly growing mutations that infest the place," I added. "And yet, where else can we take the children?"

"Perhaps they will feel at home in Innsmouth," Fortuna said from behind me, as she stepped from the staircase and lowered her eyes to avoid looking at the paintings. "They are of the same blood, are they not?"

Holmes nodded as he yanked open the front door to the Cararo mansion and gestured at us to exit.

"Mr. Hagley knows everyone and everything around here. I will ask him to ensure the safety of the children. Hagley shares the same ancestry. He will know what to do. Now, let's make haste!"

My heart picked up pace. At last, I was getting my family out of this dreaded mansion, although Holmes and I were not quite done with Innsmouth. We would be forced to return and deal with Cthulhu, Dagon, and the others; but this time, we would do it alone and from the sea.

"No! Don't leave me here!" It was Hortense. Her words were slurred. I whirled to see her fall against the door leading into the billiards-examination room. She toppled to the floor, landing on the plush hall rug, then groaned and struggled to a sitting position.

Mary gasped, and her face went pale. She clapped a hand over her mouth and stared at me as if asking me what to do.

Holmes jerked his head toward the door and also stared at me. He wanted my family out of there, so I told Mary to take Samuel and Fortuna and hurry out to the buggy, where Hagley waited. Holmes faced Hortense Cararo.

"Madame, you are shameful," he lectured her. "Get off the floor. Take care of yourself. You have children."

She wailed and clawed at her nightgown, a slinky garment with tiny straps and a cut that revealed more of her body than I wanted to see.

"Holmes!" I cried, backing toward the door.

In response, he peered more closely into the hall, then jumped back and joined me.

Shrieking as loudly as anything I had heard on the mud beach, Hortense clawed at her chest and stomach, ripping the flimsy gown. She writhed, rolled to the middle of the hall, and lay with her arms and legs splayed. Her body heaved with spasms. Arching her back, she screamed the hideous words of my nightmares:

"She tried to warn me, tried to explain
Her children were not meant to be plain.
...after the stars are gone...
...after the stars are gone...
Ch'thgalhn fhtagn urre'h nyogthluh'eeh ngh syh'kyuhyuh."

In the middle of the hall, the tentacle-and-hexagon stencils on the arch throbbed to the chant. The tentacles broke free, elongated, and thrashed across the ceiling.

"Jacob!" she cried, but Dr. Dragoon did not appear. Her eyes glazed over, and she returned to the wailing of gibberish.

As pustules popped from her flesh and pushed toward the ceiling, suckers extended from the ceiling tentacles and stretched down as if trying to reach her.

Another Innsmouth mutation of smallpox.

Holmes and I tossed our travel cases through the door and dashed out. The octopus-shaped knocker rattled as we slammed the door. From behind it, we heard the explosion.

Holmes shoved me into the waiting buggy. Crammed inside with Mary, Samuel, and Fortuna, with our bags stowed in the rear, Holmes yelled at Hagley to get the horses moving.

"Boston!" he cried, as Mary and Fortuna both broke down weeping. Even Holmes and I shielded our eyes from the dreaded house.

We knew the hall was filled with the remains of Hortense Cararo. She had died in the same manner as her husband. The only adult left in the accursed place was Dr. Jacob Dragoon, and he was welcome to tend to his lover one final time. As for the children, Hagley would surely take them among their own people, or whatever passed as people in Innsmouth. It was one of the saddest decisions of my life. To this day, the guilt weighs upon me, and yet, what else could we have done?

We had to stop several times en route to Boston to stretch our legs and attend to Samuel. Holmes spent the time lost in his thoughts, probably trying to decipher whatever he had seen in Dagon's *Auctoritatem*. Wanting to shut out the horror of Hortense Cararo and her children, I let my mind drift to Mr. Hagley, who had already agreed to look after Jeffrey and Sylvia.

Despite his Innsmouthian blood, Hagley reminded me of many a Londoner I had met over the years, those true to their word and with compassion in their hearts. Willie Jacobs again came to mind, as he often did. A man born to bad luck, Willie had died with the same bad luck; but never had a finer man entered my life and filled me with such hope for humanity. I had seen my share of soulless men, enough to make me somewhat jaded about the fate of mankind. But every now and then, someone came along who reminded me that the human heart *can* be good, if only we insist upon it in ourselves. Willie had been one such man. Hagley was not of pure human blood, he was tinged with that of the Deep Ones; and yet, he was a better man than most.

What does that say about the human state? I wondered.

* * *

After Innsmouth, Boston felt like a return to civilization and normalcy. The streets were lined with shops and cluttered with people and buggies. It was surreal to think that Boston and Innsmouth were in the same state. I doubted that the women with their shopping bags and the men with their pocket watches and pipes knew much about the lives of their Innsmouth counterparts. I'm sure they didn't want to know. If I could, I would blot Innsmouth from my own memory.

Thankful to disembark, we found a pleasant inn for my family's stay and then bid Hagley farewell. I promised Mary that, soon enough, Holmes and I would return and together, we would all journey home.

As I had expected, both she and Fortuna worried and fussed over us. Holmes was reluctant to waste time with food and a bath, but I insisted.

"For what we're about to do," I said in the dining area of the inn, tucked into a comfortable chair at a normal table, "we're going to need all of our strength."

I'm afraid that our appearance and the stink of our attire permeated the air. Other diners wrinkled their noses, glared at us, and moved as far away as possible.

"A bath won't help this," Holmes said drily, "but I shall take your good advice, Doctor, and eat. It will be a distinct pleasure... Let's make it fast, shall we?" He examined the handwritten menu and raised his finger to let the inn's owner—a craggy man with a face ruddy from the sea—know that he was ready to order his meal. The fellow shuffled over, wiping his hands on a grimy apron, and nodded at Holmes.

"What'll it be?" he asked.

I looked at the menu, skimming quickly over fish fry and grilled cod and shrimp. Buried at the bottom of the list of offerings, I found my gem, a shepherd's pie made of meat, potatoes, cabbage, and carrot. Holmes ordered a pot pie of chicken and vegetables. Mary and Fortuna bypassed the fish items, as well. We all ordered ale.

"It feels so normal here," Fortuna whispered, her eyes roving about the place: at the ladies in their ordinary garb, at the men with beards, mustaches, and top hats. There wasn't a tentacle, toe frill, or rattling larva in sight.

"You will be safe here," I told her, this time *truthfully*, unlike the somewhat half-hearted assurances I had offered upon our arrival in Innsmouth. "This *is* a normal place. It's much like London, though more crowded, larger, and American. Eat, rest, take walks, recuperate," I told Mary, squeezing her hand. "Holmes and I will be back before you know it."

"Be careful, John. That thing will crush you."

Cthulhu.

It was more likely that one of the monster's tentacles would crash down and split our boat in half. Holmes and I exchanged a glance, remembering our near-fatal incident on the *Belle Crown*. We had barely survived, and a wave on the Thames, regardless of its size, is nothing like a giant wave on the open sea.

* * *

After our repast and some rest, Holmes and I washed and left for the harbor, where we bought tickets on a boat that would bring us to the ship, the *Elysium*, that had transported us from England to Innsmouth.

"It's safe out there," the seamen told us. "The monster *sleeps* at Devil Reef."

"No, the monster—" I started to mention what Hagley had told us, that the word from Innsmouth was that Cthulhu and Dagon had left Devil Reef for the sea. But Holmes and I had no first-hand knowledge of this fact. For all we knew, the beasts from the otherworld lay directly beyond Devil Reef, ready to rise again over the bay.

"That's good to know," Holmes interrupted with a smile. "Come along, Dr. Watson. It's a beautiful day for a journey at sea. Let's enjoy it."

With more assurances that the sea was safe from whatever dwelled at Devil Reef, the sailors helped us aboard. Within the hour, Holmes and I clenched the rails of a boat as it zipped over the water toward our destination.

The sea was mild, the waves steady. The air refreshed us, the breeze cleansing our senses of Innsmouth. If only we could abandon the *Elysium* with the Killer Eshockers in its hold, then it might have been a more delightful excursion. But we both knew what lay ahead, and it was with great dread that we made that journey.

When we were again on the deck of the *Elysium*, we ceased

pretending that this was just an ordinary outing. We scrambled down the stairs to the lower hold, where we immediately went to work setting up the Killer Eshockers in the engine room.

There were only two of the machines, but they filled the room. On the Thames, we had used but one Eshocker. Each of the Killers resembled the extreme treatment Eshockers created and used by Dr. Sinclair at the Whitechapel Lunatic Asylum, but the mahogany boxes holding the Killer Eshockers' components were much larger. The difference between a Killer and an extreme treatment machine was that the former included a giant transformer that pumped out a strong enough pulse of electricity for our purposes. The harpoons, made of brass and steel, were strong enough to pierce the toughest hide. Per Willie Jacobs's instructions, ten clamps secured tightly wound copper coil to each harpoon. The cables securing the harpoons to the Killer Eshocker were also coiled with copper.

It would be difficult to use the Eshockers without Willie Jacobs, but Holmes had taught a few sailors how to operate the machines in the engine room. We tried to tell each other that the Killer Eshocking would destroy Cthulhu, but I don't think that either one of us truly believed it.

"It worked on the Thames monsters," one of our dynamo men said. "It will work here."

"Maybe," Holmes said. "It did work in the Thames, yes. We attach this harpoon—" he pointed to one of the harpoons attached by cables to the Eshocker "—to enormous electrical voltage that we obtain from the dynamo

THE ADVENTURE OF THE INNSMOUTH MUTATIONS

and transformer designed by Mr. Willie Jacobs. When the harpoon hits a creature, the electricity flows into it, and through it, the electricity flows across the opening in the sky where the creatures come from."

"Dynamite doesn't work with these monsters," I explained. "Cannonballs, bombs, bullets: nothing works. They just knock the beasts back or drill some holes into them, which we've seen heal as the beasts flit in and out of our world through that opening."

While Holmes and I had told Inspector Lestrade about the science behind the Killer Eshockers, we saw no need to delve into so much detail with the sailors who were helping us battle Cthulhu. I doubted that they would understand or care about the details. Holmes had explained it to me repeatedly before I understood the methodology, and I still wasn't so sure...

Something about pressure waves...

I dug back in my memory to that discussion with Lestrade. "An explosion from dynamite," Holmes had said, "means that chemical energy converts quickly into high-temperature gas, which expands and creates pressure waves. These pressure waves can knock the creatures back, but they cannot close the rift between our world and the otherworld. The creatures can simply duck across the rift and avoid the explosions."

The Killer Eshockers had actually sealed the rifts over the Thames. The high voltage had traveled across the rifts with the monsters, and the scientific properties of the otherworld had transformed the voltage, making it close the rifts.

And here we were again, in another engine room, attempting to use the same technique to kill Cthulhu. Cables ran between the steam engine and two huge dynamos, and from them, to the two transformers, each with one hundred coils of copper on its left and three thousand coils on its right.

"Make sure to keep your eyes on the red cord hanging from the hole," I said to the dynamo operators, who nodded nervously at the cord that was attached to the cable trailing up to the deck. "When the cord lifts completely out of the hole and you no longer see it, turn off the voltage."

"Aye, sir." The largest of the group steeled his fists, but I could tell he was as terrified as his mates. His eyes darted around the room, his face twitched.

"Let's go, then," Holmes pressed. "Take the ship closer to Devil Reef."

One of the men scurried off to obey the order, and as Holmes and I returned to the deck, the ship changed direction and started speeding toward Innsmouth.

"The last place I want to go," I said.

"Indeed," Holmes said, "and let us hope that it is the last time we have to think about that infernal village." He pulled the harpoon cables through the holes in the engine-room ceiling. The red rope curled on the deck by one of the holes. I would drop it and signal the sailors to power up the Killer Eshockers if and when we saw Cthulhu or Dagon.

Half of me prayed that the monsters *wouldn't* show up. Half of me prayed that they *would*.

Approaching Devil Reef from the sea sent waves of nausea through me. I trembled and broke out in a sweat, chilled instantly by the cold air blasting past me. The reef swelled from the water, larger and more deadly than I remembered. The rocks soared higher and dripped with flesh, fat, and mounds of the oddly colored fog. The orbs, boxes, and complex shapes that I'd seen while approaching last time no longer swarmed around the rocks. In their place, the larvae buzzed, and their brethren, still sliding from the slit between the clouds, writhed and flapped and swam with them. Despair filled me. I thought my head would explode from the tension.

"Where's Cthulhu? Where is Dagon?" Holmes exclaimed. "I don't see them here, Watson."

"It's as the sailors told us in Boston," I said, my voice cracking from nerves. "They're no longer at Devil Reef. So where are they, Holmes?"

Rather than answer, he raced down to the engine room, only to return moments later, as the ship ground to a halt, then turned and headed back to sea.

"We're leaving?" Hope surged through me.

"No," he said. "I instructed the captain to push out farther from Devil Reef. If Cthulhu isn't here, then he's at sea. He'll find *us*, Watson."

Cthulhu did not disappoint Sherlock Holmes. He did find us, and when he arrived, it was on a wave the height of our ship. I'd seen Cthulhu from the village, but never from such close proximity. He was *immense*. His tentacles soared outward in all directions, casting shadows that covered all in the blackness of a monster storm. Massive wings unfolded and spread, and the wind howled, bucking up the wave another ten feet.

Holmes and I grasped the ship rail, heads tilted back, eyes glued to the monster.

The wave curled. At the very top, where Cthulhu poised, ready to smash down upon us, the froth gurgled.

"It's about to break!" Holmes cried. He wrenched himself from his trance and raced over to the red rope and shoved it down the hole.

From below, the sailors cranked up the Killer Eshocker, and electricity screamed. I felt its power in the cable and in the harpoon I hoisted from the deck. Holmes and I staggered under the weight of the weapons and from the force of the gale.

The wave thundered down, knocking the boat askew. I slipped, grabbed at my harpoon, seized it just before it slid over the deck and the opposite rails. Holmes had the rail in one hand, the harpoon in his other. I scrabbled up and did the same. I awaited his command.

In my hand, electricity shot through the coils around my harpoon. The muscles of my hand and lower arm throbbed.

A second wave knocked the ship off course again, as Cthulhu swam away from us—too far away for our cables to reach.

Aftershocks of wave upon wave hit us, and the captain couldn't steady the boat and steer it toward the monster. Every time he tried, another wave hit. Cthulhu was slipping toward the horizon. Finally, the boat engine revved, and the ship flew over the water, chasing the flailing tentacles, the bloated head, the monstrosity that had risen from the bottom of the sea.

The beast turned, as if hearing the ship racing after it. Cthulhu was up for the fight. He charged directly at us.

He grew larger, and yet *larger*. His head loomed. The tentacles were too close. The suckers reached for me.

But he was still so far away...

How could any creature be this big?

I don't know if I said it or thought it.

"Now! Release your harpoon, Watson!" Holmes suddenly screamed.

Aiming as well as I could on that up-and-down sea, I fired the harpoon through the wind at Cthulhu's head. Pain sliced down my shoulder with the recoil, and I stumbled back. Holmes's harpoon hit the beast in the head, as well. Both harpoons fell from the hide.

We hadn't *dented* Cthulhu.

Nothing.

What would it take?

We pulled in the harpoon and cables, launched them over and over again; and each time, they hit Cthulhu's head and simply bounced off.

"It's as if we're tossing pins at him," I said.

Worse, every time we sent a harpoon at his face, Cthulhu flailed his tentacles and swam closer to the ship.

I feared another huge wave. I feared death in the jaws of

Cthulhu, in his belly, in the massive muscle of his tentacles. One sucker to my body would pulverize me.

I became aware all of a sudden that the ship that had brought us here from Boston was bobbing to starboard, far enough away to remain safe yet close enough to rescue us, should our ship go down. My brain calculated all possibilities. One thrash from Cthulhu, and no amount of ships at any range would save us. The one thing I was absolutely certain of was that *we would not kill Cthulhu.*

Holmes, also resigned to this fact, dropped the red rope for a final time, and the Killer Eshockers choked off.

"There's no rift here," Holmes said, thinking aloud. "It wouldn't have worked anyway."

"We had to try," I said.

"Look," I pointed at Cthulhu, who was swimming toward the horizon, "he's bored with us. He's leaving."

"What worries me, Watson, is where he is *going.*"

As we headed back to the Boston port, I told Holmes that it was time to take my family to London.

"We've done all that we can," I insisted. "There is nothing more we can try."

"No. We will finish the job." Holmes frowned at me. "I have one more idea, Watson. It's dangerous—"

"—and this wasn't?" I said.

"It's dangerous," he repeated, "but I think it will work. I *know* it will work."

"Then why did we attempt using the Killer Eshockers?" I asked, dismayed that he would risk our lives and those of the sailors if there was another way.

"Because the other method requires that I convince Dagon to help us."

23

We paid a driver handsomely for a ride to the outskirts of Innsmouth, where he would drop us off, procure the other half of his fare from Holmes, and race back to the safety of Boston. En route, wearing protective leather gloves, we compared the two copies of the *Dagonite Auctoritatem* that had come into our possession on our adventures: the one Holmes had taken from Olengran's shack, and Amos Beiler's book, which had led to his untimely death and brought us to the whole mystery in the first place.

The Beiler volume sat like a dead weight on my knees. The animal-hide cover was greasy, sliding about under my leather gloves, and the book was grotesquely heavy. Both volumes looked the same: bound with sinew, each containing hundreds of pages of yellowed hide inked in dark maroon.

Page by page, we flipped through the two books. Upon careful examination, we concluded that the same weird symbols were inked upon the Beiler copy and its Innsmouth counterpart.

"Do you remember, Holmes, that Amos Beiler had a separate page of ancient instructions for the table, chest, and chair of bizarre dimensions?"

"Of course I do, Watson. Only Beiler could interpret the instructions to build those deadly items. His book had been passed through the generations."

I flipped to that page now, and Holmes flipped to the corresponding page in Dagon's copy.

"It's here," he commented, as I quivered to see those jumbled geometric constructions and symbols again. Many people had died—been murdered in the most hideous ways—due to Beiler's *Auctoritatem*. Amos Beiler himself had died, exploded to bits in his own barn, which had been built according to these deadly dimensions.

On the bottom of the page, inked in what appeared to be dried blood, numbers clustered in coils.

"300000 437 500 197 207 82 79 18 16," I said softly, my body shaking.

"The door code to Willie Jacobs's tram machine building, where inside, his father was murdered as gruesomely as Amos Beiler."

I would never forget that code, most of the numbers corresponding to scientific values.

"300000," I recited, as a student of eight years old recites elementary mathematics to his instructor, "is close to Foucault's 1862 measurement of the speed of light: 299,796 kilometers per second."

"Or, as you might recall from our earlier discussions,

the 300000 might instead refer to the notion that the light from the full moon is 300,000 times weaker than sunlight." Despite the gravity of our situation and what we faced in Innsmouth, Holmes allowed himself a chuckle. "You know, Watson, that I have little faith in astronomers and their imprecise science."

"We never did puzzle through all the numbers," I noted, "finally deducing that the unknowns corresponded to science as yet undiscovered. Though," I recited the memorized values, "207 is the atomic weight of lead, and 16 is the atomic weight of oxygen."

Holmes had already turned to the next page in Dagon's copy of the *Auctoritatem*. Flustered, I did the same, and together, we continued to work our way through the two copies, seeking a difference that might lead us to a solution that would seal the deadly dimensions forever and keep the infernal creatures out of our world.

We scoured approximately the first hundred pages of each *Dagonite Auctoritatem*, finding no difference. And then, we both saw it at the same time—

"Look!" Holmes cried, pointing at a heap of complicated geometries interspersed with arcane symbols.

I stared at the Beiler version.

"Not here!" I cried. "None of it. The entire page, Holmes, it's missing from this version!"

Dagon's *Auctoritatem* contained an extra page of incomprehensible shapes and symbols mapped onto endless swirls seemingly cast into infinity.

"This is it," Holmes said. "This is the answer. As with Beiler's page of furniture notations, described in bizarre geometries and codes, Dagon possesses a page that only he can decode and understand. Olengran kept the *Auctoritatem* until Dagon came forth to claim it and to... use it."

The buggy ground to a halt, the horses reared, the driver screamed at them, and then he jumped down and yelled at us to immediately disembark. Holmes and I gazed at the bleak landscape before us: Innsmouth, with its brown scum fog, clacking flying larvae, wriggling slime-orbs, with its corpses and flesh rot. Beyond, the bay was a pot of stinking filth, and overhead, rotting clouds split and monsters tumbled to the boulders. The driver wasted no time in leaving us to our fates.

"*Flatland*. Edwin Abbott," I muttered. "The best book of the past ten years. Abbott was a genius. He guessed that life exists in other dimensions, and indeed, we now know this to be so."

"We don't know it as a *fact*, Watson. We don't know where these creatures come from or where they go through that slit in the sky. Nor do I care right now. All I care about is closing the deadly dimensions and getting rid of these damnable creatures. Now let's move—*quickly*, Doctor!"

We scrambled down the alley past the ruins of all we'd seen before: shacks had toppled, leaving jumbled boards that vaguely reminded me of the jumbles in the *Dagonite Auctoritatem*; pieces of dead villagers, ripped to shreds by the killer waves and the pickings of Old Ones; bones, shells, fish heads with gelatinous eyes. The sky dripped brown mist that smelled of decay and death. Under the weight of its burden—the opening to the deadly dimensions and the appearance of the Old Ones—the sky was collapsing.

What will happen if the sky collapses? Will it take the world with it?

"No time!" Holmes yanked my sleeve, and I tripped over skeletons and slipped on mold and slime.

The mist was sweeter with rot down by the bay. Sucking the syrupy haze into my lungs, I panted and prayed that I would have the fortitude to see our mission to its end. Holmes was doing no better, though he was putting on a brave front. I could tell that he had weakened, as had I, in the air of Innsmouth. Sweat coursed down his face, which was no longer pale, but rather, blotched with red patches. The wind raged both from the sea and the knife wound in the sky; our teeth chattered from cold, our bodies shook.

Summoning the remnants of our strength as well as our courage, we fought our way past writhing shapeless masses, tentacles and translucent spheres, past pincers, claws, and fangs. As before, the howling and gibberish hammered my skull, and my eyes lost focus. Colors spun and wrenched apart. Larvae yowled and descended upon us, jaws snapping at our faces and arms. We beat them off, Holmes with his walking stick, I with my fists.

My knuckles smashed into webbed eyes, frills blooming from mouths, clawed feet, and grasping pincers.

There were too many of them, and only one of me. I felt

myself sinking into the mud. They would crush me into that mud. I would die there.

"Eeesh-beanjzh-ig-gooolmoreunjghtzaicklefrosh g'vlag!"

It beat into my brain. The mud reached my knees. Blood coursed from my fists, but still, I pummeled those hideous monstrosities with fists broken and raw from the effort.

Holmes's stick cracked against the beasts, and his hand reached into the fray; and he hauled me up. Half dragging me while beating off the beasts from beyond, he kicked a final few, swiveled, and shoved me onto the rock slabs, which clattered rhythmically in time with the howling.

"Eeesh-beanjzh-ig-gooolmoreunjghtzaicklefrosh g'vlag!"

Waves of filth knocked me to my back. I scraped fish and gore from my face, stood again, and raised my fists. I howled with the rest of them, only my words were screams of rage and prayers to God.

Holmes's coat had been ripped from his body. His jacket and trousers were rags, blood soaking the remains. Gashes glistened on his face, arms, and hands. As I looked at him, my friend, injured and suffering, my mind hardened to the task at hand. My screaming abated, my rage receded.

"Do you have it?" I asked Holmes.

He managed a smile, winced as his lips opened.

"Yes," he said, "I have it, Watson." He tapped the front of his trousers.

It was then that I noticed the gigantic shape of the *Dagonite Auctoritatem* crammed into his clothing. Thankfully, we had both lost a lot of weight in Innsmouth.

Holmes's trousers drooped several sizes too large on his emaciated frame, but accommodated the huge volume.

"Holmes," I cried, "you amaze me!" I had lost Amos Beiler's copy of the infernal book while battling the monsters on the beach.

"Put it down," something gurgled from the filth that surged over the rock.

"What the—?" I said.

Put the Dagonite Auctoritatem on the rock. Right before our eyes, forcing us both to shake our heads to clear our vision, Maria Fitzgerald coalesced out of nowhere and nothing, recognizable, but unutterably changed.

Her flat eyes were ringed in black. She stared at us, coldly and with no trace of human conscience. Where she had once had hair, scales jittered on a barely recognizable face and over chin barbels. She no longer had arms or legs. I couldn't count the number of fins fluttering and flapping around her body, the number of frills. She hissed her words, yet her bulbous lips never opened.

Shocked, I realized that she had hissed those words straight into my brain.

Holmes gasped. He had heard the words, just as I had, and they had struck inside his brain, as well.

"It can't be," he cried. "What are you? What is this?"

My heart ached, it hurt. But then, pride swelled and with it, hope, as Holmes regained his composure and spat at the thing before us.

"Maria Fitzgerald from the great beyond, from other

spaces and times! You are not of this Earth! Return yonder, from whence you came, return and never plague us again!"

Something else probed my mind, and then it entered. With Maria's voice came another, similar but shriller, piercing my skull in a high-pitched treble.

Put the book down! the other screeched, and I recognized the voice of Amelia Scarcliffe. She coagulated from the mist and the fetid wave that flushed over me, slopping onto the rock beside Maria.

Holmes lifted his arms, as if conceding to authorities. His eyebrows rose.

"It is best. You are right," he told the hideous pair.

"But... Holmes!" I objected.

He pulled his leather gloves from his pockets, and after pulling them over his open wounds without so much as a wince, he produced Dagon's book, which was wrapped in leather. Noticing my raised eyebrows, he said, "I got the leather from the *Elysium*," then he returned his focus to Maria and Amelia. He placed the book on the rock and backed away, gesturing at me to come with him.

"It all culminates here," he whispered.

"But what will they do with it?" I asked harshly. "They will destroy the *Auctoritatem*, and with it, our hopes of saving the world."

He shook his head and helped me stumble backward. We neared the dilapidated pier; like a wreckage of broken bones, its skeleton poked from the bay.

"No, Doctor, the last thing they want to do is destroy

that book. Remember, it's been kept for the eons under lock and key for Dagon's return."

Yes, Olengran...

Maria interrupted my thoughts.

We were already gone, she said, as Holmes's eyes glazed with concentration, and I realized again that she spoke directly to both of us through our minds at the same time. *Your world is not ready for our kind. Your world is polluted with too many people. You do not live in harmony. You live to destroy.*

The Old Ones don't care, one way or the other, what humans do to each other, she continued. I noticed that neither she nor Amelia had taken the *Dagonite Auctoritatem* from the rock. *Earth is our eternal home, from time's beginning to time's end, and from there, to infinity in both directions. Time whirls and circles, and space is not what you think it is. We saw you here. We knew the time was right, the time is now.*

"For what?" I demanded. Holmes remained silent throughout, his eyes squeezed shut, his eyebrows creased. Suddenly, he opened his eyes and addressed me as if discussing the weather.

"Watson, it's simple," he said. "They need the book, not for themselves, but for Dagon."

"But," I sputtered, "but why?"

"It is what I told you earlier," he answered. "The extra page in Dagon's copy. Only Dagon can decipher, interpret, utter whatever incantations are on that page, Watson."

My spawn came, that which Koenraad sired, Amelia treble-shrilled into my brain. *Finally, after millennia, it was*

I who fulfilled the third oath of the Order of Dagon, to reproduce and birth the Deep Ones. Dagon came.

They were done with us. They left us by the pier, with their final words ringing in our heads.

Dagon will come for his Auctoritatem. *Your smallpox infects us. It makes Deep Ones and Old Ones—all who come—more powerful here. Dagon and Cthulhu. It weakens and destroys acolytes, those of weak blood. It seeps across the rifts into the otherworlds, where time is thinner, longer, different. Smallpox infection in the otherworlds, far across the dimensions, tortures us, kills us. Dagon comes.*

From the mud, Amelia's spawn slithered onto the rocks and fluttered overhead. A few villagers straggled from the alleys, slopped across the cesspool that passed as a beach, and huddled together by their vile bay. In their midst were two tiny figures that I recognized: Jeffrey and Sylvia.

"So Mr. Hagley did as we requested," Holmes said. "He gave the children to one of the last Innsmouth families for protection." As I stumbled toward the children, he held me back. "No, Doctor, leave them be. It is best this way. It is the *only* way. They are of Deep Ones blood. They must go the way of their people."

"But they are like us," I insisted, "like you and me, like Samuel!"

"Are they? Do you know how to heal what ails them, Doctor?"

"No," I had to admit.

"They will go with the others," Holmes said, and he

squeezed my arm before releasing it. Then he cringed, for his palms both had deep wounds that would require my services as soon as we returned to Boston.

I remembered Cthulhu out at sea, how he had thundered across that giant wave, and I suppose that I expected Dagon to appear in a similar fashion. But no wave rose, and if anything, the water grew quiet, barely stirring.

A dent appeared across the water's surface, trailing from Devil Reef to the shore. And Dagon rose from below: first, his giant frog head, then his forearms. Wings closed on his back, his massive muscles thrust his body up, and he sprang like an amphibian, snatched the *Dagonite Auctoritatem* from the rock, and two huge claws flipped through the leathery pages.

The spawn settled, no longer chanting and squealing. Jeffrey and Sylvia cowered upon the rock, arms raised. Dagon's voice, when it came, boomed, and it was so deep and so loud that it shook the rocks, the pier, the whole of Innsmouth. The children jittered up and down, as did the worshiping spawn. The world rumbled with Dagon, all in harmony, the drumming throttling and bouncing in my skull, and Holmes and I collapsed on the pier.

When I thought my head would explode, the booming ceased, and Dagon disappeared with the *Auctoritatem*— he did not disappear beneath the sea, however; his body splintered into a billion pieces, which fragmented into a billion more, and then he and his infernal book rose into the brown-scum mist, and from there, into the clouds.

With him went all the others—the spawn, the larvae, the monsters, Jeffrey and Sylvia—*poof*, into dust, and *whoosh*, into the clouds. I pictured a healthy Jeffrey, no longer hemophilic and starving, and a healthy Sylvia, no longer drugged and deformed. I knew that they would never look like the images in my mind, like human children; they would exist as *something else* in the great beyond. But they would *exist*, which was the important thing.

The black clouds shuddered; the opening widened as the Old Ones vanished into the beyond. And then, glowering a final time at Innsmouth, all the seething froth, the brown-scum filth that had been hanging there for so long—all of it, with a resounding boom, slammed shut. The rift was gone; sealed, I hoped, forever.

"If I hadn't seen it myself…" Holmes finally managed to say.

"I saw it as well," I said, and after a pause, asked him how he knew that Dagon needed the book to close the rift.

"Your wits are not about you, and for good reason. Few can see what we've seen and survive. You keep asking me these questions… The book, Watson," he said slowly, measuring his words, halting once, then continuing. "Theodore Jacobs used the *Dagonite Auctoritatem* to open the deadly dimensions in his tram machine building. Amos Beiler used his *Dagonite Auctoritatem* to open the deadly dimensions in his barn, where he built furniture that killed people. The *Norma* structure in Swallowhead Spring was another construct of deadly dimensions, and it, too, brought a rift. The ultimate slice into otherworlds ripped open in that warehouse by the Thames, pulling creatures into London, into the minds of our own people, Watson— into your mind." He turned, caught my eye, then dropped his gaze again. "In each case, spells from the *Dagonite Auctoritatem* breached the gulf between our world and the beyond, bringing those creatures upon us. As soon as I realized that Dagon had a copy, I concluded that he would use it in the same way."

That's when Holmes's explanation crystallized into conclusion, and I understood.

"In this case," I said, as he nodded vigorously, "the deadly dimensions were already open. The creatures were here. Dagon and Cthulhu were here, ready to blaze their way across the Earth, yet they remained at Devil Reef. And so... and so, Holmes, the only reason Dagon would need that book was to unleash Cthulhu and crush all else in the world... or, if need be... to *close* the rifts, to *escape* with his Old Ones back whence they came!"

"Admirable! You outdo yourself!" Holmes said. "And the smallpox infections, as they hit the Deep Ones and the creatures from beyond, as they dribbled into those otherworlds, the infections mutated the creatures and slaughtered them. Scientific properties differ in other dimensions, as Maria 'told' us."

"Scientific properties," I repeated. *As if...*

"Yes. Science, Watson."

Holmes and I hobbled along the broken wood slats toward the fish-processing plant, where we headed up the alleys and to the forest. I assumed that Hagley, as always, would be waiting for us. How he would know this time that we were in need of his services, I hadn't a clue; but just as Maria and Amelia had infiltrated my mind, I had a feeling that Hagley would simply *know*.

24

The water off Boston's pier looked welcoming: a wide expanse of sea, blue and undisturbed by unnatural creatures. Mary, Fortuna, and Samuel waited on a bench with our bags. My life would begin anew. I would devote myself to my wife and child, to making them happy, to ensuring their safety until my dying day. I would make sure that Fortuna stayed with us for as long as she wanted, and if she asked to leave for any reason, I would always help her in every way I could.

After Holmes and I received medical care from Boston's finest doctors—their methods were much like my own—we had all shed the clothing we'd worn in Innsmouth. At as low a cost as possible, for we had not traveled here with much, we had all acquired new garments: fresh, clean-smelling, with not a scrap of Innsmouthian muck on them. Soon, we would be home, where our unblemished attire awaited—along with our homes, our beds, and the London smog, which I would now find *soothing*. Mrs. Hudson would greet us, I was sure, with open arms and culinary delights. Mycroft would finally be forced to admit that Holmes's intellect exceeded his own. Lestrade would never question our skills and would regard us *both* as detectives without equal.

"There's our boat. Soon, we'll be onboard." Holmes gestured at a large craft that could withstand any wave the sea might throw at us, or so I hoped.

Hagley had indeed been waiting for us at the edge of Innsmouth.

"I dropped off the children," he had explained as Holmes and I begged for immediate escape from Innsmouth, "and I saw the two of you by the water. I waited, saw Dagon, saw the Old Ones go into the sky and leave." Shrugging, Hagley had displayed no reaction, positive or negative, to what had transpired. "They'll come again, when the time is right," he said. He then told us that Frederick Cararo had indeed left everything to Hortense, but she was dead, having exploded from the smallpox mutations. The old man had left no provision in his will for the children, but they had been sucked into the beyond anyway. "The estate will go to the government," Hagley had told us. And Dragoon would be forced back to Boston to earn his living in his former manner, as a pimp and a hustler. "Let him have it," the driver added. "His type never live long anyway."

"Watson, over there!" Holmes said, jerking me yet again from my thoughts. I squinted. A tall, thin man limped down a pier to a boat, where he climbed aboard. With one arm in a sling, he was heavily bruised, his face smashed and bleeding.

"I wonder how he got out of Innsmouth. He probably

attacked someone at gunpoint," Holmes muttered, "and stole a horse."

"Moriarty," I whispered. "He's heading somewhere, Holmes, but not to London. The only ship that's sailing home is the one we're about to board."

"He'll rebound quickly. He'll return to London. Mark my words," Holmes said.

Mary, Fortuna, and the baby boarded first, and we trailed behind. I wanted to make sure my family was safely aboard, that nothing would go wrong.

The Boston police had informed us that all the rifts were sealed. Word had come from England that our homeland was safe again. "London, Avebury, Half Moon Bay, the Thames: all clear," the police had said. "You're a big hero in England, Mr. Holmes."

"As, I am sure, is my associate and dear friend, Dr. Watson," Holmes had declared. "The tram machine is dead, I assume?"

Nodding, the officer had added that "it's not cranking out gold, nothing, sir. Dead. Just worthless parts now."

"And the sea?" I'd asked. "*Cthulhu?*"

"He's gone, sir," the other had assured me. "Sank to the bottom of the sea, maybe killed—we don't know, but he's gone."

"When the rift closed over Devil Reef," I said nervously, "maybe Cthulhu sank, and he's going to rise again."

"Not in our lifetimes, I hope," Holmes said. "Come along, Dr. Watson. It's time to go home."

Within the hour, the ship was cruising peacefully through

calm water. The sunset was beautiful, an ordinary orange ball sinking over the horizon, casting tendrils of light over the ripples spreading in our wake. Somewhere, the *Elysium* with its Killer Eshockers also sailed home.

Holmes and I gazed at the dying sun. It was our sun, and it was free of black clouds and slices into the deadly dimensions.

"I'm thinking," Holmes said, "that it's time for you to return to medicine. Focus on your family. I can manage my cases without you, Watson."

"I must admit," I answered, "that after this deadly dimensions affair, any future criminal cases you pursue will be child's play."

"Nothing is child's play, Watson. The human mind is capable of great travesties and abominations. It is scientific evidence that will stop criminals. *Proof.* And for that, my work is necessary."

"Yes," I said. "You are correct, and your work *is* necessary. As for me, this will be my final case." I turned from the sun, as it sank, its final strand shimmering then slipping beneath the fold of the beyond... the horizon.

"I cannot put Mary through any more of this," I added. "Never again. Never, Holmes. Samuel needs a steady life. It's up to me to take care of my family."

We stood quietly, two friends enjoying an excursion. After a long spell, he turned to me, and even in the dark, his presence was familiar; and it was comforting.

"Watson, my dear fellow," he murmured, "one can never say 'never.'"

ACKNOWLEDGEMENTS

The first book in this series, *Sherlock Holmes vs. Cthulhu: The Adventure of the Deadly Dimensions*, introduced Sherlock Holmes and Dr. John Watson to bizarre monsters and mysterious chemical reactions of other spacetime dimensions. Holmes insisted that what appeared to be supernatural was based on hard fact, the cold reality of the universe and its properties. Along with murders related to what Holmes came to think of as the deadly dimensions, he encountered and solved other murders linked to the central crimes. His expertise in chemistry proved essential, as did the skills of Willie Jacobs, the son of a murdered man who had built a deadly tram machine. Professor James Moriarty was in play, actively countering Holmes's moves.

In the second novel, *Sherlock Holmes vs. Cthulhu: The Adventure of the Neural Psychoses*, Holmes once again confronted science beyond the 1890s in the form of Eshocker machines. Dr. Reginald Sinclair of the Whitechapel Lunatic Asylum designed the Eshockers to treat his patients either in hospital mode or extreme treatment mode. But Moriarty found another way to use Sinclair's Eshockers—to give electric jolts to the public in his nefarious dens. All three types of Eshockers *could have existed* during Holmes's time. The engineering required to devise and build the Eshockers was already known—in our real world. I created the engineering schematics for all of the machines before I started writing the book. As the deadly dimensions dumped more of the bizarre monsters into London, addiction, brain disease, and death swept through the city, and even Watson fell prey to the neural psychoses. While Holmes eventually solved murders seemingly committed by supernatural entities, he also solved other crimes, including a locked-room murder. Along with Moriarty, the book features Mycroft Holmes and the Diogenes Club and my favorite character (other than Holmes and Watson) in the series, Willie Jacobs.

By now, you have finished reading the third novel, *Sherlock Holmes vs. Cthulhu: The Adventure of the Innsmouth Mutations*. This installment brought Cthulhu—as well as Dagon at Devil Reef—on stage in full force. Once I placed Holmes and Watson in Innsmouth, all hell had to break loose. After all, we were in *Innsmouth*, and the series title is *Sherlock Holmes vs. Cthulhu*. The ultimate showdown had to occur between Holmes and Cthulhu. So off I went, pounding out the pages, giving you Cthulhu, Dagon, and an Innsmouthian nightmare that almost brought Holmes to his knees. *But it didn't: of course not*. Rather, Holmes saved the day, maintaining throughout that the weird hell around him had to be based on science and logic. Moriarty battled Holmes and Watson to the bitter end.

After all of this strangeness, after years of immersion in the world of *Sherlock Holmes vs. Cthulhu*, I'm not sure what I will write next. I'm leaning toward writing a straight thriller set in modern times. And yet, the allure of Holmes and Watson remains. Perhaps Sherlock Holmes isn't done with me yet. Only time will tell.

As I close, I want to thank my editors Steve Saffel and Sam Matthews at Titan Books, and my agent, Cherry Weiner. Most of all, a huge thank you to my readers, those of you who enjoy this series as much as I do. You are the reason that I write stories.

Sherlock Holmes and Dr. Watson: thank you for such a fun time.

With love to my family,
Lois H. Gresh
September 2018

ABOUT THE AUTHOR

LOIS H. GRESH is the six-time *New York Times*-bestselling author of twenty-eight books and more than sixty-five short stories, as well as the editor of the anthologies *Innsmouth Nightmares* and *Dark Fusions*. She is a well-known Lovecraftian writer whose works have appeared in *Black Wings of Cthulhu*, *The Madness of Cthulhu*, and many other anthologies. Her work has been published in twenty-two languages. *Sherlock Holmes vs. Cthulhu: The Adventure of the Innsmouth Mutations* is the third in her new trilogy of Holmes thrillers. Lois is a frequent guest of honor author at large fan conventions and has appeared on television series such as the History Channel's *Ancient Aliens* and *Batman Tech*. You can follow her adventures with Sherlock Holmes at **www.facebook.com/lois.gresh** and **www.loisgresh.com**

THE CTHULHU CASEBOOKS
SHERLOCK HOLMES AND THE MISKATONIC MONSTROSITIES

JAMES LOVEGROVE

It is the spring of 1895, and more than a decade of combating eldritch entities has cost Dr John Watson his beloved wife Mary, and nearly broken the health of Sherlock Holmes. Yet the companions do not hesitate when they are called to the infamous Bedlam lunatic asylum, where they find an inmate speaking in R'lyehian, the language of the Old Ones. Moreover, the man is horribly scarred and has no memory of who he is...

"Lovegrove does an outstanding job."
San Francisco Book Review

For more fantastic fiction, author events, competitions, limited editions and more

VISIT OUR WEBSITE
titanbooks.com

LIKE US ON FACEBOOK
facebook.com/titanbooks

FOLLOW US ON TWITTER
@TitanBooks

EMAIL US
readerfeedback@titanemail.com